DEATH OF A POLITICIAN

NOVELS BY RICHARD CONDON

Death of a Politician
Bandicoot
The Abandoned Woman
The Whisper of the Axe
Money Is Love
The Star Spangled Crunch
Winter Kills
Arigato
The Vertical Smile
Mile High
The Ecstasy Business
Any God Will Do
An Infinity of Mirrors
A Talent for Loving
Some Angry Angel
The Manchurian Candidate
The Oldest Confession

OTHER BOOKS

And Then We Moved to Rossenarra
The Mexican Stove

DEATH OF A POLITICIAN

a novel
RICHARD CONDON

Richard Marek Publishers
New York

Library of Congress Cataloging in Publication Data

Condon, Richard.
  Death of a politician.

 I. Title.
PZ4.C746De [PS3553.O487]   813'.5'4   78-16015
ISBN 0-399-90018-7

"You say that people in authority are not to be snubbed or sneered at from our pinnacle of conscious rectitude. I really don't know whether you exempt them because of their rank, or of their success and power, or of their date. . . . I cannot accept your canon that we are to judge Pope and King, unlike other men, with a favoured presumption that they did no wrong.

"If there is any presumption, it is the other way, against holders of power, increasing as the power increases. Historic responsibility has to make up for the want of legal responsibility. Power tends to corrupt and absolute power corrupts absolutely. Great men are almost always bad men, even when they exercise influence and not authority; still more when you superadd the tendency or the certainty of corruption by authority. . . . The inflexible integrity of the moral code is to me the secret of the authority, the dignity, the utility of history. If we may debase it for the sake of a man's influence, of his religion, of his party, of the good cause which prospers his credit and suffers by his disgrace, then History ceases to be a science, an arbiter of controversy, a guide to the wanderer. . . . It serves where it ought to reign, and it serves the worst cause better than the purest."

In a letter to Mandell Creighton, Bishop of Peterborough and London, published in 1904 in *Life of Mandell Creighton*

—LORD ACTON

This is my body
Up for sale,
This is my conscience
Deadly pale,
This is my sanity
Price tag peeping.
These are my people,
Why are they weeping?

The Keeners' Manual

1 Date of Orig. Report			Date Assigned	Case Number	Unit Reporting										
Mo 8	Day 9	Yr. 64	8/9/64	255	17th Homicide Squad										

tim's Name		Address,City,State,Zip,Apt. ☐ Res. ☐ Comm.							TEL. Home Bus.	Unknown
'alter Bodmor Slurrie, Visitor, Waldorf Astoria Hotel										

vious Classification		45	48	49	50	51	52	53 Pct of Arrest	56 Arrest Number
ssification Changed To:		41							

WANTED PERSONS INFORMATION (INCLUDE PERSONS ARRESTED)

ne,Last,First,M.I.	Address,City,State,Zip,Apt.	Home Bus.	Unknown
me,Last,First,M.I.	Address,City,State,Zip,Apt.	Home Bus.	

NO	SEX	RACE	AGE and D.O.B.	HEIGHT	WEIGHT	HAIR COLOR	FACIAL HAIR	NICKNAMES,SCARS,MARKS,CLOTHING ETC.	WANTED PERSONS AL
1									
2									
3									

61 Reporting Agency	Case Number	Referral Changed From	To		☐ Open ☐ Closed	rled Number
MPANION CASES						FOLLOW-UP NUM

ATE INFORMATION ☐ LOST ☐ STOLEN ☐ REC'VD	VEHICLE INFORMATION ☐ REC'VD ☐ USED IN A CRIME ☐ STOLEN, IF STOLEN WHERE	63 LARCENY of MOTOR VEH. ONLY	ALARM NO. an
; NO.	V.I.N. _____ COLOR _____		
ATE	YEAR of VEH _____ VALUE _____	1-PARKING LOT	TIME
AR	MAKE _____ INS. CODE _____	2-GARAGE	

HOMICIDE: WALTER BODMOR SLURRIE, M-W-54, GUN (NOT RECOVERED)

SUBJECT: INTERVIEW OF RICHARD BETAUT, TENANT OF PREMISES WHERE BODY WAS DISCOVERED.

1: On this date at approximately 10:50 P.M. the undersigned with Police Officer John Kullers No. 4912 – 17thUP interviewed one RICHARD BETAUT resident at Apartment 2634, Waldorf Towers, Waldorf Astoria Hotel. He is M-W-58, widower, has been resident in above premises since August 1944. He is former District Attorney, City of New York, County of New York, former Governor of the State of New York, a practicing attorney in the City of New York who was two times the candidate nominated by the Republican party for the Presidency of the United States. He states that the murder victim, exVice President of the United States, exUnited States Senator from Texas, exCongressman from Texas, had attended a meeting at Apartment 2634, Waldorf Towers, from approx. 4:30 P.M. day and date of homicide. Richard Betaut and others at the meeting went to dinner at 7 P.M. Victim remained in Apartment 2634. When Richard Betaut returned to Apartment 2634 at 9:45 P.M. (departure and return time checked with floor clerk, Agnes Munshin) he went directly to toilet off main bedroom. When he entered the toilet/bathroom of Apartment 2634 he observed the slumped body of a fully-dressed-Male-White seated on one of his own dining room chairs in the bathtub in a pool of blood. Richard Betaut immediately reported his observations to the manager of the Towers (John Cremers) speaking from the bathroom telephone. The duty clerk (Albert Fumire) recorded receiving the telephone call at 9:55 P.M. He summoned Police Officer John Kullers who was in the employee washroom of the Towers section. Officer Kullers proceeded directly to Apartment 2634, observed the condition of the homicide victim and reported the homicide to the 17th precinct.

INVESTIGATION CONTINUING   STATUS OF CASE   ACTIVE

August 10th, 1964
11:58 P.M.

TO: Chiefs of Base (US) + Alert Psychiatric Units (Regions as Listed)
Priority: Red Urgent
Subject: W.B. Slurrie, Death of

Herewith names and addresses from sensitive areas of Slurrie's life.

Debrief as assigned: your region.

To accelerate cooperation and to insure accuracy in the time allowed, you will use chemical and hypnotic reassurances under psychiatric supervision.

Exceptions to chemical & hypnotic reassurances:

Richard Betaut
Abner Danzig
Marie Coffey

Mrs. Coffey was debriefed during WBS lifetime at his request.

DESTROY: All debriefing notes in presence of CB. One written report to me (Semley) not later than noon, August 12th.

RED URGENT

DSP

DATE: 10th August 1964
TIME: 5:18 A.M.
BASE REPORTING: New York

DSP (Semley) Only

CHARLES COFFEY

I was sleeping when Betaut called. He wanted to come right over. Betaut could concentrate on the imperative like Horowitz staring at a piano. I asked him where he was. "I just left Nils," he said. Betaut was the only one I knew, in our line of work, who called Felsenburshe by his first name. Everyone else called him Mr. Nils except, of course, where good fellows got together.

It was raining hard. Cabs must have been scarce but, being Betaut, he got here in just under ten minutes. I answered the door in my pajamas at about a quarter to twelve. He hit the doorbell so savagely that I imagined he might try to beat me up when I opened the door. Betaut is a short, solid man—all burning black eyes, with the white, whiter, whitest teeth of the television-age politician. But his package hardly reflected his spirit because Betaut is a force like an earthquake: that voice and the way he uses it, and the way he looks when he is demanding something from you which you didn't know you had. Betaut is one of Nature's intimidators and he always gives more than value for the money.

He stood there like a pit rooster at the middle of a convention of butchers, staring up at me as if I had given his wife a social disease. Then, as if he hadn't really recognized me, he shoved past into my own living room. He stood in the middle of the V'Soske which Marie had designed, wearing that gray cartoon fedora high up on the crown of his head and looking like Calvin Coolidge's bookmaker. He did not sit. He waited until I had shut the front door and started into the room, then he said, "Walter Slurrie was murdered in my bathtub."

I thought I hadn't quite caught what he had said. "Your *bathtub*?"

We both sat down slowly, staring at each other's eyes, pleading for answers.

Betaut made his voice boom and snarl at the same time, a sound like the lion house at feeding time, but that was only his normal way when something energized him. We understood each other. I had handled the State Committees for him in '48. Dick Betaut is the total politician in the ongoing sense of that word. He is as hard as diamonds, as sentimental as a hangman, and he invented all the devious questions and straight-arrow answers. Right now Betaut is only a multimillionaire Wall Street lawyer but twice he was Republican candidate for the Presidency of the United States. Once he almost made it—which I know doesn't count.

"I don't need to tell you, Charley," he detonated from somewhere below his navel, "we've got to protect the Felsenburshes on this from the Bay of Pigs all the way forward, if you know what I mean."

"I hope you're not overreacting," I said.

"Charley, do you have any idea what the media are going to *do* with this murder? And therefore the police? Everyone is going to want to get something out of this. Everybody who has a pencil and a brown paper bag to write on will turn into something called an investigative reporter."

"You're right. As usual. How?"

"I have already moved."

"How?"

"Nils concurs with me on this, Charley."

"Then let's go."

"The New York police asked me for a list of the people closest to Walter. That's what gave me the idea. I gave them your name,

2

of course. You'll probably be hearing from them tonight."

"Tonight? It's already tomorrow."

"Charley, how can they wait? An ex-Vice President of the United States has been shot to death in *my* bathtub. The most controversial politician in the entire western alliance has been murdered."

The telephone rang so suddenly that I almost wet my pajamas.

I walked out to the hall to get it. "Charles Coffey," I said into it."

"This is Gallagher, 17th Homicide Squad, Mr. Coffey," an amiable voice said. "There has been a murder and —"

"I know about it."

"When can I see you?"

"Give me a half hour to shower and dress."

"Right. How do you know about the murder, Mr. Coffey?"

"Governor Betaut is here."

As I walked back into the living room Betaut said, "This is the plan—approved by Nils, I might add. You will handle the New York police and stay ahead of what they are going to tell the press. I'll handle the Secret Police. Nobody knows New York on a local political level better than you do, Charley."

"And nobody knows the SP like you."

"Then we have our mutual goals."

"But I don't mention the SP to the cops."

"No. Never. Just lay it on until they understand that you are a factor who can get the entire police force transferred, in toto, to the 123rd Precinct. This is no time for diplomacy. Call the Mayor and tell him what you want. If he balks, call the Governor. We have to know the direction this investigation is taking."

"Dick?"

"What?"

"Why the SP? Does the SP have a Homicide Squad? I mean, to *solve* homicides, not to commit them?"

"They are national, Charley. They have fifty times the resources of the NYPD without any interference because they operate invisibly. I gave them the same list of names I gave Lieutenant Gallagher and, using their own extraordinary methods—they are deep into chemicals and psychiatry for debriefings now, you know—quite possibly they may run down the killer before the NYPD can get near any solution."

"What happens then?"

"They'll give the killer to me and I'll turn him over to the NYPD. They have situation analysts and computers. They have

3

these new psychiatric techinques and an unlimited budget and—when you come right down to it—with everybody screaming at the NYPD for an arrest, with pressure from all directions, the heads of these cops will be coming to a point. Of all the things I would not want to be, beginning about two hours ago, would be the Homicide lieutenant in charge of this case."

"Well, you certainly have it all figured out."

"This is no casual Harlem hit, Charley. The corpse in *my* bathtub was Walter Bodmor Slurrie." He put his comedy fedora on, then patted me on the shoulder as he walked past. He said, "It's thirteen to five that Nudey Danzig had Walter killed."

When he was gone I got out my address book and called the Mayor. He was fast asleep, naturally, at such a time of night, but he took the call.

"What the hell happened?" he said into the phone.

"Walter Slurrie was murdered in Dick Betaut's suite at the Waldorf."

"Holy shit!"

"Hughie, I know that you know that when I call at this time of night about a thing like this that I only do it after checking everything out with the Felsenburshes."

"Of course, Charley. Of course."

"Walter Slurrie was one of our own, Hughie, and I know you understand me. I handled every political campaign he ever made except the first one. Walter was a Felsenburshe man."

"Yes. Absolutely. Just tell me what you need, Charley."

"I want to stay on top of this case, which is *family* to the Felsenburshes, Hughie. We don't want to have to wait to read about it in the papers. I don't even want to have to call cops who will be over their heads with action to ask them what's happening."

"Just tell me what you want, Charley," he said patiently.

"The Homicide lieutenant in charge is a fella named Gallagher. I want you to tell the Commissioner that you want him to tell Gallagher to write up a special daily written report which somebody way up in the department—to impress the shit out of Gallagher—will then distribute to people like yourself with a need to know."

"Hell, that's a great idea all by itself."

"I want to be on top of that list. That's all we want, Hughie."

"You've got it. Tell Nils, please. Delivered by hand every day or twice a day."

"Thank you, Hughie."

"Not a bit. Thank *you*, Charley."

4

17 Date of this Report | File No
8/10/64
7:18 AM

1 Jurisdiction 9 Pct of Occ 12 Complaint Number
17th 1755

TEL. Home Unknown
Bus.
53 Pct of Arrest 56 Arrest Number

PLAINT FOLLOW UP ADDITIONAL COPIES FOR (PG 108-11)
17th Homicide Squad
Address,City,State,Zip,Apt. ☐ Res. ☐ Comm.

-313-081 Date Assigned Case Number Unit Reporting
8/9/64 255
51 52
50
49
Home Unknown
Bus.

Date of Orig. Report Yr.
Day
8 9 64 Walter Bodmor Slurrie, Visitor, Waldorf Astoria Hotel
45 48
Home

41
WANTED PERSONS INFORMATION (INCLUDE PERSONS ARRESTED)
Address,City,State,Zip,Apt.

Previous Classification
City,State,Zip,Apt.

Classification Changed To:

Name,Last,First,M.I.

Name,Last,First,M.I.

TO: FIRST DEPUTY COMMISSIONER VINCENT J. MULSHINE

FROM: LIEUTENANT RICHARD GALLAGHER, 17th HSQ

As per orders from Commissioner Mitgang find herewith the first of the written reports to be sent directly to you relative to the above homicide.

At 10:14 P.M., 9th August, my duty sergeant, George Fearons, reached me at the Romeo Salta restuarant, West 56th Street, to report what he called "an extremely sensitive murder" at the Waldorf Towers, East 50th Street. As I left the

5

restaurant Fearons had a car pulling up to get me to the scene. I have a good team.

John Cremers, manager of the Towers, was waiting for me at the 50th St. entrance. He told me the murder victim was Walter Slurrie and said he felt sick because of the amount of trouble the homicide was going to cause.

We proceeded to Apartment 2634 in the Towers, where Police Officer John Kullers, 4912-17thUP, was waiting with former Governor Richard T. Betaut, tenant of the apartment and the person who discovered the body, who told me he was late for a meeting with Mr. Nils Felsenburshe. I said he would have to telephone his explanations because I needed him where he was. I said this respectfully. The Governor has always been a friend of the Department, as he pointed out to me.

Then I asked him to explain what had happened in the apartment which led to the murder.

"We had a meeting of the Inner Committee of the Party at half-past four this afternoon," he said, "to discuss basic strategies to secure the Presidential nomination in '68 for Walter Slurrie."

"Who was at the meeting?"

"Charles Coffey, the ex-Vice-President's political adviser. Dr. Hugo Huggems, the candidate's foreign policy adviser, Walter Slurrie, and myself."

"What happened after the meeting?"

"Dr. Huggems and I went to dinner at the Yale Club. Mr. Coffey said he was going home to do some work, I believe. Vice-President Slurrie said he would remain in the apartment to go over notes he had been making during the meeting. He was a demon note-taker."

"What happened then?"

"I walked home alone from the Yale Club – back to this apartment, that is. Dr. Huggems lives at the Yale Club and he remained there. When I let myself into this apartment I had an urgent need to urinate so, without removing my hat, I think, I went directly to the toilet in the bathroom off my bedroom. I could have gone into the so-called powder room which is off the entrance hall. I could have gone into the one off the dining room. The toilet I chose was furthest away. It could have been that I would not have discovered the body until tomorrow morning because I never bathe at night, brushing my teeth and washing up, as I do, in the small lavatory next to my bed."

"Did you notice the body immediately?"

"No. I had this urinating on my mind, you see. But when I turned away, adjusting my clothing, I saw it. It is quite a spectacular mess, Lieutenant, as you will see. I then telephoned the Towers manager on the bathroom phone and told him to get up here immediately. I sensed that this could be a matter which would or could involve national policy."

"How?"

"Well, suppose you people determine that this was a suicide. What then? Slurrie would have been the next President of the United States. He is a statesman of world rank. He was famous even as a congressman, extraordinarily prominent as a senator. He was Vice-President for two terms and he ran for the Presidency in the last presidential elections. What I am saying is that people in positions higher than yours or mine might not want Walter Slurrie's death to be revealed as a murder or as a suicide for that matter, if you follow me."

"I don't think anybody in any position has the muscle to cover this one up, Governor."

"I told Cremers flatly that, as far as I was concerned, as far as I personally could control it, there would be no cover-up. We must summon the police at once, I said. No hotel security officers, please. Cremers called his office and told them send a police officer to this apartment. Officer Kullers appeared within ten minutes."

Kullers said, "I was using the employees' facilities, Lieutenant, when a bellhop came running in and he drags me away so fast I don't have time to button up. The way things are happening maybe I'm not buttoned up yet. I walk in here and here is Governor Betaut, two-time standard bearer. He reports the homicide to me, I confirm it by going in the bathroom where I tag the body right away with a 95 on the right thumb, filling in the time, date, and circumstances of the death. Then I call the precinct and report the homicide."

I thank Governor Betaut for his cooperation and apologize for holding him up for his next appointment. Fearons takes him out to drive him wherever he wants to go. I ask him to please keep in touch. As he left my people poured in.

I tell Weldon to have Cremers set us up with a temporary

7

headquarters in the nearest space available to the murder apartment, then to write up the DD5's. I put Bocca on the phone to notify the Manhattan Detective area to canvass all commands for personnel availability and to call Current Situations at Police Headquarters. "Give them our headquarters location and telephone. Call the Office of the Chief of Detectives and notify the Assistant Chief for Manhattan South."

I have Policewoman Garfunkel call the Medical Examiner's office and tell them that it is my own assessment that Barry Wolf should get over here personally to get the victim downtown and up on the table himself. I tell Adler to get everything ready with the forensic people and Wolf's people to get that body out of this hotel like Hugo Zucchini getting out of a cannon. I told Ribik to line up two men to go over hotel records, toll telephone calls, and descriptions of visitors at this apartment in the past twenty-four hours. I told him to get all messages and mail and to interview maids, floor waiters, elevator men, doormen, and bellhops for any notice of suspicious circumstances. Dick Richards I put on setting himself and another detective to walk around the perimeter of the hotel to take down the license numbers of all parked vehicles including cabs and delivery wagons. I told him to handle the hotel garage himself. Fearons came back. I put him on going over the apartment for doodles on telephone pads or on hotel menus and to go through all the drawers and closets for notes or anything else the killer hadn't meant to leave there.

I go in to look at the scene of the crime and bring Policewoman Schrader with me to take notes. I am beginning to turn to lead when I think about the noise the media are going to make about this case and how nobody in the PD is going to want to have anything to do with it. All I hoped was that nobody was going to get any ideas that any of this could be covered up. About seventy people knew all about it already, counting hotel people and police. There was going to be outside pressure laid on like there hadn't been since Arnold Rothstein had been hit in '29, while he was holding files that could blow up the whole city administration. My father caught the pressure on that case. It must run in the family. When we got to the big bathroom I went straight to the john to vomit without looking for the victim. Just future shock. After that I felt like working.

The corpse was seated on a red plush Victorian chair in the bathtub. Betaut had positively identified the victim as Walter Bodmor Slurrie and we would ask the immediate family for a confirmation of that. The victim had been shot through the back of the head, through the larynx and, from the blood, in the abdomen. There was no weapon to recover.

The body was fully dressed. The chair was an unusual feature, not only because people don't take red plush chairs into bathtubs, but because firing at least three times at that close a range, the killer would have had to knock the victim off the chair and each time lift him back on the chair. It was also worth wondering, I dictated to Policewoman Schrader (a facility, dictation, I have never had before but which your office provided because it felt I might possibly be busy with other things while I was required to get out this daily written report on the case), why and how the killer or killers had got the victim to sit on a chair in a bathtub. And why three shots in different parts of the victim's anatomy? Any one of the three shots would have done the job. There is hardly an old maiden aunt alive who doesn't believe that if a victim's larynx is blown away it was a Mafia hit. And maybe it was. Just the same, when the late President was assassinated, the wounds were incurred just where these wounds were: left rear parietal region of the skull and in the larynx. Some fairly complicated things were building.

Outside the bathroom there wasn't a powder mark, a blood-stain, or a fingerprint – or any sign of a struggle. It all happened in and around that tub. The point is: if someone a former Vice-President of the United States knew well invented a good enough story to get him to sit on a red plush chair in a bathtub he might do it. But what kind of a reason could anyone come up with to convince him to try that kind of a chair in surroundings like that? If his friend wasn't holding a gun on him he might sense something unusual.

The Medical Examiner, Barry Wolf, has established that the first shot went into the abdomen. This is the sequence. The victim is shot in the abdomen. He is knocked off the chair and into the tub. He grabs his abdomen. As the killer lifts him back on the chair, the victim's bloody hand touches the wall leaving a good print. In order to shoot the victim in the abdomen the killer had to step inside the tub directly in front of the victim who is still alive, not yet shot, and seated. Why no struggle? Dr. Wolf says the victim had not been drugged before he was shot. Why didn't the victim grab the killer when he had one foot in the air to step over the wall of the tub? The victim had to know he was going to be killed. He had nothing to lose by struggling with the killer.

The floor of the tub is running with blood. The killer's shoes are slippery with it, maybe the bottoms of his trousers are damp from it, but he has to stay in the tub to lift the victim back on the chair so that the killer can get out of the tub with his blood-soaked shoes to be able to get behind his wounded victim to be able to shoot him in the back of the head.

We have shoeprints on the bathroom floor. They are clear prints from unusual shoes. We are checking out this type of shoe.

The killer shoots the victim in the back of the head. The victim is now twice dead yet the killer lifts the body back on the chair so he can shoot him again.

The powder burns, the stains, and the marks from the angle of continuing falls from the chair say that this was the murder sequence.

The killer then removed his shoes. We think he wrapped them in something, probably a hotel towel, walked in his socks out of the bathroom to Betaut's closet, where he put on a pair of hunting boots that belong to the state trooper who takes Betaut hunting every fall. The killer knew his way around the apartment, had to have been there before, was known to Betaut, and probably to the victim. From his shoe size and weight, the killer was probably a male of about 190 pounds. There are possibly a number of people in the Slurrie-Betaut circle who knew the killer well.

When the Medical Examiner began to work in the bathroom – and after I had yelled at the Forensic Squad not to do their usual sloppy work on this one – I returned to the living room of the apartment where Police Commissioner Mitgang, Chief of Detectives Joseph Maguire, and the chief inspector of uniformed police were waiting for me.

"We are all here now," Mitgang said, "so let's proceed with the meeting. First, I want to say that nothing in our business gets impossible to live with until it involves politicians. And need I remind you that on this one we are up to the cheeks of

10

our asses in them. I have already had the Mayor twice tonight, the Governor once, and one U.S. Senator, but that is only the start of it. We not only have a dead politician, but it's got to be a walking twenty-eight-year headline like Slurrie. That isn't bad enough, he gets himself killed in Betaut's bathtub. Betaut! Now let me tell you men something and I am addressing this right at you, Gallagher. Whatever happened to this department before this homicide, there's never been anything that can compare in any way to the heat we are going to catch on this one. The press doesn't even know about it yet. Everybody from the President to Pravda are going to be leaning on us with this one. I hope I have made my point here."

We wait for the clincher. It comes. "Gallagher " the PC says, "you got to front everything. I am very sorry, but you are going to have to be master sleuth and issuer of all the news bulletins at the same time. The whole department will be backing you up all the way, of course, but you've got to be the focus for the heat on this case. We got to have one clear police target out in front where everybody can hit it with anything. Now—very important, Gallagher—I want a written report to go from you to my Deputy First Commissioner Vincent Mulshine every time there is any kind of development on this case so that he can send copies of it to all sensitive areas which need to know. Beginning immediately, Gallagher. I know you'll be up to your ass, but this is vital and we'll supply you with someone who will type it up as you give it. Okay?"

I said, "Why not?"

"All right. The goddam press are waiting. Organize them into manageable sections, them start to feed them bulletins. No pictures of the victim. Anything else at your discretion."

Weldon got me by the arm. He said Marty Esposito the head of the Forensic Squad wanted to see me at the scene. I went into the big bathroom. Esposito said, "Did you take a look at these footprints?"

I squatted down beside them. "They look like lily pads. What kind of shoes made those?"

"Somebody downtown is going to have to figure that out," he said.

"They have no heels. They're all soles."

"Maybe the killer was an Indian," Esposito said. "They look like moccasins to me."

11

"Are you going to be able to tell me the probable weight and height?"

"If the killer had stood in soft mud or cement, I could do that, Lieutenant. But on a tile floor, I can't even tell you if a woman or a man did it."

"A woman? With feet that size?"

"She could be wearing somebody else's shoes on purpose."

"But the body was blown off the chair at least twice. The body weighs about 195, dead-weight. The floor of the tub is slippery with blood. How could a woman make those lifts?"

"Come on! My mother-in-law could dribble this guy across a court."

"So it could be a man or it could be a woman. But you will probably agree that it wasn't a midget."

"Two midgets could have done it, Lieutenant."

Barry Wolf called me over to the tub. They had the body undressed, face down. "How about that for a back?" Wolf said.

I squatted again and studied it up close. From the base of the neck all the way down the back and across the buttocks, it was covered with heavy welts, old and new; some of them white with age, some still oozing blood.

"This guy had himself whipped before he was killed," Wolf said. "This guy has been having himself whipped for about twenty years. The chest is the same."

"Now I have to call in a police psychiatrist, for Christ's sake!" I said. "What do you think, Barry? Could the same person do both – the whipping and the shooting?"

"Why not?" Wolf said, "If Slurrie paid enough."

I stood up. "A suicide?" I asked him. "I could have a suicide? And not the most sensational murder of this month?"

"You could have the most sensational suicide of the year, pal," Wolf said. "How about it? Two circus midgets flagellate, then shoot the former Veep to death. Now that's news."

"Aaaah, shit!" I said.

TO: FIRST DEPUTY COMMISSIONER VINCENT J. MULSHINE

FROM: LIEUTENANT RICHARD GALLAGHER, 17th HSQ

It looks like today's big clue is that Mrs. Walter Slurrie thinks her husband was killed on orders from the Kremlin and Peking.

The body left Apartment 2634, Waldorf Towers, at 11:58 last night in a bakery truck inside a basket of hotel laundry. It was downtown on a table before the media knew it was gone. So far four television crews have tried to climb up my nostrils.

13

We held 56 media people in a hotel reception room while we held a press conference for the N.Y. dailies, the wire services, and two news magazines. I brought the rest of the media up-to-date right after that. Everybody tried to yell at once so I told them that unless everybody calmed down I was only going to issue written bulletins right through the case. They got quieter but not much. I told them the outline of the facts as we knew them. I said that photographers and TV people could photograph different chairs in the bathtub but that we had the murder chair downtown. They had already done that in another suite. I said the Medical Examiner's report would be made available at the next press meeting which would be held at noon every day at the new Police Academy on East 20th Street and that Policewomen Schrader and Garfunkel would pass among them with information sheets. We got through the first press conference.

Of the people on the Betaut list of Slurrie intimates, only Betaut, Coffey, and possibly (we will know soon) Nudey Danzig were in town at the time of the murder but we are now checking everybody out for alibis. I called Coffey at about 11:45 last night at his apartment. Betaut was already there (so he must have had a very short meeting with Felsenburshe). Before I left to see Coffey I got my people together and told them I wanted the most detailed set of 5s they ever turned in. I took Sgt. Fearons with me to Coffey's apartment at 227 East 57 Street.

Charles Coffey is an authentic kingmaker. He has been in charge of the political interest of the Felsenburshe family since 1947. He handled Slurrie's campaign for the Senate in '48 and managed both of Slurrie's vice-presidential campaigns. He was in charge when Slurrie ran for President in 1960, though no king was crowned that time. Slurrie and Coffey were roommates at Coomber Law College in Malthus, New Jersey. Coffey has been a professional politician all his life, as is his father Martin J. Coffey, now a State Supreme Court Justice up for retirement. Charles Coffey is 54 years old, 5'10" but heavyset so he looks shorter, one of the "Spanish-Irish" left over from when the Armada went aground. He looks like a man who doesn't intend to give anybody any change. He talks with a thickened, nasal, monotonous New York Irish accent like you and me, except that his voice carries further than

14

mine. When he smiles, by split-second chronograph, the way politicians smile, it is just an instant grimace which pulls the ends of his mouth toward each ear, showing us stained teeth, then drops the curtain back so that his face expresses nothing. He has dry-sad eyes. In my experience when people show moist-sad eyes like a hound dog's, they are usually just myopic. But dry-sad eyes is a rare enough thing because that is despair or, in the old Victorian style, the heart has broken. But Coffey has a jolly, hearty voice; an instant cajoler.

I asked him about his movements after the meeting at the Waldorf that afternoon, remaining aware at all times that this was the original of the fellow who can actually have a cop transferred to south Staten Island. He must have read my mind. He told me he had no intention of throwing his weight around but that it wouldn't do any harm for me to remember how much he weighed. He said, "Governor Betaut invited me to dinner with Professor Huggems but I had a lot of work to get done so I decided to go home and hit the dictating machine. Walter Slurrie called me here at about six-fifteen. He wanted me to jog his memory about something which had come up at the meeting."

"Can you tell me what the meeting was about, Mr. Coffey?" I asked him.

"It was an informal political meeting. I wasn't paying much attention but we were there to agree on strategies to advance Walter Slurrie's candidacy for the Presidency in '68."

"Mr. Slurrie called you..."

"I went back to the Betaut suite to bring a file that Walter said he needed. I didn't stay."

"What time did you leave?"

"Oh, about twenty after seven. I'd lost my momentum for work so I walked up Lexington through the heat to the Gaiety Delicatessen, got a sandwich and brought it home, ate it with a bottle of beer, read through a few files, took a shower, and went to bed. I was in bed at ten-twenty."

"Anyone in your family at home?"

"No. The kids are at school in Berkeley, and my wife is in California staying with her mother who lives in Berkeley." That was when I noticed his dry-sad eyes.

"You were alone here?"

"You mean can anyone verify my story?"

15

"If possible, Mr. Coffey."

"The doorman and the elevator man saw me come in. They saw me go out with the file for Walter, then they saw me in again."

"Do you have any idea who might have killed Mr. Slurrie?"

"Killed or wanted to kill?"

"Can we run down this list of names of people close to him?"

"Nobody was close to him. But go ahead."

"His wife says she thinks either the Soviet government or the Chinese had him killed."

"I would have said Walter was one of their best friends in this country. He made such a mockery out of Red scares and investigations, he had McCarthy moving so grotesquely, everything that whole crowd did was unserious and ludicrous. He was certainly never any danger to the Russians or the Chinese, for heaven's sake. A lot of people got the feeling that if Walter and McCarthy and that gang were against the Communists, that they must be all right. I say that with hindsight, seven years after it was really fashionable to carry on as Walter did."

"What would Mrs. Slurrie's own position be in this case?"

"You mean as the killer? Out of the question. An impossibility, Lieutenant. The fact that the Slurrie's two sons were not his children might indicate some difference between Walter and his wife. She could have resented that Walter couldn't give her children and that he forced her to turn elsewhere but that stuff is for psychologists, and at any rate it is academic because Walter told us this afternoon – well, yesterday afternoon – that his wife was at home in Dallas."

"Who is the father of the Slurrie children?"

"Cardozo, the business partner."

"There could be a joint motive?"

Coffey shrugged.

"How about Horace Hind?"

"Hind could have had it done. God knows he has the money. But Walter was the only man Hind trusted. Walter was Hind's lawyer. But Hind is – ah – too remote. He doesn't live in this world."

"How did Slurrie stand with you and you with Slurrie?"

16

"We've been friends for almost thirty years. We've made each other prosper. We didn't agree on everything, but we agreed on most things."

"Tell me about Slurrie and Cardozo."

"They were close business partners. But you could say they ran those sort of businesses. Even investigators might be hard put to find out what they were. You could say that Cardozo and me – and a man named Danzig – were Walter's only friends. Except his wife."

"Hind wasn't his friend?"

"Hind was his client."

"The Felsenburshes weren't his friends?" That was a shot in the dark.

He became cooler and more deliberate. "Walter Slurrie and the Felsenburshe family have never met. They have no place whatever in this investigation. I want you to believe me that that is a good thing for you to remember. It is an important and relevant statement from me."

"Slurrie had a relationship with them."

"Not with them. With their interests. I am the Felsenburshe political representative – in a way – actually I am a member of the in-house legal department. I scouted Walter on behalf of Felsenburshe enterprises because they are determined to encourage stable, nonradical candidates who are interested in government. Walter and I were school chums, so I was able to speak to him frankly about possible common interests with my own work. I see to the Felsenburshe family's interests just as Governor Betaut sees to their legal interests. In short, we protect the Felsenburshes. Is that clear?"

"Yes."

"Good. Then let's try to keep it that way."

"We were talking about Cardozo."

"Yes. Well, they had met years ago when Cardozo was on the fringes of the Mob in Miami. Cardozo has worked for Nudey Danzig much longer than he has been in business with Walter."

"What kind of work did he do for Danzig?"

"That's not my neighborhood. But I suppose the Miami police can help you there."

"Any reason for Cardozo to kill Slurrie?"

17

"I can't think of any. But they were sitting on a prodigious pile of money, remember. Walter Slurrie, who always cried the poor mouth, was a very wealthy man."

"How much?"

"Tens of millions. Maybe more. Cardozo holds and hides the money for Walter, in their own bank and in God knows how many dummy businesses. Whenever Walter wanted to buy something, such as an elaborate house or the New York apartment, he would apply to his own bank for a loan, then borrow his own money while he proclaimed to the press that it was breaking him. So, if they had a falling out over the money, then Cardozo would have a motive for killing Walter in order to obtain total control."

"So, a lot of people could have dreamed of killing Slurrie."

Coffey shrugged. "By and large, that's the way he affected people. And we haven't even mentioned Nudey Danzig yet. Danzig started Walter in Washington. Danzig put Walter into the Navy. Danzig started him in elective politics. Danzig put Walter at the head of that Wall Street law firm where he never handled a case. Danzig financed Walter's Red Crusade after Danzig had secured the congressional nomination for Walter in Texas. Danzig has made hundreds of millions for the Mob because he controlled Walter. He has saved the skins of labor leaders, caused mergers, gotten top defense contracts, fiddled with big income taxes and heaven knows what else because he controlled Walter. Walter put him at the top of the heroin industry indirectly. Danzig owned Walter. Danzig is also a known professional criminal and a killer. If Walter crossed Danzig, and I am not saying he did, then Nudey Danzig put out a contract on him."

"Jesus, I voted for Slurrie twice," I said.

"If you were one of those, Lieutenant, you probably would have even if you knew then what you know now. There is one other possibility we mustn't overlook. Not that you could touch them."

"No? Try me. Who?"

"The SP."

"Who?"

"The Secret Police of the United States of America. They had the greatest motive of all."

18

DATE: 10th August 1964
TIME: 7:26 A.M.
BASE REPORTING: Dallas   DSP (Semley) Only

MRS. WALTER SLURRIE

I told the children last night. I told them that the whole world
is as hurt and as heartbroken as we are. People die. That has to
be. Everyone accepts that. But they die, they aren't murdered. I
spoke to the police lieutenant in New York who is in charge of
the investigation. He said it is certain that Walter was murdered,
it couldn't have been suicide. But I can't get it through my head
that a man who was Vice-President of the United States, inside a
luxury apartment in the best section of one of the biggest cities
an hour after it was decided that he is going to be the next President of the United States, that a murderer could just walk in off
the street and shoot Walter down as if he lived in some cold-
water flat in some slum. I don't think so. I'm sorry. I asked that
police lieutenant whether he had checked out the SP and the FBI
and the State Department and the Department of Defense to get
their investigators and analysts working on who had to have
killed my husband. The murder has a Communist core because

19

Walter was the greatest enemy of Communism that they have ever faced, in peace or war. Walter actually invented the Communist issue in this country in 1947. Walter trained and coached and developed Joe McCarthy to take his place in the front line when Walter moved up to become Vice-President and to direct the Cold War. Walter was responsible for more Soviet and Chinese setbacks than any other force or individual. Their intelligence services are alert, you can be sure. Walter taught us that. They knew that their mightiest foe was being prepared, by the people who care in this country, to assume the Presidency in 1968 and they knew that would mean an end for a lot of worldwide plans for them.

I say that Walter died for us. He was murdered at the direction of either the Soviet government or the government of Red China. I hope there isn't going to be a cover-up on this. Walter often warned me it could happen. I have to say it. I feel compelled to tell you the truth.

Walter lived for his duty. He wasn't a happy man. I will never be sure whether he ever passed a single happy day. He talked to me. He told me all the things he had to say because he was never able to talk to anybody else because he had no way of being himself with anybody else.

I loved him. He never let me down. He never—not once—hurt me, or raised his voice or did anything that we know other men do to their wives. He had big problems but he had a big heart. This country woke up this morning realizing what a great man they have lost forever because they didn't value him enough to protect him. He never got back what he gave this country every minute of his life.

Walter loved me and I am proud to say he trusted me, a unique acceptance by Walter. He might tell Charley Coffey what was on his mind politically. He could tell Eddie Cardozo what he wanted to say about business. He was like a son to Nudey Danzig, no matter what certain people might like to make out of that. Nudey Danzig is a man of honor, just as Walter was, and they knew what it meant to have enemies. Walter could talk anti-Communism with a man as powerful as Horace Riddle Hind, one of the richest and most glamorous men of his generation. But, about the things that lived deep inside his heart, Walter was only able to talk to me. He went through life thinking that he was a greatly disliked man, something on which I would never agree because Walter had courage and character. He didn't know the meaning

20

of fear and he had to work to earn every cent to pay for his education.

My husband was the oldest surviving of five brothers and I think that could have given Walter a morbid cast of mind. After he passed the bar (number 103 among the 178 people who took the examinations) he was taken on immediately by an old-line law firm in Lubbock, Texas—O'Connell & Chambliss. He had no connections. He got that job on merit, to do divorce work and land development cases. I tell you this so that you will know how brave he was. He told me, weeping—and they were the real tears, not the kind he could pump out for the media and when you were as close to anyone as I was to Walter you can certainly tell the difference—he said he never understood almost anything to do with the practice of the law. The entire *thing* baffled him. But he rose above that darkness, something which takes enormous character.

Walter knew that the practice of law was the only shortcut to success in this country. He based his entire credibility as a politician on having been a lawyer. He just put his faith in old Dean Coomber's back-up procedural books. Walter was always grateful to Dean Coomber.

Everything Walter accomplished he did by himself. "I did it my way" he would sing in the shower after days when he and Eddie had made a particularly good deal. That spirit from a man whose father had deserted the family many years before, when Walter was a little boy of ten! Walter's mother, who lives in El Paso and whom I don't know very well, kept the family together with a scratchy little grocery that sold seconds and damaged can goods to the Mescalero Indians around the Salopado foothills. They had been brave warriors once, Walter often told me, but our breakfast foods and other nutritional disadvantages had softened their teeth, causing them to drink too much. The store was on the ground floor of a house on a knoll over an irrigation ditch. Walter hated that house. It couldn't have been an easy life. Walter said he didn't mind the work—he loved honest work—but he resented its lack of promise. But he found a way. He made it to Texas Tech on a Religious Minorities scholarship—he posed as a Druid—and later when we married we planned a Conservationist ceremony (though it didn't quite work out) because Walter had a great respect for the ecology and knew that was a sound stand politically. Politics were never too far from Walter's mind.

His yearbook picture at Texas Tech said in its caption that

when Walter smiled it looked as if he had bitten into a cupcake full of thumbtacks. That was a joke because they didn't know Walter the way he let me know him. He had many kinds of smiles. All of them except one were pained, forced smiles that he dealt to all the strangers in his life. His real smile, which he kept only for us—for me, the two boys, and Eddie—was really a wonderful, sunny, almost open thing to see. No one could have resisted that smile. It was filled with much of the love that made up Walter.

Walter earned thirty dollars a week at his peak as a lawyer in Lubbock, possibly more than Abraham Lincoln made in Illinois. Walter gave twenty dollars of that to his mother. He would tell me when we were alone that, from the time he was able to understand what money meant, he knew that only money would ever free him from his slavery in that scratchy little grocery store. He explained to himself that he was not meant by God to live out his life in a used food store selling to scruffy Indians in west Texas. Not that he didn't love Texas! Oh, quite the contrary.

Walter admitted to me that his family's total dependence on those poor, ragged Indians was what made him hate blacks, Mexicans, Catholics, Jews, and foreigners. The only explanation for that one weakness in his character is that since he rarely ever saw anyone but very poor Indians when he was in his forming years, and only heard about people like blacks, Catholics, Jews, and foreigners from his father, well, although Walter despised the poor, he hated poverty more, if you get the distinction. Poverty was not just a vote-catching issue for Walter. It had real meaning, going back to his childhood.

Walter's mother was such a driven woman that he told me she never smiled once during the years he lived in Salopado. He had to resort to pranks to make her react. He would drop a ten-pound sack of flour on her from the loft above the store's counter, then, as she crashed to the floor, he would drop from the loft window, sprint around to the front of the house, and go running through the front doorway of the store to be fulfilled as she called out weakly for help.

An example of his stick-to-itiveness: when he was a freshman at Texas Tech he found a little paperback book from Racine, Wisconsin, called *Magic Tricks With Cards.* Even years later Walter could make playing cards do anything he wanted them to do and, no matter how odd it may sound to you when you first hear this—before I can explain his point of view on it—Walter was able to work his way through Texas Tech on what he earned at poker games because of the skills he had taught himself. This was not cheating. Walter worked as long as four hours every night to master the effects in that little manual, rehearsing with the cards until his fingers ached. If the other players in that poker game had had Walter's will-to-win enough to sacrifice their time for it the way Walter had, they too could have worked their way through college by games of chance.

I was telling you how well Walter could weep at will. He said it was just a knack he had that he discovered could be used to emphasize many points he was trying hard to make in politics We had many a good laugh when the media would write about Walter's "wounded eyes." Walter was an actor everywhere but at home.

After he joined O'Connell & Chambliss in Lubbock, Walter was able to put aside over seven thousand dollars from the weekly poker game held by the poultry and cotton shippers and the cheese producers of the region in the backroom of McCarry's Pharmacy. Counting what was left out of his salary after he had paid his mother, on the day he left for Washington he had banked over nine thousand dollars thanks to *Magic Tricks With Cards.* Walter was determined not to be poor and he never let himself down in that resolve.

Walter's mother had wanted him to go into the grocery business with her, and she put up a lot of resistance to his going to Texas Tech, but as hard as it was for him to say it, he flatly refused to relive her life and Father's. It was hard for Walter to comprehend Mother's attitude to higher education. She had been a junior at college when she met Father, a day laborer who worked in the irrigation ditches. Not that Walter was ever ashamed of him for that. Mother and Father married almost as soon as they met. Walter told me it was common talk about Father that he could not so much as dance with a person of the opposite sex without becoming sexually aroused beyond self-control. And Mother loved dancing. In any event it was Walter's private feeling (expressed only to me) that Mother could not have respected education or she would not have married Father.

Two months after the Japanese struck at Pearl Harbor, Walter acted. He loved his country above all else, he explained to me, but he did not wish to jeopardize his place at the Texas bar by being drafted into an army of citizen-soldiers. He told me that many young lawyers, instead of reasoning that their specialist

23

educations should cause their government to use them as soldier-lawyers, would just find themselves in the trenches and need to undress and bathe in the same room with a lot of burly, sweaty men like Father.

Walter was the second most fastidious man I ever knew. He also hated the crass and the physical. Also, he knew it would be very wrong if that were permitted to happen to him. So he wrote to his old roommate at law school, Charley Coffey, who was then at the U.S. Marine boot camp at Cherry Point. I have Walter's letter right here in the file. Let me read it to you, just the pertinent part.

It is not if I would ever shirk my duty. It is not, and we may be sure of this, that I have any fear of combat or of death. It is solely because my country is in danger and, since it has been made crystal-clear as to where my own skills exist after arduous training and professional experience as a lawyer, to serve my country best I write to you in an unashamed and forthright manner to ask if you would ask The Leader, for me, if he can see it within his power to cause me to be cast into a wartime role where my skills as a lawyer may best serve this blessed nation.

It worked out as Walter said God meant it to work out, except the end. Charley was able to set Walter in the Interpretations Unit of the legal section of the Tire Rationing Division of the Office of Price Administration in Washington. It was no easy berth for a man as uneasy about his footing in the law as Walter was. Dean Coomber had not published a back-up book on how to interpret tire rationing. Walter was totally at sea but, as he told me and I certainly agreed with him, it was better than having a Jap grenade explode under his privates or having to undress in front of all those hairy, smelly men.

DATE: 10th August 1964
TIME: 8:10 A.M.
BASE REPORTING: Miami   DSP (Semley) Only

EDWARD CARDOZO

Lemme tell joo one thing. If I ever get my hans on the bahstair who kill Wullair I am firsz gun estoff him opp his own *culo*, then I am gun work on him with a axe. When you buss jawr ahss with a man for twenny years then some cogswawker come in an hit him you blow your rug. Oh, jess. It walk up an kick the cheat out of me. How coo anyone do that to one of the greatest Americans of this century? I am gun tell you everything I know because not only is Wullair *el honcho de los honchos* but I also think you slip something in the coffee to make me talk.

A long time ago, in 1942, Harry Danzig call me in Larranaga's office at the dogs. He tell me Nudey, the boss, his *hijo*, want to see me in the coffeeshop of the Jakarta Motel, North Miami, eleven the next morning. I can feel this is beeg chance for me. I been honggeen arronn maybe twelve years, since I was a li'l *pachuquito* from Aguascalientes who swim across the river honggeen on the shirt of his father when I am six years old. I am in Miami since my whole life after that an I am not even a Cuban. So I

25

dress opp with my white suit an my brown-an-white shoes an a brown-an-white tie and a Panama hat like I am a fahkeen yacht owner.

I wait in front, at the counter, an talk to the little gorl who bring the food. I can see she like me and I am practically ready to ask her if she would like to make *pinche* with me some night when Harry stan up at the back an call me over to the booth. Nudey an Harry just come donnstairs fron the big Wednesday meeting when Nudey split the skim from Vegas, an the Caribbean. Every week Nudey's end is abaht four hunnerd gran, everybody know that. When Nudey come donnstairs it mean that the courier leave for New York where what is left is gun get cut again until some little pieces go to Chicago an Cleveland.

Harry is an old frenna mine from when I run a crap game with his okay. He get me the heart trouble papers which keep me out of the draft. He get me the laundromat territory for Nudey's numbers in North Miami. I go right back to the booth. I stan beside the table until Nudey tell me to sit donn because I want to espress that I am *caballero*.

He tell me to sit donn an have a glass of tea. "You are a neat dresser," he say to me. "A jacket is an important item no matter how hot out."

The gorl bring the tea an leave.

"I talked to Al Carifoli," Nudey say. "He thinks you might be right to front up a shopping center for us." The real name of Al Carifoli is Schmalowitz but sometime it pay to make people think joo are a Sicilian. I smile at Nudey an nod my head.

"But that's later," Nudey tell me. "Harry told you to come over here because used tires are gonna be very big. I want you to go to Washington for me an look around. Take your time. Get it right. But the sooner the better."

"I unnerstan one hunnerd per cen'."

"Harry will tell Dom G. to set you with a nice place. Make friends with some smart little broad in Used Tires at the OPA so she can set you with the paper handlers there. I wanna bring in some tires from Cuba."

"Whatever joo say, Nudey."

"Do a nice job an I'll talk to Carifoli."

I drink a glassa gwatter. I don like tea.

When I go to Washington the next night I take with me twelve dozen pairs of nylons in all the sizes and colors. Dom. G. put me in a nice apartmen with a li'l bar, 2101 Connecticut Avenue. Maybe some people coo find booze, gas, steaks or sugar while the war, but nobody but Nudey coo find nylons. Even without nylons I am lucky. Women like me. But even if they decide they hate me, they are gun fall in love with the nylons.

Dom G. knew a gorl who turn tricks on the side but who was a typewriter in the day in the OPA pool. I take her to dinner at Dom's place, then I screw her, give her some nylons, then let her pass me to a li'l redhead who is in the Tires section. She is Betsy Ginzler. She is secretary to the head honcho for Tires in the whole Southeast.

"Walter Slurrie is your man, all right," she say to me. "Too bad he don't wear nylons."

"Jussa same, *niña*," I tell her, "maybe he nidd a frizzer full of esteaks or a twenny poun' bag of esugar."

"I doubt it, Eddie."

"How come?"

"This is the most suspicious fella I ever saw. He is convinced everybody in Washington is a Jew. Starting with Roosevelt."

"Joo espend a lot of time with him?"

"All day."

"No. I mean . . ."

"After work?"

"*Si.*"

"Eddie, he hates OPA people. He says everybody is always angling for something."

"What does *he* want?"

"Everything movable."

"He sound like a rill country boy."

"Correcto profundo."

"He likes you?"

"It's very hard to say. I couldn't even tell you if he likes steak."

"I want to mitt him."

"Listen, Eddie—"

"For six pair esheer gun metal, long length nylons, I want to mitt him."

"I don't think he goes out with *any*body."

"You can figure it out."

"Well, maybe if you threw a party or something and had somebody there as bait . . ."

"What is bait?"

"Slurrie gets drunk on names. Not names to you or even to my kid cousin—but like a Coast Guard bandmaster? Or a fellow who works in the White House garage?"

"How about a senator?"

"He would cream."

"Where this *maravilla* come from?"

"West Texas, he says. But this one has to be a liar."

"Amarillo?"

"He says Lubbock. A lubbock sounds like a Yiddish word for loafer. You sound very well connected, Eddie. That's very nice."

"It's a living."

A fonny thing I never get Ginzler off my mind. She stand like a li'l *reina*. She never bother about thinking, which is very good in a woman. Sex is important to her. Her eyes are the part. Her eyes look at herself the way she would like to be someday, not right now. Her body was the only small thing about Ginzler. It vibrate. It send out promises that she will only feel the things which are *monumental* but she don know yet which is *monumental* an which is *nada*.

I call Harry from Washington an tell him I could use a congressman. Harry set everything with Dom G.

On the day of the Used Tires fiesta, Dom G. send over a whole case of New Jersey champagne, a big roass beef with a *gato* to carve it, a nize, li'l wayress, two hookers for decoration, the ambassador from Haiti and Congressman Ueli Munger from West Texas.

Ginzler deliver Slurrie. He is wearing a black body bag, which make him look like he rent it at the morgue. Ginzler look *estupendo* in a gold dress which I get Dom G. to borrow from a gorl her size.

The Used Tires *espantando* stand in a corner like a marzipan trademark at a candy convention, while the men cluster aronn the two hookers an Ginzler cluster aronn the men. She tell me later that Used Tires cannot move because he is so impress to look on his own congressman. But he is careful not to look at the Haitian ambassador. He was in shock that a *negro* coo be invited to a Washington party with such distinguish people. Poor fellow. He celebrate his own joylessness. Life got to be serious with him to have a meaning. Hoppiness is jost something they estoff inside a song.

28

I move Congressman Munger over to the Used Tires department.

"So y'all ur from Salopado?" the congressman say to him, *muy harto,* with a black moustache.

"Yes, sir," Wullair say.

"Rancher or are you in the cheese bidniz?"

"No, sir. My family are the fine grocery distributors for the region. I'm just a country lawyer."

"One of the Lubbock firms?"

"Yes, sir. O'Connell & Chambliss."

"No kiddin'? Heard they had a young lawyer over there who was almost disbarred."

Wullair get very red, very quick.

"Before my time," Wullair say.

I say to Wullair, "You make me very honor that you come to this li'l party tonight, counselor," which is the signal to Dom G. to move the congressman back to the two hookers.

"I am sincerely happy to be here, Mr. Cardozo," Wullair say to me. "I really enjoy the occasional Washington gathering."

"Well, you with a rill lady. We have much respeck for Miss Betsy Ginzler. Her Dad is quite a man—as you know." That should set Betsy with the OPA. He is very impress. "Yes," he say, "oh, yes. He is quite a man."

The wayress hand me a plate of beef an a *copa.* I give it to Wullair. He dig in like he is not itt since Christmas. "Call me Kiddo," I tell him. "Everybody call me Kiddo."

"Are you—ah—related to the late, great Justice Cardozo—ah—Kiddo?"

"Distantly. What kind of work joo do at the Navy Departmen, Wullair?"

"No. I am with the Interpretations Unit at Tire Rationing, Used Tires Division, of the OPA."

I go in like a cannonball for Nudey.

"OPA? Well, well. I know the whole gang over there. If there is anything I can do for you at OPA, Wullair, joo got to call me. Any frenn of the dotter of Biff Ginzler is a frenna mine."

"I suppose you know them all at the Navy Department, too," Wullair ask me experimentally.

I shrug. "Is that kind of tonn," I say.

The wayress bring more meat and wine. I take the empty plate and glass from Wullair an give him the new estack.

29

"Thank you—Kiddo. Who is the colored man?"

"That is the Haitian ambassador. Very rich, an very French, although he do a terrific American accent." Armand was the fry cook at Dom G's place.

"Fine tailoring," Wullair say, an he chomp the meat again. I see he is scheming. All I got to do is wait.

After dinner Wullair tell Ginzler he got a toothache an he wonder if is all right he don't take her home. "That would be terrific, Walter," she tell him with genuine pleasure. As soon as Wullair leave, Dom G. get everybody out with what is left of the case of champagne, then Ginzler and me take a shower together before we get in the sack. After a while Ginzler say, "He is taking off his shoes now, wondering how he is going to surround you."

"I give him all the openings."

"He probably wants to be an FBI man. He is exactly the type."

"I think maybe the Navy Departmen."

"Not a chance. Walter knows a fellow could get killed that way."

"We not gun have a long gwait to fine out." I turn off the light.

"I like it better with the lights on, Eddie," she say. "Is that all right?"

I switch it on again.

"Eddie?"

"Si, niña?"

"Would you mind wearing your shirt and tie when you do it tonight?"

"Como no?"

"I'm a pervert maybe. But, you know, it appeals to me."

"Listen, it's okay. If that's how you like it, that's how we do it."

At the water cooler the next day, Wullair ask Ginzler if she could have lunch with him an she almoss drop her paper cup.

"Why?" she ask him.

"I would like to show my appreciation for last night," he tell her.

She can't figure it out. She know a lunch will have to coss him abaht five dollar but when they leave the building he tell her how crowded all the restaurants are an that itting outside is like a picnic so he buy them two ham sandwich an two milk an they itt on a bench where he tell her, she swear he say it, "Hitler is not as bad as people say. He is only trying to get a little more room for his people."

"Or maybe less people in the room he already has," she tells him. "Are you trying to kid me, Walter? Hitler is a fucking monster."

She say he make a big face when she use that language an I don blame him.

"Well, perhaps personally that is true about Hitler," he tell her. "I wouldn't know. Historically, he is only trying to get justice after the treaty of Versailles."

"Why should you be for Hitler?" she ask him.

"Because life is unfair," he say.

"Are we going to sit out here in this cold wind and talk chit like this, Walter?"

He changed the subject right away because he can't stan the language an I don't blame him. He tell her how I am a great admirer of Biff Ginzler.

"Biff Ginzler?" she say, then she catch on that I must have a rizzon for the con. Wullair cross-examine her abaht me an she tell him I am a very imporrant lobbyist. He tell her he don wan to go over her head to her father's frenss but that he rilly had to see me and would she set it up?

"So call him."

"Well, a man like Kiddo . . ."

"Come *on*, Walter."

"You have no objections?"

"What do I have to do with it?"

"Will you give me his phone number?"

"Certainly."

"I am very grateful to you, Betsy. And I want to say that when I leave the OPA I am going to put a very complimentary letter in your efficiency file."

"Gee, thanks," she tell him. "I really appreciate that. A lot of guys would have just sent me a quart of perfume."

Ginzler and me got a good laugh out of that. "He is a rill hick," I say.

"Well, Eddie, I don't know what you want from him but you've got it."

"Where you gun put all the nylons, baby?"

"He needs a favor bad and I hope that's good news for you."

"I think you like me, Betsy."

"I like you."

"I like you," I say to her. "Allow me to tell you that I mean it." I don remember anybody who get to me more than that little *chica.*

Wullair call the next morning, a Sarrurday. We were asleep. It was only like five to nine.

"What?"

"Ah—Kiddo? This is Walter Slurrie? At the OPA?"

"Yeah?"

"I was thinking about your—ah—kind offer?"

"Yeah?"

"You said—at your very enjoyable dinner party the other evening that if—ah—I ever needed counsel I should call on you."

I grin at Ginzler, the sleeping angel. Well, I have score for Nudey. I throw my legs out of the bed. I say to the phone, "If you nidd help, I am honor that you call. Any frenn of Elizabeth Ginzler is a frenn of mine."

Betsy open her eyes but she don say nothing.

"Be in the lobby of the Carlton at a quorr to one," I tell him. "We grab lunch an talk." I hang up.

Ginzler roll over in bed. "Eddie?"

"Digame, niña."

"You wanna fool around?"

"Today is different," I tell her. "Wullair wan to do business so I stan in the chower for a while an get my head clirr."

"That's okay. Boy, that Walter. What a schemer."

He sit on the edge of the chair in the Carlton lobby staring at Bernard Baruch, who was way over on the other side. Wullair look like he sit at the center of the worl, three blocks from the White House, in the classiest hotel in tonn, in the capital of the whole enchilada, in the middle of the big war. He jump out of his chair when he see me. The way he shake my hand I decide he must sell life insurance on the side.

Wullair was a hick so I order red wine with the lunch to hypnotize him. I never see a man itt the way Wullair itt.

A long time later he tell me since he was in Washington he live mostly on hot dogs which he like very much. He get a wholesale contract for the franks through the Meat Prices Interpretations Unit at the office. He also itt cabbage an store cheese an he use

32

ketchup to make a second vegetable because he want the diet to balance. He eat the same thing every day for two years because he want to save his money so he can put it in a two-a-week poker game.

We finish the lunch. I light a *puro*. "What's up, Wullair?" I ask him.

I look at this guy an I can't treat him bad because no matter wha hoppen to him he is never gun know anything about the real life. He is a big, dopey blond guy who sit there like he done something bad, but his eyes say to you that he deen know he done anything bad, they tell you he don know if he done good or bad. All he has between himself and the real world is *mucho formale*. That is never enough.

"May I speak to you sincerely, Kiddo?" he say to me.

I personally never answer that kind of question.

"In my determination to leave the OPA—they are all Jews over there and everyone is trying to grab something for himself—I am not turning my back on the legal profession. I have to make that understood. I will never do that, Kiddo. The law is everything to me."

"A good field," I say.

"Rather—if I may expand this thought, and it is my sincere belief that this thought is worth expanding—rather I would like to continue to use my skills as a lawyer but—and this is important—but I would like to see those skills used more directly to help win this terrible conflict which has overtaken mankind than I can see them presently being utilized by the OPA, if you see what I mean."

"I don follow you, Wullair."

"I have this gut feeling, Kiddo. I cannot—simply *cannot*—waste the years that were poured into my highly specialized education at a time when my country needs as many lawyer-warriors as it can muster."

"Wullair—what joo *want*?"

He take a deep breath, then he say, "I want a commission in the Navy, which would let me use my gifts as a lawyer to benefit our fleet in the Pacific."

"Not in the Atlantic?"

He shake his head. "When the war is over people will think more glamorously of the Pacific, perhaps because of the South Sea islands."

"I am not gun to tell joo tha this cannot be done, Wullair," I

33

say, "but I got to say to joo that life iss very fonny. Here joo nidd a very, very big favor while—at the same time—*quel coincidencia*—I hoppen to nidd a li'l favor which joo can do for me."

"Mutual agency," he sing to me.

"Wha?"

"How can I help you, Kidd? What little favor? Go ahead. Just try me."

"I nidd a li'l muscle over at Used Tires."

"Used Tires?" he cry out with joy, "why—but that's my *command*! I am in *charge* of Used Tires."

"Joo are?"

"Yas, yas."

"How abott that? Well, I have the chance to bring in some very good tires from Cuba and that can help a lot of Americans, believe me. But the OPA says strict controls an to hell with the pipple."

"You are talking about my *domain*, Kiddo."

"I just nidd a li'l help. I am okay in Miami. I have four good *amigos* on the Dade County Defense Council Allocation Board."

"As I recall, there are only four members on that board."

"Oh, jess. But they nidd approvals from Washington."

TO: FIRST DEPUTY COMMISSIONER VIN-
CENT J. MULSHINE

FROM: LIEUTENANT RICHARD GALLA-
GHER, 17th HSQ

We have received 194 "confessions" to
the Slurrie murder from different parts of
the country.

The Dallas police questioned Mrs.
Walter Slurrie at her house.

Mrs. Slurrie confirmed that Edward
Cardozo and her husband were unequal
partners (Slurrie 70 percent, Cardozo 30
percent) in a wide variety of businesses
that involved the ownership of a number

of cash bank accounts, the values of which were not stated.

Mrs. Slurrie readily confirmed that Edward Cardozo was the father of her two children, although she told me that she had confidence that neither her husband nor Edward Cardozo would have given that information and that she would not. She asked me who had told me. I explained that everything to do with private information obtained through police investigations could not be divulged. She asked me how could anyone leap to such a conclusion then. I said perhaps the children resembled Mr. Cardozo. She smiled broadly and said that was very good instant detective work, that the children were quite the images of Mr. Cardozo. She asked me how the information we had discussed about the business partnership and the children would be or could be interpreted from a police standpoint.

I said the facts could confirm her position and Mr. Cardozo's position high on the list of suspects. Mrs. Slurrie said she would explain to me why that was impossible if I would explain to her how such suspicions could take shape.

I said, "Suppose only the two partners knew what all the assets of all their holdings were, and where the assets were situated for reasons of taxation, possible illegalities, and political considerations. Also suppose you and Edward Cardozo, father of your children, saw that you could obtain all of these assets, in cash and otherwise, by murdering your husband."

"That is tidy enough as far as it goes," Mrs. Slurrie said. "But the value and whereabouts of my husband's assets held jointly with Mr. Cardozo are listed, item by item, in my husband's will, which leaves his entire estate, with minor exceptions, to my two sons, whom he saw as his own sons. That will left me an annual income of $150,000 a year plus our two houses. Edward Cardozo was my husband's devoted friend. He could gain nothing from my husband's death. Then, there is also the question of my availability. I was in a community center meeting at Vizcaya Cove with fifteen or more other people at the time Walter was murdered."

We will follow up on all of this information and check it out without delay.

36

DATE: 10th August 1964
TIME: 7:30 A.M.
BASE REPORTING: New York

DSP (Semley) Only

CHARLES COFFEY (continued)

Walter Slurrie knew politics as he sidled out of the womb, picking his nose and resenting the world. He knew, to make an unlikely parallel, that all effective political action is like bringing a woman to orgasm. There aren't any orgasm-producing nerves in the vagina of politics either, it is the indirect pressure that does the trick. Walter was born knowing where to apply the pressure using the tool of the lowest common denominator.

I've been in politics all my life starting with practical, straight-ticket politics in midtown New York. My father was a Municipal Court judge in the 30s, a hard-line Tammany man like his father and grandfather before him. Pop was a stocky, pie-faced man with straight white hair parted in the middle as if he had done it with a piece of pink chalk. It made him look as if he had been packed in two halves, my brother Dennis always said. Dennis repeated the same few banal things all his life. He was a dull fellow and a pain-in-the-ass. My mother was dead by the time Walter spent those few days with us, allowing Dennis to repeat again, "When you are dead for a second it doesn't matter how long," always concluding with, *"Finito la musica."*

The way Mom died was typical of the way she had lived. Dennis and I were nineteen and eighteen respectively when the roof of the church in Queens fell in on her while she was on retreat with St. Moganna's sodality. Dennis said (frequently) that the event had changed his life. Dennis and Mom were fairly doctrinaire people. Not Pop. Pop, maintaining shifting bases of comparison of everything with everything else, on a *quid pro quo* basis, always knew where the cash drawer was in any burning building. Nothing panicked him. He would figure that he had wasted his life if he didn't know the guy who could fix it.

We lived in a five-story brownstone house that Pop owned outright, on East 31st Street between 2nd and 3rd. My lifetime memory of the house is walking up and down the stairs on errands for Pop. Dennis said Pop made us do it as a way of paying rent, Pop not being able to accommodate anything that did not involve *quid pro quo*. Dennis would mumble that Pop ought to do his own stair climbing. "He oughta let his nose fly him up," Dennis (always) said. Pop had a nose like a pitted toy balloon. But some germ did it and I am not just saying that to be loyal.

Pop was an interesting man. He had dozens of phobias, not all of them known to me. He would never pass a bathroom door by walking at right angles to it. As he approached the door he would turn so that his front faced the door, then sidle past it, staring at it warily. When Dennis asked him about it, Pop tossed a glass of beer over him by way of explanation.

In 1935 I was twenty-five years old, the same age as Walter Slurrie. I had been graduated from Fordham and I was studying at Coomber Law College in Malthus, New Jersey, where, Pop said, one of the great dental chewing gums had been made. Walter Slurrie was my roommate at Coomber, which offered a "pragmatic" approach to passing bar examinations: advanced memory techniques backed up by "special" law books. Just say that Coomber was a specialist sort of law school with advanced grind techniques and no discussion, debate, or theory. Old Richard Coomber was a natural born publisher but, being an extremely devious man, this was how he made his way round to selling books. The entire college was contained in one building that looked like a car barn at the end of a suburban tram line. The building had a red tin roof, which could cook up intense interior heat in the late spring.

Walter came from Salopado, Texas. Years later my wife told me that *salopado* means sneaky in Spanish, so the town definitely left its mark on Walter. Not that he would have anything to do with Spanish. He feared and despised everything that wasn't American, such as blacks, for instance, who were Africans to Walter. Jews were Litvaks. Chicanos were South Americans, and all foreigners, in a threatening way, were Communists to Walter excepting Irish and German people—to a certain extent.

Walter detested people no matter where they came from. He never lost that. As he advanced in politics he reserved his most scourging vengeance for the American people. Walter despised all people so deeply that ultimately he had to charge them very large anounts of money for having to associate with them and, even more, to represent them in their governments. There were qualifications. He hated me except when he could use me. He loved his wife as a woman (his mother had been a woman, he told me), yet that was hardly Walter's highest rating. He liked his two sons. He loved his two business partners. He would do anything for those five people if it didn't cost him money.

Walter was as easy to dislike as he said other people were. He had a grating West Texas voice, so close to being a Gullah cum Aleutian dialect that it could be incomprehensible. He was very tall, with sharp bones like lookouts—front, rear, and sides. He shambled when he walked, always smelled a little gamy, and when I roomed with him for the sixteen months course to get a (Coomber) law degree he wore a marigold-yellow Zapata moustache. He looked like a hick because he was a hick. A funny thing was, in later life, whenever he controlled who was to photograph him, as often as possible he hired a broken-down, poor-mouth, whining ex-*Time-Life* staffer who looked and sounded (around those horrendous West Texas raw edges) just like Walter, cowboy moustache and all.

Pop made me go to Coomber Law College. I suppose everybody but Walter had an alibi for going there at all. Pop said, "The main thing is to qualify for your profession, which is politics. A law degree, or let's say a license to practice law, gives you great clout with the sources of power in this country. Power isn't what seems to make things happen but the voice that ordered those

39

things to happen. You just pass the bar, that's all, Charley. Politics will take care of the rest." He asked me if I wanted to throw away four years at some regular law school when I knew I was never going to practice law anyway. "You bet your bottom dollar you don't," he answered for me.

Pop was a self-made lawyer and he did pretty well. When he was thirteen years old he started as a law clerk/messenger boy in the old St. Paul building near City Hall with specialists in Papal law, Engelson & Knauerhase, who got rota divorces for rich Catholics, and knew every Cardinal in southern Germany and Poland on the intimate pronoun basis. Pop qualified for the bar when he was twenty. Not that he practiced much law after that. His Tammany district leader, the legendary tennis innovator, Big Tom Buckley, set him on a letterhead with twenty-six other "lawyers" in a firm that did special work for the city. After that the organization ran him for Alderman, then sent him to Albany as an Assemblyman, made him Motor Vehicle Commissioner, then State Bill Drafting Commissioner, then got him elected to the Municipal Court, where he served the Party for eleven years. What with his salary and this-and-that, Pop cleared about $35,000 a year before the dollar went off the gold standard and they sent it off to the wars.

The Tammany district clubhouse was uptown from our house, at 53rd and 1st Avenue. The Party wanted to make a real show of power in 1935 to impress Franklin Roosevelt with how much he was going to need them in '36. Pop said to me, "It's gonna be a real push this year, Charley. Margaret Feeney told me they're layin' out two grand to bring hoodlums up from the Lower East Side, and the Honest Ballot Association boys have agreed to look the other way, she says."

Margaret Feeney was the invisible secretary to both the Fire Commissioner and the Parks Commissioner at $8,200 a year from each job which she never went near. She also had the doorknob concession for all city and state buildings. In more ways than one if you wanted to get a door open you had to see Margaret. She also expedited getting licenses to use the city tennis courts in the parks, as a wholesale source naturally.

The District Leader was a bumbler. "He's no Tom Buckley," Pop said, "but he's like a dowsing rod when it comes to gettin' money in. That counts, of course, but thank God for Margaret's brain. It keeps us goin'." Margaret asked Pop to tell me to bring along "another young lawyer" as a volunteer worker on Election

Day. "Young lawyers are good for this," was her theory, "because the voters think they can trust them. If there was a way to do it I'd use priests."

Pop wrote this to me at Coomber. He did not believe in telephoning because of the electricity. Pop never touched electricity if he could help it because he knew it could cause cancer. He had me (and Dennis) to turn on the lights in the house. Pop sat under an awning in the parlor because of the electricity flowing through the house. He was sure the electricity had turned his hair prematurely white. When he was forced to use the telephone or to flip on a wall switch he wore a barbecue mitten.

It took some negotiating for me to get Walter into New York as a volunteer because he resisted spending money. New York City was only 42 miles from Coomber but Walter had never been there, even though he had never seen a big city in his life, because he could not make sense out of spending money for the journey. I explained that the clubhouse would pay him five dollars for the two days and that I would pay half of his bus fare. He would stay at our house in New York so there would be no cost to him for meals or rooms. The largesse offered made Walter suspicious of me and Tammany Hall. Dean Coomber had told Walter he was the most suspicious student ever to attend the law school, itself a wary nest of paranoids determined to get something for nothing so they could worry about the consequences. Walter never entered a room without looking up at the top of the door to check whether someone had balanced a bucket of water up there to deluge him. He said such a thing had not happened to him personally but that he had read about it. The Chinese box effect was that Walter wasn't protecting himself or his clothes, he was protecting his dignity. Walter's dignity was his most precious possession. He stood vigil over it like a sea lion protecting cubs. Walter had two other qualities, I now see: bleakness and concealed grief. With the cloying hindsight I now possess I think it was Walter's grief for his future. He dreamed enormous dreams but he seemed to understand that, no matter how close he might approach them the malevolent thing which would always stand in the way of his ever finding them would be himself. Walter seemed to know too well what he was. He was morbid and unhappy but his rejection of suicide (which his deeply depressed presence suggested was an act his dignity would never permit him to commit) forced the alternative: he seemed to be plotting to cause outside forces to destroy him.

41

As a young man Walter was as awkward then as when he became Vice-President. He worked desperately to gain control of his physical movement, which continually threatened his dignity. He stood like a policeman over his faltering coordination but control eluded him. Walter was too self-conscious to be self-contained.

Coomber Law College had been reconstructed within into a beehive design, so that the greatest number of students could be packed into the available space. We left our cells only when we were required to eat. We were there to learn how to pass state bar examinations in sixteen months of legal education. The walls of each cell were hexagonal, fitting into the other identically shaped rooms at all sides and on different levels. There were catwalks along inner sides of the interior walls. Dean Coomber's wife had run off with the architect of this contraption.

We were penned in that room. When we weren't swotting we were talking politics. Walter loved to talk politics, and in those days he got them wrong. He would say, "One of these days the right man will be elected President and the newspapers are going to be taken in hand and controlled by a government that really cares about free speech. Do you think European countries, which have a damned sight longer history of freedom, don't keep control over their newspapers?"

"You're as half-baked on that as you are on everything else," I'd say." In Europe most newspapers began as platforms for political parties or for Catholics who considered themselves a minority. They're just a business proposition here. Do you think any politician could tell those merchants how to run their business? Or would you want it that way?"

"Newpapers have got to be taught respect for authority. Hitler has their respect in Germany and he's only been in office for two years. Mussolini has their total respect. Our papers act as if they were the masters."

"What would you do?"

"Well—I'd take over radio and put it under the post office department where it belongs. They even do that in England, for heaven's sake. Then I'd make radio the principal news source by holding news back from the press. Then I'd give the people great entertainment on the radio but to get that they'd have to listen to my news."

"That will probably always be your trouble. You look at America and see Salopado, Texas."

After days of negotiations about whether or not he would go to New York with me, Walter accepted with grave pleasure. "I love to travel," he said expansively, considering that he had hardly ventured past Lubbock. "I prefer hitchhiking,. which is why I have accepted your one-way bus fare in cash. It is cheaper and, if you want to make real time on the highways you should dress the way any conservative automobilist might imagine Horatio Alger's heroes had dressed, clean, dark clothes, a sensible tie on a white shirt, and fedora hat, which you must take off as each safe, conservative-looking car approaches. I utilized everything but knickerbockers. I could have crossed this country in one-third less time if I had worn knickerbockers and high shoes."

"Why didn't you?"

"Where could I wear them afterward? In court? In my chambers? No, thank you."

"Don't you run into freaks, hitchhiking across the country?"

"Oh, well. Sometimes you get the unexpected love-that-has-no-name sort of driver but I can cope with that. I don't let that bother me."

Even then, Walter was a forceful and convincing actor who could weep on command. He had disciplined himself not to "mingle with women, at least until I have established myself in the practice of law." To practice law was Walter's great commitment. It meant everything to him. It made him more than his father had been or any of his brothers would ever be. With an intensity that is still painful for me to remember he would screw the seat of his pants into his desk chair in our tiny cell and stay there for as long as ten hours, learning the law by rote. He did it. He overcame those books. But he never gained the slightest understanding of law or what it stood for. He was able to follow neither its functions nor its meanings. He only knew that the license to practice it had advanced the ambitions of other people and he was determined to make it advance his.

The Sunday before the weekend Walter came to visit was a standout day. After Mass Pop called Dennis and me into his study, which had one window. He had hung a framed four-color reproduction of a painting by James Richard Blake of Ratti, who became Pope Pius XI, on a wall behind his desk. The Sacred

43

Heart of Jesus, in an imitation walnut frame complete with half walnut shells, hung on the wall facing him. Three (short) bookshelves held old almanacs, a Douay Bible, an incomplete set of Zane Grey, and back issues of *The Pullet*. There was no carpet and only hard, straight wooden chairs except for Pop's which was cushioned and comfortable. This was the room where Pop displayed his public self.

He flashed his nose at us under the straight, white, pink-parted hair. "You may remember," he said, dropping each word like a raw doughnut into hot fat, "how I have told you over the years about my boyhood friend, Eddie Tierney."

Dennis groaned just loud enough for Pop to hear him.

"As you well know," Pop continued, "Eddie Tierney was a man who lived out his life waiting for his father to die so that he could inherit the money. That's all he did with his life, and the father lived to be one hundred and one years old and was all over the radio for it. There was real money there once—the father made it in iron shovels—but having to support Eddie and the lazy sister for all the years certainly subtracted from the pile. Besides, the father was a horse better over the telephone. Nothing big, but it mounts up. Well, when Eddie was seventy-six years old—he was considerably older than me, with no skill for annything—the father died with nothin' to leave him or the sister because there was nothin' left. Eddie Tierney, I am ashamed to remember, committed the immortal sin of leppin' off the Weehawken Ferry, leavin' a note behind, blamin' Roosevelt. He was eighty-two years old. The sister had just dyed her hair red and she was seventy-nine, and I want to say that neither I, who was to have gotten 3 percent as executor of the father's estate, which Tom Buckley put me into, nor annyone else, could find it in their hearts to attend the funeral. Eddie Tierney was buried in Potter's Field, boys."

"I got to get uptown, Pop," Dennis said.

"No doubt," Pop answered. "Well, I am going to save you boys from the irreversible mortal sin that happened to Eddie Tierney. I gave this lots of thought, boys. Instead of having my two sons wait for me to die to get at the money, I would take another course."

I looked sideways at Dennis, wanting to cry out a warning.

"Are you going to give us the money now, Pop?" he asked, liked the dummy he was.

Pop looked across the desk at him, pitilessly. He waited until

Dennis was aware of the silence. "You are not gettin' a penny outta me, now or later," Pop told him. "Every cent I own, a matter of about a hundred and forty six thousand dollars, is goin' to the Sisters of the Precious Blood."

"Oh for Christ's sake," Dennis said appropriately.

"But I won't leave yiz out on the street. Whoever gets married first gets this house. The other one, and I think I know who that is, gets the chicken ranch in Jersey." Pop took his time lighting a big cigar. "I hope yizzle agree that I am doin' this for the sake of yer immortal souls but, whatever you think, that's the way it's gonna be."

"Well, I think you musta went nuts," Dennis said. "You must be some new kind of sadist—if I thought you knew what that meant."

"Whatever it means, it's better than what you are, son. Thank God your sainted mother never knew."

Dennis rushed out of the room repeating "Oh, shit!" very shrilly.

"Do you want to say anything, Charley?"

"It's your money, Pop."

"Well, I'll see you through until after you pass the bar, Charley. Then you'll be on your own."

I walked uptown with Dennis who was working on himself. We were after some steak sandwiches at Costello's on Third Avenue. It was a cold wet day. The Third Avenue El looked like some giant's dog had peed all over it. Dennis mumbled and moaned all the way uptown but I stayed out of it. When we stood at the bar he ordered a scotch. I had a small beer.

"Well, that's that, Charley," he said. "I get nothing because I wouldn't be found dead at the stinking chicken ranch."

"Why shouldn't you get the house? You're out working"—he was an auditor for a hotel chain—"I'm still in school. You'll probably get married first. Why shouldn't you get the house?"

"Because I'm queer," he said.

"What?"

"I'm as queer as they come, Charley."

"Queer? You mean like a *fairy*?"

"Yeah," he said bitterly. "That's what they call us—fairies." He snorted. "You didn't know I was queer, did you, Charley? Well, I didn't want you to know."

"This is some conversation."

45

"You heard Pop. He knows."

"*Pop?* You talked this over with *Pop?*"

He snorted again. The snort was now in his repertory. "The cops told him—somebody did."

"The *cops?*"

"I got pinched in a raid on a queer bar."

"Oh, no!"

"I was wearin' a woman's hat."

"Come *on*, Dennis!"

"I didn't know anything like this about myself until after Mom died under that falling roof. It was such a dramatic way to go that I was like drunk on it. I don't know. Everybody coming around at the wake, grabbing me, and patting me, and squeezing me because of the miraculous manner of Mom's death. The day after the wake I went right into a public terlet with one of the elevator men at the Foley Square Court House and that was that. I just went queer. I can't explain it."

"There was no miraculous manner of Mom's death," I told him. "Some crooked contractor put sand in the cement and the goddam church just collapsed."

"Well, annyway, it was miraculous in the way it changed me."

"Stop kidding yourself, Dennis. Why kid yourself? Were you one way on a Wednesday, then on Thursday because a roof caves in in Queens, did God reach down and change you into a fairy?"

"Well, it's true. It happened. It's hard for you to understand that I'm queer—because we're Irish."

"*We are not Irish!*" I yelled at him, banging my fist on the top of the bar, which was a terrible thing to admit in Costello's. Tim's brother, Joe, working at the far end of the bar, looked up at me in pain and dismay at the blasphemy. "Let's not bring any of Mom's alibis into this," I whispered to Dennis. "She was a German. Pop's two grandmothers were Norwegian and Greek and he never saw Ireland in his life either—if it exists."

"Well, just the same, I'm queer. I'm as queer as they come so I'm not marryin' annybody so I'll get nothin' out of Pop."

"Give me a minute to think, will you, Dennis? Please?" I sipped the beer and watched Ernie serve steak sandwiches in the bar mirror. I tried to figure things out. People die from shark bites, I told myself. They become flagpole sitters or marathon dancers. What's the difference what my brother does? I certainly couldn't change anything. People are either feeling objects or

46

they're just statistics. Maybe they are only a bunch of labels they found somewhere, the way Dennis found his inside a woman's hat. Whatever Dennis was, that was his response. Otherwise he was the same as he had always been—a quarrelsome, repetitious human mystery who lived on soup. All through the later years what I thought that Sunday in Costello's stayed with me, got firmer, ten harder. And through all of my life in politics that's how I saw the people. Quarrelsome, repetitious mysteries who deliberately contrived not to vote and cheated themselves out of a right to keep things from getting worse. They were all flagpole sitters and marathon dancers. What was the difference what happened to them? They didn't want to change anything and I certainly could not.

"All right," I said to my brother. "I'm used to the idea now."

"I swear to God, Charley," he pleaded. "I tried it with a girl once but it was as disgusting as Pop's nose."

"Spare me, Please."

He began to blubber. He fled to the john. When he came out his eyes were red.

"Listen," I told him, "the house is too far downtown for me. You can have the house."

"No. You're gonna be a lawyer. You gotta stay in the district. Look what it did for Pop."

"I'll stay in the district but I'll move uptown."

"Charley, lissena me. I am simply not going to take my kind of friends into the house where Mom lived. It's too much. I'm sorry but she was Irish."

"She was as Irish as Anna May Wong."

"People can't help where they're born, Charley."

"Whatever. But I won't live there. If Pop happens to die in the next sixty years, we'll sell the house, then split the money and I'll move uptown."

"Hey! And I'll sell the chicken ranch and we'll split that. Okay. If that's the way you want it, I can use the money."

Walter stayed with us for four days. He was a totally different kind of decoration around the house, particularly for Pop. Walter had a high mop of brassy blond hair and teeth like a fist. The wet density of his eyes was so packed that their gravity prevented light, or perhaps anything else from escaping except those instant wax tears he could manufacture. His permanent expression was one of evasiveness.

47

"Jesus, his eyes bounce around like stones in a baby's rattle," Pop said. "If he licks his lips once more he's gonna bleed."

Away from the Coomber Law College (I like to say the name, it is such a mockery), I had to marvel at Walter's rigidity. He seemed to be trying to move through thick lard. He spoke very little. He seemed to be studying Pop as if Pop was modeling the lawyer's line. Before Pop left for the chicken ranch with two buddies from the NYPD Bunco Squad, he said to me, "When I was on the bench in Night Court I had to look at a lot of peculiar lawyers. This guy Walter is a genuine Night Court lawyer."

Saturday afternoon I told Walter I would call up a couple of bimbos I knew and we could all have some laughs. He looked at me with dismay.

"No thank you, Charley," he said. "I understand the need for marriage, yes. I understand reproduction as a race responsibility. But with this sort of one-time, frivolous little flirtation which you are suggesting, one thing always leads to another. Demands are made. Lusts are generated. I don't think we have time for things like that in the schedules we have set for ourselves. However, you go, by all means. I will remain right here and read." Now you have to hear a speech like that in its original sand-and-rattlesnake-shit West Texas accent poured out at the rate of minus two miles an hour. You've got to see those little eyes looking past you at something which has to be maybe eighteen or twenty years ahead. You have to realize, too, that he didn't have any idea of what he was saying. He was probably too shook up by the big city to want to venture out at night, but whatever he felt he knew he just couldn't not do it without giving reasons as solemn as a summation to a jury.

"You don't like to dance?" I asked him.

"Dancing is not what it is represented as being. Women like to rub up against you when they dance. My father was a great ballroom dancer." He made a disgusted sound.

We went uptown to Broadway to the Mark Strand to see a Warren William–Kay Francis movie about her going blind and him being a doctor. I didn't know, of course, that—a lot of the rest of the plot aside, but not all of it—I was watching the center of the story of my own life to come.

Dennis came in late Saturday night so he slept late on Sunday morning. He didn't go to Mass when Pop wasn't there anyway.

48

When I left for Mass I asked Walter if he wanted to come but he said that he had been raised in such a simple, direct religion that he didn't see how he could understand mine. "You aren't supposed to understand mine," I told him. "That's the whole point. It was designed that way as a continuing test of faith."

"Dishonest to me," Walter said. I left him reading the Bible in Pop's hideous study, which was just off the front door at the top of the brownstone steps. After Mass I shot two games of dime-a-way rotation with Arthur Moergeli, a block captain who owned an Italian restaurant in Canarsie called Zurich East. He thought Zurich was in Italy, I found out. I picked up a dozen water rolls on the way home. As I let myself in the front door I was almost knocked down by Dennis as he came rushing out of Pop's study, red and breathless.

"What's going on?" I asked him. "You sound as if you'd run a mile carrying an anvil."

"I was seeing your friend," he answered softly. "I hope you don't mind."

"Mind?"

"I like him very much. He likes me, too." He ran up the stairs.

I went into the study carrying the bag of rolls. Walter was still reading the Bible with the same expression of suspicious gloom. He gave no sign that anything untoward had happened, so I decided I had read all the wrong things into what Dennis had said, the oddly girlish way he had said it and the way he had posed there with his pajamas wide open. "Lunch in twenty minutes," I told Walter.

"I will help you, Charley," he said.

We got to the clubhouse at 4:45 A.M. on Election Day. There was plenty of noise, hot coffee, and buns. About sixty election workers had turned out. They kept moving, talking, and practicing politics on each other, slapping backs and laughing at anything as hilarious as a greeting, most of the men smoking cigars even at that hour.

At 5:30 A.M. The Leader addressed the volunteers. "Yiz all know yer job," he told us. "If there's anny trouble, pass the word to yer driver on jooty. There won't be no trouble from the Party across the table today, that's all handled. No challenges. If anybody challenges yer voters tell yer driver on jooty, then look the other way. We don't want nobody claimin' yer a witness. The

49

cops is cooperatin' today so, if you gotta call yer driver on jooty, tip off the cop so's he can get outta sight." He stepped down to heavy applause.

"What did he mean?" Walter asked me.

"How?"

"I don't know what he meant."

"Next year is a national election year, so we have to roll up a big plurality today so we can bargain for our share of federal jobs next year."

"Why should the Republicans cooperate?"

"Why shouldn't they? We take care of each other. Nobody loses. When Hoover ran they rolled up the plurality. The first time around anyway."

"Then what are we doing here?"

"We vote the drunks and the drifters. A vote is a vote."

"Charley, please don't kid about a free election in a democracy."

"Who's kidding?"

"And what is—your driver on duty?"

"They are hoodlums sent up from downtown. The leader only asked for them because it makes his district sound like an action center."

"What are they for?"

"They get people not to mill around and congest the polls."

*"Hood*lums?"

"It's not as bad as it sounds, Walter."

"Not as bad? It's a travesty."

"It's politics. Most voters don't bother to vote so we've got to get the vote out to protect ourselves with Washington."

"Charley, we'll only be cheating ourselves if we go along with this. If we bring one false voter, if we allow one citizen to be intimidated, then what happens to the system? What happens to the democratic process? We would be inviting tyrants in."

"If this is how tyrants get in they've been in since the Civil War. This is what machine politics is—very straightforward stuff. Maybe that's what bothers you, Walter."

Margaret Feeney came up grinning, carrying stacks of small brown envelopes, packages of twenty each held by rubber bands. "Charley," she said, "your driver on duty is Sam Giana in the blue Buick. Your driver, Walter, will be Shecky Fein in the yellow Dodge." She gave us each two stacks of envelopes, then hurried away.

"What are these?" Walter asked with dismay.

"Two bucks in each envelope. For the bums. They're waiting for us in the saloons. Let's go. Your driver will tell you the routine."

"I'm not going, Charley. I will have nothing to do with this."

"Don't be a horse's ass," I said angrily. "Where do you think a grandstand play like that would put me with Margaret?"

"And where do you think all this will put this democracy if we go through with it? Here," he gave me back his stack of envelopes. "Do whatever they trained you to do. I'm going back to Coomber and work. But I will still be your friend. And I will pay you back for that treat at the movies."

DATE: 10th August 1964
TIME: 4:35 P.M.
BASE REPORTING: Miami

ABNER DANZIG

Considering what you got on me in the files this is a waste of time. But since you ain't got as much on me as I got on you, I'll talk to you about Waller if that's what your owners want.

I am a busy man all my life and I work hard to be generous because the other guy thinks he can't afford that. I am an old, short, white-haired Russian immigrant who does the thinking for the Sicilians. I multiplied the efficiency, cash flow, funding, reinvestment, and operations for our syndicate by making all the families follow the basic organizational rules of all successful American big business. We are a bigger business than any of them except the telephone company.

What is the Syndicate? It is not the Mafia. It is only 20 percent Sicilians, who are so noisy the public thinks they are the only ones who are in it. The rest is blacks, Greeks, Jews, and guys at your country club, who are as American as a twelve-dollar bill. I am the Chairman of the Board. Most of our families do what I recommend for them.

You want to know how we all feel about losing Waller Slurrie? We not only lost a partner, I lost a friend. It was like losing a son. I never thought I would outlive Waller but then I never thought I would outlive Benny Siegel until I had to have him taken out. That was really losing a son. But they were two entirely different people. They both had a thirst for nobility, expressed only slightly differently. Waller was a sad man – maybe a tragic man. He wanted to be a great man but he was addicted to money. He couldn't get enough of it and he never would if you gave him Fort Knox.

I suppose you are tryna find out who took Waller out. I don't know. Waller had so many deals going that he could have loused himself up. If we have to know in my business who killed him we'll keep it to ourselves.

DATE: 10th August 1964
TIME: 9:58 A.M.
BASE REPORTING: Miami   **DSP (Semley) Only**

EDWARD CARDOZO (continued)

I call Harry in Miami an tell him I am all set with the tires. He says he get back to me an he call in twenny minutes. "Nudey says bring him down here," Harry tell me. "We fix you up at the Wofford."

Wullair is tiggle to go to Miami because the government owe him time off an because we pay for it. On the plane he ask me if I am Italian. I tell him I am a Mexican an I can see his eyes change. He ask me if I take out citizenship. I see this is an imporrant thing to Wullair because with him, if I am a foreigner, he can't truss me. If I am American everything is okay. "Oh, I see wha joo minn," I tell him. "No, no. I am born here. But my father was very big in the oil business in Mexico so we live in Mexico when I am a little boy." His eyes say he feel good about me again. I am not a lousy foreigner for Wullair.

He say, "Less play a li'l gin to kill the time." He take a pack of cards out of his pocket. We are playing the third han when I reach over an grab his wriss and say, "Wullair, don't ever play cards with my boss because he will have a fellow come to you an break every bone in both you hans."

He look at me with a blank face.

"I don't understand," he say. "What do you mean?"

"Wullair, you are maybe a good card mechanic when you play in the poker game in high school but you outta you head to try it with me."

Now come the words. Wait till you hear what he say to me. "Do you mean that there are a lot of other people who read *Magic Tricks With Cards*?"

"I don get it," I tell him.

"You speak as if card manipulation were a fairly common thing in Florida which, frankly, astonishes me. I thought—well, I found that little book. It was dog-eared and battered. I didn't think there were many copies of it still around and I certainly didn't think that there would be many people who would be willing to go to the trouble which I have undergone to learn how to manipulate playing cards so that, by application of science and hard work, the outcome of a game of cards could be more or less controlled in the manipulator's favor."

"It is an industry," I tell him.

"How do you mean?"

"Wullair—what you do with the cards is sheeting. You don't ever hear the word—card sheet? You are a card sheet, Wullair."

He turn to cold stone. "If I practiced piano playing for five thousand hours," he say, "and I had the gift for playing that instrument with feeling, and if I earned five thousand dollars a concert because people everywhere wanted to hear me play, would you dare to call me a piano cheat?"

"This is something you got to figure out for yourself. I only tell you that if you do that to the cards in a game with strangers, you get yourself insult, beat up, knife or shot because what you do with the cards is what they mean when they say sheeting."

"My God, think of the years men like Bobby Jones and Babe Ruth and Jack Dempsey put into their art. If others applied themselves the way they did, others might be champions in their places. But only they took on the pain and trouble of training and practice. This is very, very upsetting, Kiddo."

"Just figure it out, Wullair."

"Well, I am probably confused because I have only played in

three regular card games in my life." He leans back and changes the subject as if we never play cards. He tells how his father used to take him to Palm Beach but how he never been to Miami, shit like that.

The Wofford was Nudey's hotel. It was one of the two hotels the government allow to stay open in the wartime. Harry set us with two bedrooms connected on each side to a big living room. The first day I leave Wullair on the terrace in the sun an go to see Harry. "When you wan him?" I ask.

"We're up to our ass. They tryna draft Nudey."

"Holy cheat."

"No sweat. It just takes a lotta time onna phone. Hey—thanks for the two pounds of pastrami fom Gitlitz. Marvelous. So listen. Bring him out to the Jakarta at two in the afternoon on Thursday. Is he drivin' you outta your skull?"

"Oh, Wullair is all right. He is a schmo but he got something. I don know what it is, but he got it."

"Nudey'll know what it is. I'll send you over some broads."

Harry send two women to the Wofford that night. After they leave, Wullair tell me a long story which, I fine out, is to proteck me. I ask him, "Who want to be protected from women?"

He say, "I am not opposed to fellatio but I will not permit intimacies beyond that." He is obb-so-lootally straight when he say that. "She was a pleasant woman and pretty in her way. I wanted to be a good sport so I let her go ahead. When it was over, I asked her what her name, Mickey, was short for—just making small talk, you understand. She didn't know. 'My name is Muriel,' she replied. 'Some big shot called me Mickey on a party. We were all on this boat. After that everybody called me Mickey. I hate it. I think it's a cheap name.' The point here is, Kiddo," he say to me, "a man must always insist on fellatio."

"What is fellatio?"

"You know—the mouth."

"Oh."

"In wartime there is the constant danger of contracting a veneral disease, I just don't believe in boffing. Think it over."

I get a lot of mileage out of that story over the years but that is the next-to-the-last time I ever hear Wullair talk about sex in twenty-two years.

* * *

The next day we drive straight out Collins Avenue to the Jakarta. Nudey an Harry are in the booth. Nudey is paying off the Cheriff of Dade County. We wait at the counter in the front until Harry give the sign. The li'l gorl behind the counter come right over. She put her han on top of my han. She smile a rill dorty esmile at me an she say, "How can I do for you?" At this second the Cheriff leave an Harry call us. I make a fonnee face to the gorl an she got to laugh. I bring Wullair to the booth an Nudey tell us to sit don.

"Busy day today so I gotta be quick," he tell us after I introduce Wullair. "Okay. We got a deal here? You get me the permits for the tires an I get you a commission in the Navy?"

"In the legal department of the Navy," Wullair say. "In the Pacific."

"Whatever."

"What is the procedure, Mr. Danzig?"

"You work for Kiddo. Next, we need the tires more than you need the Navy and this is gonna be a long war anyway."

"How long?"

"I give it three more years."

"Well!"

"So you stay in the OPA two years more. Then we transfer you. You'll make a nice dollar out of it."

"No, sir," Wullair say. "You can take care of my food, shelter, and clothing while I'm in Washington, that doesn't come to much—just as the Navy would take care of it at sea—but if I took money for this it would be wrong. I have thought it all through about accepting a naval commission from you people. That *may* not be right but what keeps it from being wrong is that there are no real elements of personal gain in it, and there are even certain elements of loss for me if I should be killed in a naval battle, et cetera."

"I am talking about maybe sixty or seventy grand as your end here."

"The amount has no bearing on the morality of the case, Mr. Danzig. I would be making myself a party to criminal procedure so let's not continue to discuss money. I will guarantee that you get your tires for eighteen months or more. At that time I will expect you to have arranged to have me sworn in as an officer of the U.S. Navy."

Nudey look like he might throw a couple dishes but he say, "Lemme think about it, Waller. Drink the tea."

"Where can I find the little boy's room?" Wullair answer him.

58

Nudey don't know what he is tallking about. I tell Wullair, "Secon door on the right, then first right," I tell him. "An take you time, Wullair." He get out of the booth and walk away.

"What is this?" Nudey ask me.

"He is a fonnee fellow."

"Listen—Harry ran a sheet on him. He can hardly make a living. An he was almost disbarred the first year he practiced law, so where does he get all this honesty shit? Right out in the court the judge says to him that he has serious doubts whether this guy has the ethical qualifications to practice law. You know what your friend here makes in a year—a whole year—before he got that cockamamie job with the OPA? He makes eighteen hunnert an twenny dolliss a year—a *year*, Kiddo."

"All I can say to you, Nudey, is that he is the one who okay the tires for the whole southeast United States."

"But what kind of a lock do I have on this schmuck if he won't take money?"

"Well," Harry say, "we need the tires."

"Yeah. All right. I'll take the deal. But there is something wrong with this fella."

Wullair go back to Washington the next day an I get to work. When I begin in the tire bidniz for Nudey I have one gas station. When the war is over I front three hunnerd an forty-seven as far west as New Orleans and I supply six hunnerd an four others. We get them any kine of tires because of Wullair. We get them counterfeit gas rationing coupons, hot auto parts, an Nudey gives me the punchboard concession an I do all right. When the war is over my end come to $113,588.63 plus another $38,294 from the punchboards. Nudey give me the spot to front the big, new chopping cenner in North Miami. Then he tap me to be his man with the Batista Cubans in Miami real estate. I am a Mexican but they like that. They espeak Espanish very, very fast so I espeak very very slow an make them laugh. We have a good time.

We get action everywhere. Guillermo Peña, used to be the Cuban Secretary of the Treasury, back up a big truck to the Treasury Department in Havana two days before Castro come in an load it with eleven million dollars in cash. Nudey took care of flying the money out for him and put it in one of his two banks Nudey own in Miami, then he lay it out to Peña how he could hide all the money in Miami real estate, which Nudey sold to him, to wait for the land boom which is never goeen to estop. Nudey get me into some very estrong real estate situations.

59

DATE: 10th August 1964
TIME: 9:27 A.M.
BASE REPORTING: New York

DSP (Semley) Only

CHARLES COFFEY (continued)

I don't know know why I volunteered for the Marines. If there is another war I am going to be a cook. Boot camp is torture, then all that miserable ocean across the south Pacific and, as soon as I set foot on dry land, I got hit. That ended the bad part of the war for me. The rest of it—well, that was the wonderful and beautiful part of the war. A lot of guys were cut in half that morning, us and the Japanese. Going in from the sea we watched them fall out of life on the beach. Our landing got it just as bad but I don't know much. I sprinted about eleven steps, counting to stop thinking, then it all stopped for me. Guys on both sides of me were blown apart and yet, out of all that, the terror and death and screams delivered unto me the most important part of my life, which has shone, in one piece for me, all the way through until now. I found my wife and she found me.

I lost my left eye. It was the best trade I ever made. All the great love stories have to start somewhere.

Marie was inside her fifth island assault. She was a Navy nurse who always got ashore hours before she was supposed to be there, and I never knew anyone who was less deserving of that much pain and death. What it did to her—those five assaults, then that last terrible landing—didn't simply change her, it transformed my life, giving us, together, a new life, restoring that passion which people of our ages were supposed to be able to feel.

She got me out even though everything cracked wide open for her—five was too many. I awoke at a base hospital in tropical Australia. My eyes were bandaged and I didn't know where I was. I was scared. I spoke the fear. Then her voice, as clean as running mountain water, said, "I'm here, Charley." I had never seen her or heard her before but I knew she was something significant of which I had had glimpses in books and in music. I must have been taut with fear, marbleized and whitened by it, shaking from it because her hand went under the blankets on my bed and under my bed gown. She held me gently and with expert interest. "You know everything is going to be all right," she said.

"Is this modern medicine?"

"Pretty ancient."

"It's great."

"I can tell," she said. "I am treating the symptoms."

"Is it day or night?"

"Night."

"Are we alone?"

"No."

"Are there any screens?"

"I can get them if you need them."

"I don't need them."

She took her hand away from me. I heard quick rustles of clothing falling off, then she was under the blanket beside me, and we didn't talk any more for the rest of the night.

The bandages didn't come off my eyes for a long time, it seemed to me. Marie taught me how to walk without being able to see. Most important she taught me how to listen. She so excited my senses that I can say she taught me how to smell, touch and taste. She brought me into a world that combined four senses and the mind as if she were an obstetrician. She stayed near. "Why me?" I said into her ear one night.

62

"You are mine," she whispered back. "I found you on that beach, Everything else had died or gone away but you waited for me until life, which I thought had gone too, gave you to me."

That sounds morbid maybe to anyone who was not on that beach that morning. She had stood there as if protected by a force field and watched Death stuff young lives into a bottomless sack. She was on her feet and observing even if she had wandered in her mind. I was breathing: young, blood-soaked, and blind—and gone from that place, too. Years and years later, Marie still had the power to conjure up those minutes for both of us. Marie was a mystical erotic.

She spent two days convincing me that a great good fortune had protected me. I had lost only one eye. I would be able to see, che oong to mo. She extracted all self-pity. She made me a golden winner. I was an astounded one-eyed winner and Marie was proud of me.

As soon as she could be sure that I permanently accepted that everything she was telling me was true, Marie collapsed. She was sent from Australia to a naval hospital at San Diego. I was sent to a specialist facility called Bancroft House in Northampton, Massachusetts. I wrote to Marie every day for six weeks. Then I explained all this to the Navy doctor in charge of my eyes and the doctor said she would get me some answers.

It didn't take long. Dr. Neil telephoned someone she knew in San Diego: officer country. Marie had had a heavy kind of mental breakdown and she wasn't responding. She had withdrawn, away from the pain of the war, which would have destroyed her if her mind had not rescued her and banished memory. She sat quietly and watched the sea. She slept. They fed her. She sat quietly and watched the sea.

I told Dr. Neil that I had to go to San Diego. She knew what Marie had done for me, that I was convinced that we both knew we hadn't been allowed to survive that beach just to lose each other because Marie's pressured mind had gone aberrant. Dr. Neil got me compassionate leave on a straight trade-off basis. She would make it possible for me to get to California if I would agree that, no matter what, I would return to Northampton for a final eye operation.

All I wanted from the Navy was to show me to Marie's room. Anyway they did it, because Marie had been a combat Navy nurse and I was a one-eyed ex-Marine. They put me on a MATS flight out of Boston. There were two transfers en route. I got to San Diego forty-four hours later and it was 3:20 P.M. when I got to the hospital.

Neil had told me to ask for Admiral Abraham Weiler, who Neil said was the greatest doctor in the U.S. Navy and a legend. He couldn't have been a legend because he didn't keep me waiting. He was a grizzled old guy but he must have been in love with Marie, he had me sent in so quickly. He turned out to be a very nice New York fellow who knew Al Smith who was an old friend of my family and was also my godfather. I showed Admiral Weiler my lifetime pass to the top of the Empire State Building and all that settled the difference in our rank. He lit an old pipe, then he began to talk about Marie.

"I want this meeting to work, Corporal," he said. "She's a beautiful, sensitive, fine girl. But it isn't going to work. She is gone from us. Gone just as much as if she had died and crossed over, which maybe she has."

"Yes, sir. Lieutenant Neil explained that to me, sir. But with all respect, patients are shipped into hospitals by the thousands and doctors don't cure all of them who are cured just the same. What I mean is, sir, you don't know Marie the way I know her."

"What do you have in mind?"

"Well—maybe if you'll just leave me alone with her for a couple of hours. That's all. After that I'll know whether it's any use going ahead. And if there isn't, then—well—I guess that's the end of it."

"The end of it?"

"I'll go back to Bancroft as soon as I can get a flight."

He blew smoke in my face. "All right," he said grimly. "Begin the treatment."

He took me to Marie's room. She was sitting in an armchair, looking out over the sea. He sat me in a chair facing her and told her who I was. She was looking at me but she didn't really see me. "All yours, son," the Admiral said. He left the room.

I locked the door. I turned down the bed and got undressed. I lifted Marie in my arms, carried her to the bed and lay her down. I undressed her. I got into the bed and pulled the sheet up over us. I held her in my arms. I gave her time to get used to the new warmth of a body touching her body, then I stroked her breasts and spoke softly to her. I stroked her back and her thighs. I kissed her behind her ear and I imagined I felt her body answer me. "We are on the beach at Ruaroa now. The noise is terrible. Boys

64

are being cut in half by rapid fire just a few yards away from us and there is no way out of here. The bullets kick up the sand and make those thunking sounds which we will never forget as they hit the boats. A ragged line of Marines is eight yards ahead of us, running into the jungle toward the firing. They disappear. The sand is soaked with blood around us. I have been hit. Marie! I am hit! I have gone blind! You sit on the blood beside me and tell me I am alive. You hold my head across your legs and beside my head, resting on the sand, is a young man's hand wearing an Academy ring."

Marie screamed.

She screamed again and again and again. She clung to me and gradually—moment by moment, second by second—it seemed to take hundreds of years—the recognition came into her eyes. She had agreed to come back.

"Make love to me, Charley, please," she said.

Admiral Weiler looked at me as if I were both Mayo brothers. "How did you do it?"

"I talked to her. What happens now?"

"What do you want to do?"

"We want to get married, Up there. In her room."

"Why not? Why not? When?"

"Tomorrow morning at about 09:37 hours. That's when we met."

"There isn't much I seem to be able to do around her," he said. "but I sure as hell can arrange that."

We were married. I went back to Bancroft for the last operation. Admiral kept Marie at the base hospital for sixty days to fatten her up, then we met in New York and began to live.

Marie and I were like the ducklings in the Konrad Lorenz experiments. Marie was imprinted on me and I was imprinted on Marie. Perhaps it was a bad thing but our children, in a certain way, were outsiders. The way we saw it, we had given each other back our lives and we were terrific for each other, just sitting around, or in the sack or in the kitchen, on the dance floor, in a fine shouting argument, drinking wine, choosing each other's clothes, budgeting money, going to church, disliking my brother, loving her mother—well, in everything except one thing.

Marie's mental problems seemed to be gone except that she held close to her sanity a virulent hatred of politicians. She

65

blamed all politicians for the brutal deaths of all those young men on the beach at Ruaroa. No matter how she tried, and she tried, she could not accept the fact that my family were politicians and that politics was what I had been trained to perform. We talked about it until we could not stand continuing to avoid looking at each other.

In essence, I said to her: "My great-grandfather was a politician. He helped to settle thousands of confused people in this city. My grandfather, my father's father, was a Tammany leader who saw that the poor were fed, housed, and clothed and not just at Thanksgiving and Christmas either. My grandfather caused the enactment of vital child labor and sweat-shop legislation. My father, Pop, has served the community on a dozen levels. He understands what can be done from the inside by a professional politician who can turn and shape government for the greatest good of the most people, regardless of race or religion. Politics is the only thing I understand, Marie. I was drilled just barely enough in the law to pass the state bar examination but I could never make a living as a lawyer. I am the kind of professional politician who doesn't run for office. I don't have to perform compromising acts to get reelected. My work will be to steer and influence to keep this complex structure of government stable and moving. That's what I have to do. It's the only thing I have."

In essence, she said to me: "The gangrene that infects history was put there by politicians. They seek havoc for personal gain. They serve only a handful of masters and abandon all the others to die of the gangrenes they fostered—the wars, the inflations, the unemployment, the suffering, the corruption, the shame—but most of all war. It is humanity's most degraded work. Since you told me what you work at when you leave this house, I have felt as if I were married to a hyena who drags home carrion each night for us to feast upon. You tell me we can't change anything, so since we love each other the only thing left for us to do is to pledge to each other that we will not ever talk about it. What happens outside this house does not happen insofar as we, together, are going to try to survive it."

That was the gist of it. We left it at that. I thought it was a Solomon-like solution at the time and I took the joy of it into my chest like a spear.

When I passed the bar in 1936, Dick Betaut was America's most famous gang-busting District Attorney: the implacable enemy of organized crime with a glittering record of accomplishment. While he flailed away, beating gangsters and whores (who had fictionally romantic criminal names), he kept his eye on higher things and on still higher things. Then one afternoon, to my good fortune, he had a quiet meeting with Pop and "borrowed" me as his advance column to set things going for his future gubernatorial campaign in Albany, downtown, Plattsburgh, Buffalo, and on Long Island. I was in charge of making sure that the groundwork would be so well done that Betaut would seem to march effortlessly to the Governor's chair. There was one anomaly. Our family had been professional Democrats for three generations. Betaut was a whalebone-corseted Republican. But Pop, as usual, looked at all sides of the question. He said, "You know and I know that it makes no difference which party we work for, any more than it makes any difference which party is elected. We all make out either way. It gives the voter a feeling of contest and binds him to politics through partisan loyalty. True, once we have you cross over it would be silly for you as a professional to cross back. But the point here is that you won't be crossing over. You never started with either party, so in a public sense you don't exist politically, It only goes to show how smart Betaut is that he would quietly come over to our side to line up the best muscle. If you go with them Charley, we are going to want you to make good in a big way, because by blood you are one of us and in times to come, when there might be a clinch, you will be able to see the advantages to being useful to us quicker than a born Republican. That's why renegades-at-the-top always get by. Start thinking like a Republican, Charley."

Betaut liked my work. The war intervened and I didn't get back in time to work on the first Betaut presidential campaign in '44, but when I was discharged (a married man) and Marie and I settled into the only apartment we ever had, at 227 East 57th Street, where we stayed because it was in the election district, I was invited to lunch by Pop at the Metropolitan Club. Dick Betaut was the other guest. They took a lot of care explaining to me that Betaut had interceded on my behalf to get me what, potentially, was the best job for a professional politician in the country. Betaut was willing to recommend that I be hired to take over as political affairs executive for the enormous, international, and wholly, blandly inscrutable Felsenburshe Enterprises. Incredibly—because Dick Betaut recommended it—the job would pay

67

$42,500 a year to start, plus expenses, but Betaut said the sky would be the limit once I proved to Nils Felsenburshe that I was everything Betaut said I was.

I was just this side of being gratefully maudlin, which is what Betaut had in mind for future reference anyway. Pop kept shaking Betaut's hand, then my hand, and after ten minutes or so starting all over again.

Nils Felsenburshe and his family—the brothers, sisters, uncles, nephews, in-laws, sons, daughters, nieces, nephews and counselors—a greater population than any ruling tribe in Saudi Arabia but many times richer—owned lower, southeastern, and eastern Manhattan; western Morocco and western Australia; held northern Venezuela and the entire south (sunny) side of the American over-communications industry. They owned oil fields, gold fields, uranium piles, and miracle miles of titanium, aluminum, nickel, cobalt, and molybdenum. They had ocean-wide holdings of undersea nodes, El Dorado lodes, rag-trade modes. They owned Titians, de Koonings, Degas, Rothkos, and James Richard Blakes, as well as great mind expanding areas of the international pharmaceutical industries.

They controlled principal, secondary, and tertiary banks in the major cities of the world, and many brokerage firms, personal loan companies, and bookmaking establishments. They owned thousands of square miles of timber, cotton, agriproducts, and freezing plants. They held aerospace, insurance, automobile manufacturing, telephone, satellite, and organized crime companies and cartels.

They directed rent-a-mob facilities, owned law firms, churches, and astrologers, universities, secret police organizations, and whole bodies of legislatures internationally. They possessed, as succubi possess: prime ministers, senators, cops, presidents, fleet admirals, congressmen, diplomats, assassins, labor leaders, educators, and scientists. It was all benevolent from the Felsenburshe point of view.

They operated textile mills, shoe factories, construction firms, conglomerates, defense contractors, organized sports units, undertaking chains, and television networks. Their interests encompassed mortgages, leased heavy equipment, credit card companies, bond issues, and sixty-seven racehorses, which seldom ran out of the money. They had greeting card companies to provide the get-well cards to service the 107 hospitals they owned and operated and linen and laundry companies, carpet factories, and wholesale butchers to service their chain of 172 hotels. They went forward through four national insurance companies and three Swiss banks. At all times they walked softly while carrying a big knish; play-acting, as firmest family policy dictated loudly, ceaselessly, and mournfully, that all of their wealth and alleged power had never been able to lift Nils Felsenburshe into the dream of his life—the American presidency—because that would be against the wishes of the American people.

The fact was that if by some unspeakable flaw of fate, he ever was threatened with having to accept that job, he would have fled the country until the election results could be recalled by the family and adjusted to more desirable favor.

Nils Felsenburshe didn't want anybody's job except his own. He had a man for everything, who had several men for everything else, including all the Presidents of the United States beginning with Mr. Nils' grandfather's acquisition of Chester Alan Arthur. He had curators to curate his museums, thinkers to ponder, and shaker/movers such as me to fix, patch, and make arrangements for the election of enlightened leaders and sun-filled legislation, to make connections among other reasonable men, audible moans not permitted.

Felsenburshe sweetheart unions lent, his ruffians collected and possessed, and his godly men prayed for all of us. He had shadowy specialists who knew how to talk to other people who would cheerfully do the things that Nils Felsenburshe, as a Christian gentleman, simply would not do but that had to be done if the Felsenburshes were to continue owning the steel, the public utilities, the downtown real state in the high-rent districts of the planet, the coal, solar, nuclear, oil and wind tide energy advantages; continue to hold the outstanding call notes on the two prime American political parties and to cherish Mother's Day.

The first advice I gave the Felsenburshes was about that political affairs title they had in mind. Instead they made me the in-house special assistant to the senior partner of the Wall Street law firm that counseled the family, in this case Dick Betaut. He was a lawyer and a politician, but I was a technician so he rarely tried to second-guess me.

Beyond everything else, the most preciously important of all, was what a flood of relief this brought to my life with Marie—and hers with me. It was established by me, by Pop, and by Betaut, theWall Street lawyer, the man who was my new boss, that I had turned my back on politics (for the sake of our marriage?) by going to work as a lawyer for the world's most respectable family. I was out of politics. Marie was happy and we could look into each other's eyes without evasion. More than that, it kept Marie healthy.

DATE: 10th August 1964
TIME: 11:27 A.M.
BASE REPORTING: Miami

EDWARD CARDOZO (continued)

In 1953, when Wullair is the Vice-President of the United States, Harry call me to go see Nudey at the Jakarta. Nudey was back in the booth working out something with the link man for the Sicilian families in New York, so I finally get the chance to jive the li'l gorl behine the counner. She give me a glass gwatter an tell me how las' night her mother finish making her number one thousand lamp shade with fringes for the piecework bidniz. I tell her, "I bet you got some beautiful li'l fringes yourself, *niña*, I would like to estudy them up rill close."

She has a beautiful esmile. She is hoppee with me. I know that as soon as we both have the mutual time I am going to get into her fringes. "I can tell you nothing about my fringes," she say. "That is no place to hold a mirror."

"I would be honor to afford an opinion."

"I would have great respect for your judgment."

"Then I will telephone to joo as soon as I know what is wanted by *el patron*."

71

"Bring food and wine to stay alive," she say. "I am *una tigrina.*"

The link man leave the booth. Harry nod his head to me. I go over.

"Siddown," Nudey say. "Have a glass tea." I sit across from him.

"I got something I want you to tell Waller."

I don't ask why he doesn't tell Wullair.

"Tell Waller that Harry told you I am now back in business with the SP to put me back in Cuba. Then I want you to sell Waller the idea that, if he plays it right, you guys might be able to get me to give you your own casino in Havana."

I tell Wullair. You don't have to sell him if there is a chance he win a casino. "That would be almost as big as the time Nudey got us our own bank. Except that this would be entirely tax free. It is a *tremendous* opportunity, Kiddo."

"A casino like that can bring in a net of three four hunnerd thousand a week," I say. "But, like always, you got to be the one to get it for us, Wullair. You are the top man with Nudey."

Wullair bring out his thinking face and put it on for a li'l while. We wait maybe six, seven minutes. He finally talk. "Nudey is coming out here tomorrow for some of Betsy's famous bean soup. We can put it to him after he has some of that."

"Joo put it to him, Wullair."

Nudey's cabin cruiser bring him in at ten o'clock the next night. Wullair meet him at the dock so the Secret Service don't have to worry, then he take him out on the terrace. I bring in the bean soup. Nudey eats it and he loves it. He says it is the best soup in Florida.

That is Wullair's signal to talk and he can't wait. "Mr. Danzig," he says, "I have top secret information that the SP plans to overthrow the Cuban government and I thought that information might be useful to you." Nobody have nerve like Wullair. He is handing Nudey's own information right back to him.

"Useful to me?" Nudey say. "Why me?"

Wullair deen esspect that. "Well," he say, "if Cuba is reopened to American free enterprise, I just assumed that you would want to return to Havana to reopen your gambling casinos and the—ah—other things."

"Oh, that," Nudey say. "Yeah, I got the SP to agree to throw Castro out. Sure, we'll reopen there."

"*You* got them to do it?" Joo got to know Wullair, he is a rill hick. He go for the bait like he was betting on the shell game outside a carnival tent. "Why would they do it for you?"

"Because I do for them."

"What do you do?"

"As Vice-President of the United States, I don't think you wanna know about it. Heroin? Out of Asia? Theirs? We sell it for them?"

Wullair get pale. "You're right, Mr. Danzig. I would rather not know."

"Whatta you so innarested in Cuba for, Waller?"

"Mr. Danzig, the three of us have been quite successful with the general, loose partnership among us and, frankly, I thought it might be possible for you to arrange a chance for Kiddo and me to buy into our own casino in Havana, when the right time comes, of course."

"I could do that, Waller."

"Kiddo and I have capital we'd like to invest. And you would, of course, have your usual 51 percent of the deal."

"Waller, tell me what do I need 51 percent for when I already have one hunnert percent."

"There has to be some way we can work this thing out, Mr. Danzig."

"Waller, I like you an I like Kiddo." He look solemnly at me an I nod as if we are in chorch. "I say *maybe* a thing like that could work out but you got to realize that what we are talking about here is numbers like five, six million a year. Maybe more, because if I give you the office for the casino I gotta cut you in on the shit and the broads and the sharking we move there. And maybe you are gonna get a couple pernts in Cuban real estate."

"No need for any extras for us, Mr. Danzig. Our own casino will be ample for Kiddo and me."

"Sure," I say, waving a big cigar, "let the other guy bahss his ass."

"Waller, lissana me," Nudey says, and I figure here is where he makes his move. "Betaut set you as the SP's man in the White House. The SP would be dead if their stuff went through President Kampferhaufe."

"True," Wullair say.

"So I got an idea. It figures if you start to sell the Cuban proposition to the SP from your end that the whole thing will happen sooner."

"I don't think they'd expect to hear about gambling casinos from me, Mr. Danzig."

"Don't be a schmuck, please. You will tell them that they got to take Cuba because of national security. You tell them that you, the Vice-President, would even be willing to be the Action Officer on the operation if they mount a military operation. Once they mount the operation they'll have the White House in so deep that it would be political suicide for a President to try to pull out. When you talk national security to the SP and I talk money to them, they got the right reasons on both sides to go ahead. What the hell, Waller, you been committing the White House on things as big as this anyway. What's the difference one more, except that you and Kiddo will own your own casino."

"It probably could be done," Wullair say slowly.

Wullair rilly work to sew up the whole Cuban invasion. He don't have no trouble to get the SP to commit for the Cuban take-over. They tell him they'll be ready in '56. But they don't do it in '56, or in '58 or '59, because they fuck up. They get caught trying to throw out Sukarno. They almost ruin Kampferhaufe by getting caught with the U-2 over Russia.

Nudey take it very hard. After they doublecross him in '56, he let them know that they made a big mistake and maybe they get the message and maybe they just don't give a cheat. Nudey forget about Havana. He go to work and organize the same thing in the Bahamas, which is like the same thing except Wullair an me don own any casino there.

By the time the SP decide to run the invasion to Cuba it is 1961 and there is a new man in the White House, which means Wullair is out. Nudey pass the word to me that no matter what else he do, Wullair got to be sure that he stay as Action Officer whenever the SP pulls the Cuban invasion. The SP cost Nudey a lot of money so I wouldn't want to be them. As far as the other families in the Syndicate go they tell Nudey in a Council meeting they expect him to make sure everybody get even with the SP.

When the invasion start out of Central America and the Florida keys, Wullair was the Action Officer. He work out of Dallas. He control landings and air cover. Nudey set everything with Wullair an he make a terrific dill with us for a piece of the heroin, cocaine, an marijuana action out of Colombia, which he tell us is going to grow into a very big thing. So that Nudey can pay off the

74

SP for crossing him up, Wullair never tell the air cover to get off the ground, and he send the landing boats off in the wrong sequence so that the leaders of the invasion and all the best fighters are in the last boats to go in.

The SP blame this all on the new President who has been bitching them about the operation anyway. Nobody think to blame Wullair because he is on the SP team since 1948. What help to blame the new President is that he is so mad that the SP set him up with this thing that he move right in on the SP, just the way Nudey figure he got to do. He fire the Director and the two other top men. He take the SP out of the command in southeast Asia. He announce that the SP gun be broke into three different agencies, then—the mos dangerous thing of all for him—he tell the country he gun withdraw the troops from Vietnam.

So naturally the SP have their people kill him the first chance they get—in Dallas.

DATE: 10th August 1964
TIME: 10:20 A.M.
BASE REPORTING: El Paso   DSP (Simley) Only

MRS. VICTORIA SLURRIE

Father and I had five sons. Only one is still alive. Camillo died when he was nineteen. He had tuberculosis. Sylvan, the second boy, got an infected foot when he was twelve and I couldn't afford a doctor. The panel truck was broken again so we couldn't get him to the hospital. He passed away in terrible pain. Druidie, our fifth son, was killed in an automobile accident that may or may not have been my fault, when he was twenty-two. Walter, our third son, died violently in the East, as you know, because you are here.

I had to give so much time and attention to Camillo and Sylvan before they passed on, particularly Camillo who had to be taken away and needed me with him, that it was hard on the rest of the boys. I also believe it finally turned Father away from us. And I believe it was the basic cause of Walter's suicide.

I know it was announced as murder. He was a very important man. But Walter showed, from the time he was a little boy, that he felt what he considered to be rejection very keenly. Of course, it wasn't rejection at all. I had four other sons, two of them very sick. Walter was the son who wanted all of my attention and then felt I hadn't given him any.

He always thought so much about money, but even more than that he was always desperate to get my attention. I just didn't have much attention to give anybody. We worked all the time. We were just about able to scratch out an existence from that little store. The Indians were terrible credit risks. Father had gone away. Druidie and Chester were too little to help and Walter was just waiting to make his way out in the world. I couldn't spare much attention for any of my boys. Still, Walter was a fine boy. He didn't carry his share of the weight for as long as he might have but that was because he knew he had it in him to be a great man.

Salopado was a hard place to live. The house was very cold all through the winters. We had no money for fuel. We'd burned all the firewood for miles around, whatever the poor Indians left us. Salopado was very hot in the other months. We did the best we could.

I do not speak against Father. He is gone. I love him still. He was a rough man with his sons, but many are of the belief that this is good for boys, although I do not agree with that. In nothing he did did Father try to set a good example for our boys. The others weren't the stars blazing across the skies that Walter became, but they were cheerful. There is no such thing as a "better" son. If they do their best they are all miracles. My boys did their best all through their lives.

That could not have been easy for them. Their father was a failure. He failed at everything he did and I confess it embittered me because he did not ever try to do his best. Sometimes I think that the reason Walter worked so much at trying to make me smile was that he sensed my bitterness at Father's welcome to his own failure.

When Father and I were young there was a strong interpersonal attraction between us but, soon enough, the Job's comforters who are everywhere among us were happy to bring the news to me that Father felt a strong physical attraction to all women. That did not make me bitter but it made it a matter of no interest to me whether I smiled. I think, I always did think, and still do, that smiles are the lovers' language. Children need to smile but they need other, more important things from their parents, good examples most of all. They need stability, discipline, and unselfishness. Father gave our children none of these.

Walter often told me what it was going to be like when he became his own man. He would tell me how much he admired my self-control. I did not answer that my control had been paid for at too high a price. I exchanged my youth for it. But, I *am* controlled and I am glad that set an example for my sons to serve them throughout their lives.

I have felt deep guilt over the times when I lost all control. That guilt has never left me. Yes, I had self-control except at night in the darkness of my marriage bed because of the strength of the interpersonal attraction between Father and myself. I lost all control there. Control of my voice and of my body. My sons could hear me. They could not see us but they could hear us. I will always carry that wound with me but I could do nothing to stop myself when Father took me into his arms. When day returned I would have control again but I would be unable to smile because of my guilt. Humans must smile. What we did at night before Father went away took its greatest toll upon Walter. It must have filled him with shame as it filled me with guilt until that shame filled the chasms of his soul and he murdered himself. What happened in the nights upon my bed is what made Walter grow up so tense and alone, so morbid in his speech, so guarded in his expressions of gesture and of face. But Walter stayed on with my guilt and his shame in that house long after Father went away. He said to me, with so much love, again and again and again, that he wanted to grow up to be like me. Somehow, I knew, he would have to find some way to transfer his life from one container to another so that he could cope with his distrust of his own worthiness and—somehow—be able to value happiness. But he killed himself.

Walter showed contempt for people who spoke of happiness—as if it were a radio to be switched on or off. He must have thought of happiness as being a melting snowman that other people believed could run on ahead of them forever.

I gave religion to my sons. When Father went away Walter's faith was not shattered, *he* was shattered. He became confused by our religion's insistence that money opposes nature. Walter cherished a separate personality, remote from his true self, where he was able to live for money and its acquisition as if, years hence, he would need all of it to defend himself against something he could not understand.

79

DATE: 10th August 1964
BASE REPORTING: Los Angeles

N.B. *The following autobiographical text was transcribed from cassettes found in the Bel Air, California house of Horace Riddle Hind. An audio copy has also been made. The original cassettes have been returned to the Hind bedroom in Bel Air.*

HORACE RIDDLE HIND

In 1913, when Horace Riddle Hind was thirteen years old, he invented the Boomerang Box Kite. In 1973 the design, at this time manufactured by Hind Aerospace, had become a 2,600-square-foot plastic film sail coated with aluminum reflecting layers on the side facing the sun (being painted black on the other side), and carried the same furled principle of Hind's original Boomerang Box Kite into outer space to sail outward at 124,000 miles per hour, 60,000 miles above the earth, taking television pictures and delivering instrument readings to expand human knowledge and to make Horace Hind still a greater scientific figure. That was the imprint of the pattern of Horace Hind's life: to repeat, in greatly embellished form, the great feats of his life as a young boy.

Has Horace Hind once again stumbled upon one of the deep secrets of all human behavior here?

His father, Big Horace, patented the invention of the Boomerang Box Kite for his son, in his son's name. By the time Little Horace was a grown man the royalties from the sale of his kite had earned $372,854.19 in the approximately fifty years since Hind had invented it. The lad was so proud of having earned his first dollar from his own invention that he never spent one penny of this income in his life. He invested the money so that it could remind him, with a purity of meaning, of what the earliest creative product from his brain had yielded. Creative is the key, operative word to describe Horace Hind. The thrift was not characteristic of Horace. It was the single thrifty act of Horace's wantonly creative life.

In his lifetime, 117 inventions were patented in the name of Horace Riddle Hind, inventions which he had outlined, or sketched in carefully, so that his special technicians could carry them forward to the routine inventing phases. His other inventions went beyond the field of kites into electronics, rocketry, jet liner passenger toilets, glove storage, and the development of the cantilevered brassiere.

Horace Hind also established the Hind Foundation, which, although opposed to charitable works, is dedicated to the advancement of science through technology, to which the founder had dedicated his life. The Foundation has a small Humanities section, for reasons of public relations, to which funds have been allotted for the study of chicken pox and other diseases from which Horace Hind suffered as a child.

Big Horace passed on to his son a love for the American West. Both father and son rejected the American East, with its shoddy contents and preposterous people, as an extension of Europe, nothing more. It was not American in its thrust.

Big Horace sustained his son with the shelter of this knowledge. He proved to his son that Presidents originating in the East had become insane with power. They had demolished the oil-depletion allowance. They were soft on Communists. They had turned the country's back on Asia and on the Pacific, which was an American lake. They had pleaded for national humiliation at the Bay of Pigs, the Big Steel crisis, at the Berlin Wall, and had agitated the pinkos of the country to scream out for civil rights for niggers and women which, had the Constitution wanted it that way, would have included it there.

The Boomerang Box Kite was a compact stick to be hurled into the air to gain instant maximum altitude. The first one Little Horace ever made worked to perfection. It was made out of stiff red paper and thin wooden struts. When it was aloft the automatic timer would snap the struts apart to make a box kite that was attached to a string which was a part of a reel held in the thrower's other hand. It was a fool-proof kite. Any man could look great to his grandson with a kite like that, the advertising said. It was an important seller. In 1914 one of these cost $4.95. In 1962 the kite sold for a flat $19.

I would like to make it clear that Big Horace did *not* invent the Boomerang Box Kite. This was *entirely* Little Horace's invention.

Despite his progress as an inventor, Little Horace was a sad boy, quiet and reclusive, whose friends by choice were the occasional pieces of machinery that might inspire him to repeat his success with the Boomerang Box Kite. He was well able to amuse himself silently in a corner of his daddy's workshop in Dallas, but he did not talk very much because he did not hear very well due to a disease that Daddy had acquired before Little Horace was born. He went to the Methodist Church on Mockingbird Lane at Hillcrest. He went to many schools.

When Little Horace was fourteen he built his own ham radio set, then a motorcycle out of a storage battery and a self starter motor from a junked car, but the biggest thing that happened to him was his discovery of the silence and privacy of working at night. While everyone else was fast asleep in Dallas, Little Horace tinkered or talked with radio operators on the Gulf oil freighters. This welded him to electronics on one side and to oil cargoes on the other.

Little Horace did not graduate from any school. Big Horace was a graduate engineer from the Massachusetts Institute of Technology. Big Horace was a big fish in a big pond. He had reasons to be noticed by Eastern bankers. In 1908 oil drills could not penetrate thick rock shale. Oil seekers were only tapping easy oil that lay in puddles close to the ground surface. They wanted the riches waiting for them far under the ground, but only Big Horace did something about it. In 1908 he invented BOVE (Bite Oil Vacuum Engineering), which in 1951 Little Horace changed to SHOVE (Simple Heliocentric Oil Vacuum Engineering). Big Horace's system measured whether there was any oil under the drilling site, delivered the means for getting to it, then provided a back-up vacuum system that took up all the debris out of the hole as the cutting tool tore deeper into the ground. The system was to earn Big Horace's little family more than one billion eight hundred million dollars.

At MIT Big Horace roomed with one of the five Felsenburshe brothers, an Eastern family. Big Horace was in love with a girl named Clara Ann Minkell. For two years they planned to marry, then, without warning, she married young Felsenburshe instead. Big Horace never recovered from this terrible blow. Clara Ann's betrayal changed his life and his attitude to women. They became whores to Big Horace. The East itself, represented by that mocker Felsenburshe, became a nest of seducers. Big Horace's most deeply inflicted wound upon his son was leaving Little Horace in perpetual wonderment as to whether women were really neurotic, money-lusting whores or whether they were saintly women like his mother.

Big Horace chartered railway cars and plied them back and forth to Canada, Los Angeles, and Mexico City, filling them with fast women, booze, gamblers, and admiring customers. Big Horace was the most popular ladies' man in Texas. He spent money on fun and tried his best to see that Little Horace watched a lot of it.

From the time he was fifteen, Little Horace would be summoned to bedrooms where his father lay with naked women who pretended to be asleep with their backs to the company. Big Horace would prolong these meetings just to give the boy a treat because he knew, sooner or later, the naked women would need to get out of bed to relieve themselves. It always made him laugh but it never made the women or Little Horace laugh. Little Horace was too easily disgusted to be shown that women could expose themselves like that. He made an issue of it. "Mother is at home meeting every one of her responsibilities," he said. "She is always cheerful, kind, loving, and happy. But you are in beds with naked women. I would like you to help me understand this."

"I worship your mother," Big Horace said.

"Then why do you flaunt naked women? Is it a medical necessity?"

"I lay with other women because your mother is the single exception that proves the rule. I hope you are as lucky as I was. But the odds are about 375 to 1 against you. All women, except your mother and a handful of others, are whores. They will betray a man every chance they get. You've got to believe me on this. I

84

don't know why God blessed me with such a wife. And I know, because I have had her watched day and night since the day we met and she has neither faltered nor failed me once. Your blessed mother is the only woman—and I have tested hundreds and hundreds—who has ever passed my simple tests of love and trust. But I go on testing. I will not damn womankind out of hand."

Big Horace's convictions had a profound effect upon Little Horace because his daddy was one of the most successful men in the United States. Mother was more difficult to love because she loved all things equally: rocks, Jesus, the birds of the air, the Girl Scout movement, Little Horace, chicken fried steak, opera, doggies, and snapshot albums. She engulfed Little Horace with her love, causing him to develop asthma.

Little Horace was sent to Europe for the Grand Tour when he was seventeen. He never got beyond the Municipal Casino at Deauville. He did not bet. He watched and marveled that people would drive up to the building from far away and be so pleased to hand over great sums of money for the illusion of pleasure.

He began the tests of the strength of his money, which were never to end throughout his life. At first he only had people removed from dining tables while they were eating in order that he might sit there. For $2,500 he persuaded a man and a woman to leap overboard from a transatlantic liner in midocean in the presence of a ship's officer who then needed to put all the ship's rescue machinery into motion, delaying the ship by nine hours.

Little Horace discovered that his money could do anything. His money bought him Walter Bodmor Slurrie. He, Horace Hind, owned a Vice-President of the United States outright. Quite soon he would own himself a President.

TO: FIRST DEPUTY COMMISSIONER VINCENT J. MULSHINE

FROM: LIEUTENANT RICHARD GALLAGHER, 17th HSQ

Abner "Nudey" Danzig and Edward Cardozo were both in New York on August 9th, the day Slurrie was murdered. Danzig states that they were in New York on business and that they left for Miami aboard a National Airlines flight that leaves La Guardia at 4:27 P.M. We are checking the alibis out.

The Miami Police questioned Danzig in the coffee shop of the Jakarta Motel, North

Miami. He is a little old man with a ruffian's face and eyes like dry ice. He stated that he and Cardozo had attended a meeting in a rented "directors' room" at the Calumet Bank & Trust Company at 34 West 51st Street. He would not discuss the nature of the business meeting nor who else had attended it "unless absolutely necessary." He said bank officials would corroborate his presence at the bank. The bank hired a car to take him to catch the National flight. He went alone because Cardozo said he was going to stay over for dinner in New York. Danzig said he was a frequent enough passenger on National flights to Miami that the check in desk or members of the crew could confirm that he was aboard the flight. And so could AVIS, he said, at the Miami airport.

He made this statement about the Slurrie killing:

I had respect for Walter Slurrie. I met him years ago, a long time ago. Edward Cardozo introduced me, I think. I knew Cardozo because from time to time he would bring Cuban business into our bank. That's all I can tell you about the Slurrie thing.

Asked if he could think of any motive for the crime, he said:

What would I know? Cardozo is the father of Betsy Slurrie's two children, but in my experience, it's always money that gets people killed. Cardozo's money and Slurrie's money were very much mixed up together. Partners fall out. Sometimes they want the other partner's share and even figured out a way to get it. You want to play "motive, motive who's got the motive" with me, that's a motive.

Cardozo agreed to see the police in the lobby of the Wofford Hotel in Miami. He says he did not know Slurrie was in New York on the day of the murder. Cardozo says Slurrie kept his business life and his political life entirely separate. He stated that after the meeting at the Calumet Bank on the afternoon of August 9th he had gone to the New York Athletic Club for a swim and a massage, then he had had dinner with William Egerton, a National Airlines pilot, and his wife, Francine Egerton. They are Cardozo's neighbors in Vizcaya Cove, Dade County, Florida. After dinner all three of them went to the airport where they boarded a National Airlines flight to Miami with William Egerton at the controls as chief pilot.

This is Cardozo's statement:

Nobody would hurt Walter Slurrie. He had political enemies but those are more competitors than enemies. I hope you catch the killer tonight or tomorrow. I pray for that.

Miami Police asked Cardozo if he could think of someone close to Slurrie who would have a clear motive for killing him. He said:

God, nobody knows those things. Motives are such emotional vague things sometimes. I mean, take Nudey Danzig. He was close to Walter. And Nudey Danzig is capable of having anybody killed if you believe what they printed in the papers in the 30s and 40s. I can't help you there. In theory maybe, but what's that? I hear, but it is just a rumor, that Walter and Danzig were in some kind of a deal, that's all I heard, so I can't help you there. But if, say, they were in a deal and Walter disappointed Danzig, then there could be trouble.

My estimate is that Danzig tried to turn us toward Cardozo because Danzig is just beginning to take heat on this in the newspapers. He would rather they worked over Cardozo. My estimate is that Cardozo tried to turn us on to Danzig to keep the public heat on Danzig and off himself, his shadowy relations with Slurrie, and with the Slurrie family.

Sargeant Fearons reports no luck yet on the shoes or on the gunsmiths, but we know this is only a matter of routine follow-up.

The SP team was waiting for me when I got in this morning at about 7:25. They say they are certain now that Chinese agents murdered Slurrie, want me to hold everything until they get their case together, which they guarantee will be ironbound. I congratulated them and said that was very nice.

They asked me to make an "indirect" announcement at today's noon press meeting, just saying that the case may have assumed international proportions but that a definite announcement would be made shortly.

89

I told them I was always happy to cooperate with them when they had hard evidence to back me up. I said that since we would be making the announcement, not the SP, that I would pass until they had their ironbound case all together.

DATE: 10th August 1964
TIME: 1:48 P.M.
BASE REPORTING: Miami   DSP (Semley) Only

EDWARD CARDOZO (continued)

When Wullair go in the Navy I gradually forget him. We deen nid him an I have so many dodges going that I harlee have time to make *pinche*. But it still bug Nudey that Wullair wun take money on the Used Tires dill. When Nudey sen me to Washington, to tell Wullair what we nid, Nudey tell Harry to give me a slip to show Wullair how much he could be making. The first slip show $13,472.19, then after a while $41,822.73—whatever Wullair's end is.

Wullair look at the slips like they are stage money. He say to me, "This isn't what I want my life to be." Another time he say, "You fellows only think about making a profit out of everything in life. That can't be the way it was meant."

Nudey see he cann temp Wullair so he preten he forget it. "He must be sick in his head," he say. I agree. If you head izzen pack with *frijoles* you got to agree. It is hard to figure Wullair in those days. He wun take money but he deen see nothing wrong in setting up a black market for us. He say, "Just because it's a law that doesn't make it right, you understand. I am a lawyer, as you may be aware."

He wun touch Nudey's money but when we senn him plane tickets to Florida and set him with a suite at the Wofford, and wun let him pay for anything including three, four suits, shoes and a buncha shirts, Wullair grab it. I minn he give you the filling he would take a house, a car, a ferry boat from Nudey—but no money.

About eight months before he go in the navy he say to me he wunners if Nudey could fix him up with some lessons at card tricks from whoever is the best so he could improve his game with cards.

"You mean a card mechanic?"

"Whatever the slang term is for those people. But, I thought, with Mr. Danzig's undoubted connections with illegal gambling, he must have *one* dealer who is skillful at manipulating playing cards."

"Why?"

"Well, I'm going into the Navy. If I can improve my skills I can clean up out there."

"You want to cheat your buddies?"

"They are not my buddies. And I will *not* be cheating them. Let's get this straight, Kiddo. For once and for all. I have given up hundreds of hours of my life to acquiring championship status with cards. If anyone, on any ship to which I am assigned, has put in a greater number of hours and has achieved a higher status, then he is entitled to win my money. I *worked*. The men I will be playing against wasted their time. Gambling is only another sport."

Nudey look at me with his mouth hanging open. "This guy is a real freak, right? Am I right? Is he a freak? He won't take my semmenty thousand dollars for legit work but he wants me to get him petty larceny lessons. How do you figure that?"

"He wants to be very good with the cards."

"Listen, say *anything* about this guy and I'll believe it. He won't take the money because he don't want me to have it on him. But he hates people so much that he can't wait to sit down with a deck of cards and gaff them."

"What I tell him?"

Nudey moves both hands like he is saying byebye. "He's entitled because of the tires. I'll send Apples Harris over."

Harold "Apples" Harris is the greatest bustout man in the

business for thirty years. He had no nerves, beautiful with the hands, terrific low-key patter, and the best mover I ever saw. When Wullair go in the Navy he take $1,200 case money with him. He come out the other side with $42,000.

Nudey get Wullair assign to the legal staff of CINCPACFLT, Admiral Gordon "Buffalo" Manning, where he go wherever the Admiral go because he is pick to be the Admiral's partner in the bridge games. Because of his natural bounce, the Navy give Wullair the nickname of "Mournful Max." Actually, Wullair never look that hoppee.

In January 1945, I get a letter from Wullair that I show to Nudey. It say:

Dear Kiddo:

My mother and one of my brothers were in a bad car crash. The expenses are more than I ever thought such things could be. My own funds cannot cover this. I have been remembering the success of our past business transactions. I write this letter to ask you to ask our friend if he would authorize a payment to me of $30,000 to cover the remainder of the accumulating medical, hospital, legal, and liability bills. This sum would be less than half of what he had offered me as my "share" of our past transactions.

I have been granted leave to visit my family at Lubbock General Hospital. Although the crash happened four days ago I could not get here until yesterday. Please leave word for me at the Pioneer Inn at Lubbock where I am staying.

Please extend my regards to all concerned.

Sincerely,
Walter Slurrie

"No way," Nudey says, pushing the letter away from him. "This is an entirely different proposition. The Used Tires is ancient history now. I give him a good shot and he turned it down."

"Wullair is a good property, Nudey. He never ask questions. Give him a good shot an he do it."

"Kiddo is right, Nudey," Harry say.

"Yeah. All right. But if he wants that kinda money he'll hafta start up with a whole new deal for me."

"I could lend him the money if you okay it," I say.

"You stay outta this," Harry says.

"If he does what I want, he can have the money," Nudey tell us.

So Nudey send me to Lubbock, the rill boondocks. When I check in at the Pioneer I ask for Wullair. He is at the hospital. I give the desk a bock an tell him to say to Wullair I am in the coffee shop.

Wullair get back an hour later. He look terrible, even for him. He order franks an french fries.

"Anything to drink?" the wayress ask him.

"A bottle of ketchup," he say. He look at me with those sad eyes. "I certainly didn't expect you to make the trip all the way out here," he tell me. "But I appreciate it. I will treasure it as an act of friendship."

"You think Nudey just mail the check?"

"Well—yes."

"You hear of the statue of limitations?"

"Yes."

"Nudey believe in that. With Nudey every dill is separate. He say you get your shot with Used Tires but you wun take it."

"You mean he isn't going to let me have the money?" He get very pale.

"Is no easy. You rilly shake Nudey opp when you wun take your end."

"Kiddo, the accident wiped me out. I am going to lose every cent I won in the Navy. My family didn't have a cent's worth of insurance. The crash was my mother's fault. If I don't come up with the rest of the money—about $30,000—those lawyers are going to press criminal charges against Mother."

"How much you win?"

"About $40,000. I offered it and they took it. Now I have to come up with what looks like about $26,000 for the doctors, the hospital, and the undertaker."

"A funeral?"

"My brother, Druidie. We haven't told Mother yet." He ate his hot dogs but not with the old-time gusto.

"Wullair, how come you don't figure out that maybe Nudey send me all the way out here with a proposition?"

He stop chewing. "A what?"

"We coo have phone you. Or jus forget about you."

"What kind of a proposition?"

"The same as you do at OPA for us. Only this time, instead of Used Tires, it is defense contracts."

"That's all?"

"One dill at a time."

"And I get thirty-five or forty thousand if I need it?"

"Sure. Plus your end."

"The thirty-five or forty will be enough for me, Kiddo. I just have to get out of this hole."

"You got to start to catch on, Wullair. Nudey want it very clear that there is no dill unless you take your entire piece."

"But why? He'd have his lock on me as he calls it with his thirty or forty."

"If you work for Nudey, you got to share."

"Kiddo, please understand me here. I am practically all set to go into politics. I have it all worked out with a priest on the flag-ship. There is a big chance for me in politics and I can't get mud on that. If I take exactly what it comes to on all Mother's bills then that will be an explanation which the public would accept if this ever became public. But if I take one cent more then I'm through."

"So? What is the prollem, Wullair? Let them send your mother to jail."

He push his plate away. He begin to cry but I already know about that. He is wearing his lieutenant's uniform and he is cry-ing in a coffee shop.

"Drink up you ketchup, Wullair," I say. "You be all right."

He stop crying.

"Wullair, you crazy? What can happen? You can work in uni-form at a Navy yard. Just like you were back in the OPA."

"I can't say yes until I get a few things straight, Kiddo. With all respect for you, I feel that I must ask for a personal meeting with Mr. Danzig."

TO: FIRST DEPUTY COMMISSIONER VINCENT J. MULSHINE

FROM: LIEUTENANT RICHARD GALLAGHER, 17th HSQ

When Edward Cardozo had dinner in New York with Mr. and Mrs. William Egerton, it was at the Waldorf on the night Walter Slurrie was killed there. Also, Cardozo did not attend the meeting with Danzig in the hired room at the Calumet Bank. Danzig implied they had been together from the time they had left Miami. Cardozo, when asked, said he had attended the meeting. When asked by the Miami

97

police this morning, Cardozo said he had attended so many meetings at the Calumet Bank that he had gotten his dates confused but he refused to say where he was in New York at the time of the meeting.

Danzig knew we would check everything out and may have figured that it would put heavier suspicion upon Cardozo if he implied Cardozo was at the meeting when he was not.

We have spoken to Mrs. Slurrie by phone to Dallas. She put on a strong show of grief. She agreed to come to New York as soon as she can after the funeral and will talk to us.

We have nothing solid to hit her with yet. This is what we have relating to Mrs. Slurrie and Edward Cardozo. (This is by no means the only "possible suspect" file.)

Charles Coffey and Abner "Nudey" Danzig have stated that Edward Cardozo is the father of Mrs. Slurrie's children. That, if it is confirmed, could be contributory to an arrest.

Edward Cardozo was Walter Slurrie's business partner. Among other interests and properties they own a bank together in Vizcaya Cove, Florida. Edward Cardozo was the either/or beneficiary on a $2,500,000 life insurance policy held jointly with Walter Slurrie.

Cardozo has put forth his "evidence" that either Danzig or the SP or both together could have killed Slurrie.

Cardozo and Mrs. Slurrie could have plotted Slurrie's murder to gain ownership/control of the joint interests which were 70 percent Slurrie's, 30 percent Cardozo's, and to collect the $2,500,000 insurance.

I am not rushing Mrs. Slurrie by asking the Dallas police to talk to her and I am not in a sweat about moving in on Cardozo or both of them until we nail down the identification of the owner of the shoes that made the footprint on the murder scene and establish who ordered the special ammunition for the murder weapon. Cardozo's allegations may be fantasy and may not. He told the Miami Police a hair-raising story about the involvement of Betaut, Coffey, and Danzig with the SP that I am going to check out with Betaut. I will not set down here any of the details of Cardozo's allegations. If Betaut confirms them I will deliver them to you verbally for a decision on procedure. Again, after all the details have been considered, what Cardozo is saying is that Walter Slurrie betrayed and compromised the SP to the extent the SP had Slurrie murdered.

DATE: 10th August 1964
TIME: 5:10 P.M.
BASE REPORTING: Miami

ABNER "NUDEY" DANZIG (continued)

When Kiddo got back from the tall grass he told me Waller will take the deal, so I tell Harry to set up Waller's transfer with the Navy Department. When I think of Waller with those eyes going through life like pigeons are always dumping on him, I gotta say it is typical of him to get killed on a chair in a bathtub. It was Waller's kind of safe and dignified exit. Nobody could criticize him for sprawling all over the place.

Waller looked conservative but actually he was a tinhorn personality. He made the big time in the history books but inside his head he stayed a hick and a grifter. Just the same, he was a grifter with the nerve of fourteen Apaches. Waller and Benny Siegel had more moxie than anybody I come across but neither one of them ever understood that this is a group thing, life.

You know, when I first met Waller he was different about money. Money killed him. When he first worked for us he wouldn't take money. He is the only one who ever did that to me. But he did what he was supposed to do. Then he goes in the

Navy. Then he needs money quick. So we make a new deal and he agrees to take the money.

That was when he started to change. It didn't happen all of a sudden but it was like the fella who never touched a drop of booze in his life who then has one drink and it sets off something so nobody can stop him. Money was booze to Waller. He got one close-up smell of it, then he has to have more than a hundred average millionaires combined. He was a junkie about money, that's all. In the end, he would do anything for a fix but away back, when Kiddo goes out west to see him, he says very unwilling that he will take the money but first he's gotta talk to me. What he wanted to talk to me about shook this country up so hard that it will never be the same again.

We had the meet upstairs at the Jakarta because he was wearing the uniform and it wouldn't look right downstairs in the coffee shop. I give him a cigar—$1.65 wholesale—and I ask him what's on his mind.

He wants to talk about the future. He asks me if I ever fooled around in politics. I ask him how he thinks he got to be a lieutenant in the Navy. Waller says he wants to run for Congress. He tells me about his gimmick.

"This is a very big gimmick," I tell him. While he was telling me about it I got a whole lot of feeling about America that I didn't even know I had. "Why shouldn't the American people be warned about that goddam Communism," I said. "You think I want a lotta Commies coming down here to Florida and trying to change a system that works better than any system in the world? Where would I be today if my father had stayed in Russia? I'd a been a fuckin' Commie peasant with holes in my pants. This you gotta do, Waller. And it will be a terrific thing to hear a little patriotism from a politician for a change. Where you gonna run from?"

"Salopado, I suppose."

"How many people there?"

"About 160."

"Forget it. Pick a city and run from there. How about New York?"

He shakes his head. Waller was always scared shitless of New York.

"L.A.?"

"I'm a Texan, Mr. Danzig."

"So how about Dallas?"

100

"I've never been there but I like what I've heard about it."

"All right. When you finish the job in Newport News, I'll set you up in Dallas."

"If I can get the nomination for Congress," he says, "and if I can get elected on this new, vital anti-Communist issue, that will mean the rest of the country is ready to receive the same message—if I take it to them directly. The way I see it, if I can tour this entire nation like a modern Paul Revere I will become such a national figure that the Party will have to give me the nomination for the Senate within two years from now."

"Tell me what you got in mind." He lays out his idea and I am knocked out. It is tremendous. I order us two more glasses of tea to give me a chance to get a lot of things straight in my mind, then I sit him down and talk to him on the emmis.

"There is also a terrific buck in your plan, Waller," I tell him. "But you are gonna need us to organize it. It's gonna take ball parks and stadiums. Eighteen or twenty local committees. You gotta have very good showbiz talent to stage it, to make the record albums, and to lay out the souvenir programs and the big street parades. You gotta have people who know how to light anything to milk the effects, so you gotta have deals with the unions. You need press agents and fixers. It takes a lotta money. If this is what is gonna send you into the Senate, it hasta be built like a machine which travels from town to town and never misses an angle. Give the people a great show, something new, and they'll pay gladly. They will pay at the gate, they will put money in the collection boxes, and they will make big public pledges at big lunches and dinners that our people will set up before the show hits town. Also big industry will pour money into this. Why? Because this is the first completely organized shot to scare the shit out of the people and keep them manageable, grateful, and buying. I can feel it in my shoes that you got something here, Waller. All right. I will go along with you. I will set everything up, advance the cash, get you the nominations and put you in the House, then in the Senate *if you absolutely gorrontee that you will take your piece according to Hoyle on every cent of the action, no matter how it is set up?* You unnerstan that, Waller?"

He grabs his whole face in one hand. He holds it tight while he bends over inna chair an stares at the floor to let me know he is thinking. Finally he says, "How much—ah—do you estimate my share of this Red Crusade would be, Mr. Danzig—an estimate."

"This is what I'm gonna do fa you, Waller. For the first time in my life I am gonna take the short end. I am gonna cut this operation fa 49 percent. We gotta give 22 percent to Kiddo because he's gonna have to cut in other people out of his end for organizing and operating. That leaves 29 percent for you, net to you because you don't have to cut anybody in."

"Do you have a round figure in mind, Mr. Danzig? Just a guess?"

"I'll hand you a figure—a very rough figure, but probably on the low side—that your piece for about two years' work on this would come to about a million nine plus a seat in the Senate, give a little, take a little."

He turned to mush in fronna me. This musta been that famous first taste of the booze I was telling you about. This time his hands were shaking too much to grab his face, but he bent over double in the chair again and looked at the floor. When he talked he had to make a big effort to get it out, as if another part of him had the other end of it and wouldn't let go. He is finally able to say, "If I take money from this I'll never be the kind of a leader I want to be."

"Waller, show me one of those kind of politicians, will you? I don't know what you are talking about. Just tell me who is the poor but honest politician who is leading his people to a perfect life, so I will understand what you are tryna tell me."

What could he say? Nothing.

"Waller, before they can get elected they gotta get nominated. But they don't get inside one mile of the nomination unless they make their deal with the people who are putting up the money which the system makes the candidates spend to get elected. The bigger the job in politics, the bigger the money deal that has to be made first if this politician we are talking about is gonna be nominated at all. The bigger the job in politics, the more the financial backers have to eat off."

"Do you mean Presidents of the United States would—"

"Yeah."

"No matter what I try to do," he tells me, and the life has drained out of his voice, "there is always something about it that I can't—do. I wanted to be a lawyer more than anything else but I couldn't seem to learn how. I really studied this Communist thing—you have no idea how many books I read—but I can't get a grasp of the politics of it."

"Don't be a schmuck, please. We are talking about two different things here. You are a natural for politics with this gimmick, but you gotta pay the price of admission. Go along with what we been talking about and watch them all climb aboard your bandwagon. We'll be up to our asses in deals. You and Kiddo won't know where to put the money."

"I need time to think."

"No. Either you wanna run for Congress or not. Either you wanna sit in the Senate or not. If you don't wanna go along I'll even find you a legit job someplace after you get out of the Navy—and I'll run Kiddo or somebody else with your gimmick. Make up your mind."

He watches me like a cat, which is a waste of time. "Okay, Mr. Danzig," he says, "I'll run for Congress from Dallas."

"And you'll take the piece that is coming to you?"

"Everything. Yes, I will."

Then it came to me. All Waller had been waiting for since the day we started him along at the OPA was for somebody to talk him into taking his piece! His fighting against taking money, his fix, was the closest thing he would ever come to a conscience. I was glad I got that part of Waller clear in my head.

"Now the basics," I tell him. "No bachelor gets far in politics in this country. You gotta get married."

"But I've been fighting a war. I don't even know any women anymore. I mean, not even well enough to ask them to dinner, much less to marry me."

"Don't worry about it. Kiddo will take care of it and you got a whole year to line it up."

DATE: 10th August 1964
TIME: 11:10 A.M.
BASE REPORTING: New York

                    DSP (Semley) Only

CHARLES COFFEY (continued)

Walter got in touch with me again the year after he ran for Congress from Dallas and won the election. He was married, he said. They had a little boy. They were living in the 3500 block on Potomac in Highland Park, Dallas.

A Dallas Citizens' Committee had chosen him as their candidate and had backed him to get the nomination and, despite the fact that Walter ran as a Republican and that Texas was a traditional Democratic state, he had been elected by a large plurality. We had watched him run from the 66th floor at Felsenburshe City in New York. Probably one of the dirtiest campaigns ever staged in American politics. Also, Walter's Dallas Citizens' Committee would not stand up to any close examination. But candidates have to find money somewhere and we are told that a lot of hoodlums are hat-over-the-heart patriots. The real question was:

Where did the Citizens' Committee find Walter? Another good question might have been: Why did they find him?

The Dallas Citizens' Committee had advertised for a candidate who was "a married man with a good war record and experience as a lawyer who wished to dedicate himself to public service." Any applicant had to be Texas-born and under thirty-five. Two hundred and eleven people applied for the job. The committee chose Walter.

The year Walter ran there were a half-dozen crucial contests going on around the country. Walter's was mildly interesting because he was a Republican running against a Democratic incumbent in a Democratic situation. What I couldn't put together with all the years I had known Walter was the filthiness of the campaign he ran. He just wasn't that sort of fellow. I considered that, of the two of us, Walter was the more purposeful about how he wanted politics to be run. I was a mercenary. I was the turncoat Democrat who was now hustling the Republicans for a buck. My job was to hustle both parties but make it look as if the Felsenburshes were committed Republicans. To hustle both parties I used elected politicians, of which Walter was now one.

Walter's Dallas campaign was so low and so degrading to the electoral system that I wanted to hear him tell me about what made him do it. He couldn't have needed to be elected that badly. But there were· too many other campaigns spinning around the country.

Then he called me two months after he had been installed in the House. We made a date to meet in Dallas, but before I go onto what occurred at that meeting just let me lay out what Walter's campaign had been like.

His incumbent opponent was Fred Carl Haskins. Haskins flew his own plane, was on the board at the Dallas Country Club, and was personally as well as politically popular. He had a good record in Congress after three terms in office. He was a solid citizen, old-family, who may have taken one or two drinks too many, around whom Walter built a fantasy.

Walter smeared him with an almost untested issue in American politics. Churchill had made his Iron Curtain speech at Fulton. Harry Truman had gotten the country's toes wet in it by setting up his Loyalty Boards, but the thing had never been presented as a direct threat/choice at the voter level.

The issue was threateningly foreign, something the voters had

106

heard of vaguely before but found it hard to evaluate in terms of their own lives, because it was such a remote and improbable phenomenon. But Walter brought the smell ot it and the fear of it very close to them. Ho rubbed their faces in its foreignness, its distinct probability.

It was also vaguely familiar because in the 20s Hearst had shrieked against the Wobblies and Palmer had thundered that America must be saved from them. But there had been Babe Ruth, C.C. Pyle, Dempsey, and flag-pole sitters available too, and so much more on the side that celebrated life. Anyway, Americans hadn't shown any interest in politics yet beyond the courthouse. They turned to politics with a bang when the Bomb was dropped and Walter had the great good luck to drag his malevolent issue in almost immediately after that.

Walter's "Save America from Communist Infiltration" issue was redhot and unexploited. Russians were as foreign as any foreigners could get. They had a sick alphabet, morbid writers, and a very low regard for human life. They had been shaky, undefined allies during the war but everybody knew that Uncle Joe was pretty tricky, except that Walter didn't let it lie there just like that.

He used a pendulum response. He nourished fears: fears that the peace wouldn't last. He filled the vacuum created by the disappearance of the Nazis.

I was given the privilege of a preview of how Walter's axe would fall, splitting the country in half, while he was still in the Navy, at some desk job at Newport News. We met by chance in the lobby of the Carlton, always glad to see each other as two surviving pseudo-lawyers. Walter went to great lengths to thank me for having had something to do with getting him a job early in the war with the OPA, something which I couldn't remember at all at the time. Walter actually invited me to dinner that night, a famous first for Walter, something that is nearly certain to happen in anybody's lifetime. He was in full uniform, which most grandly would have outranked my discarded Marine corporal's stripes. We went to an Italian restaurant called the Villa d'Este, where he astonished me by introducing the proprietor, a thug named Dom G. Everyone is an insider somewhere. Walter was not given a check for the dinner, but on the other hand neither was I. The food was on the ouch side for anyone who had ever eaten with Marie; a red sauce joint.

Walter hadn't changed. He was the same, plodding, intent grind who preferred to punish one idea at a time until it lay bleeding. He was always willing to settle for less.

He said he wanted some professional advice. "I have the chance to go into active politics, Charley," he said. "I've been talking it over with a priest in the Navy and with some other people."

"A priest?"

"Yes. He was my—chaplain. He isn't a professional politician, of course. I'd like to confirm a few points with you."

"Why not?"

"I am a lawyer. I have a good war record. I am wearing the leadership stripes of a lieutenant-commander—I was promoted yesterday, by the way. I am devoutly interested in doing a job for constituents and I think I have discovered a new and vital issue for the American people as they face the unknown of a post-war world."

"Is that so? Where will you run?"

"Texas."

"Salopado?"

"No. One of the cities."

"Congress?"

"Well, that's the idea."

"What's the new issue?"

"In strictest confidence?"

"Why not?"

"You can talk it after I start to use it," he said gravely. He leaned forward. "Charley, this isn't off the top of my head. I've read a lot of books—and you know how I go about studying a book—about political ideologies and economics and propaganda and I have proven the whole thing to my satisfaction—in theory anyway."

"Proven what?"

"Proven that there is a demonstrable, incipient danger of Communism taking over the government of this country."

"*Whaaaat?*"

"Right at this moment it might not seem so. But I have solid information that the Russians are pressing us for an exchange of intelligence teams, for example, which would be deadly if it is allowed to happen. They are going to try to infiltrate our government at every level. If they can penetrate our intelligence organizations, and Colonel Donovan has already endorsed the idea, then they can infect other American institutions to which access is so much easier."

"Like where, Walter?"

"Well, name it. Our communications industries. Our churches. The new visual radio medium which may grow into something important. It would be easy to worm into our educational system and our political organizations, including Mr. Truman's United Nations. Bribe and conscript. They will come to us pretending to be friends until they can fill their Trojan horses to capacity. Then they will strike in the dead of the night to overthrow our government to replace it with Communism."

"Jesus, Walter, I thought the war had bankrupted the Russians."

He took a deep breath, then expelled it carefully as he spoke. "Charley, through channels that represent one of the strongest, most cohesed organizations in the world, a unitary force with access to hidden plans and facts inside Europe, Asia and sources deep within this country, I have been privileged to study this thing from every direction. What I have been told, what I have read and remembered, has convinced me that this country is now facing a terrifying Communist peril."

I didn't doubt that Walter believed he had fallen upon a treasure of truth, what I doubted was his judgment in unraveling it. Walter wasn't an intelligent fellow. He was shrewd, he could imitate and simulate all the attitudes of cogent wisdom, but he had no judgment and no selectivity.

"Still—no offense, Walter—but it *is* an election gimmick, isn't it?"

"Well, yes. In the confining sense it is the lever that will put me into Congress where I will be able to fight and protect the American people from what then goes far beyond the gimmick stage and becomes a national peril. What I propose to take over will become the core of our national security."

"But are you going to use this in *Texas* of all places? Do you have any reason to believe that they know what Communism is or give a damn if they do?"

"If they don't know right now, they will," he answered calmly. "And, by God, the entire country will know within the next two years. When I campaign on this issue, it is just possible that people who are soft on Communism might get hurt, but I'll even do that gladly because it has to be done."

I tried to see Walter from the new perspective he was offering me, but I couldn't. He was the same faltering Walter who was sure to botch up another shot at the dignified eminence that meant so much to him. He was telling me that he was going to get himself elected against an incumbent *Democrat* in *Texas* on an issue that would have him warning a country which had just won a world war. He was going to try to tell those people that he would be protecting them from total infiltration and possession by a foreign power that had just lost 35,000,000 people in the same war and was lying gasping on its back from need, perhaps ten thousand miles from Texas.

I tried to talk around his nonsense, hoping it would go away. "Walter, can you remember how upset you were when you discovered that we were going to pay a few dozen drunks two dollars apiece to vote the straight ticket for us, using the names of other people who had died before they wouldn't have bothered to vote on Election Day?"

"Yes. And I remember the gangsters you hired to intimidate the voters who did turn out. And the police you paid to look the other way. That will never happen in my kind of politics." His voice had found its natural self-righteousness. He held my forearm. He was waxing eloquent, which was Walter's single talent beyond his pale innocence. "It was because of politics like that, and the Eastern bankers, and the Eastern establishment press that we were dragged into war. Hitler had right on his side. Ask any military man. He would have whipped the Russians for us. So the rest of us, my people in Texas, had to fight that Easterners' war in order to keep America for Americans by standing off foreign ideologies and loathsome alien conceptions. Yes, Charley, I remember that Election Day in 1935. Why do you ask?"

"Did you vote in 1935, Walter? Or in '36? Or in '40?"

"What about the gangsters?"

"*I* was the one who told you that. Did you ever *see* anybody being intimidated by a hired gangster at the polls? We had outgrown that even by 1935. Forty years ago they used hoodlums in ghettos to force people out to vote when they didn't even understand what voting was. They were disenfranchised people who had fled their governments, who feared and hated governments, who couldn't speak, read, or write English. So the Organization had people they could recognize, slum hoodlums who spoke their languages, herd them out to the polls so that they could turn their kids into doctors and police chiefs. How do you think this country works, Walter? It is an ongoing struggle to persuade

110

the people to reason out a government that can make better lives for them."

"B-movie stuff," he sneered. Walter even sneers when he is praying if he thinks God doesn't agree with him. Anyone can imagine how easy it is to want to punch him right in his mush when he sneers.

"And Americans can not only speak, read, and write now—because of strong laws—but maybe they can even think. By voting more they have less to complain about."

"We have gotten off the subject, Charley."

"Right. Now—you want my professional opinion on whether you have a good election gimmick. I say—sure. It is a great election gimmick. But what I was starting to say is, this time it really is buying drunks' votes and hiring those gangsters you object to so much."

"I don't understand that."

"You will be lying to them, won't you? You are going to tell them that some cockeyed theory is absolute gospel fact, as if you held documents in your hand which proved how many Communists had infiltrated the government, which you do not have. You will be saying in effect that you are a liar, therefore they should buy protection from you with their votes to save them from being burned in their beds."

"Do you really see it that way, Charley? Will voters see it that way? I knew you were just testing my thesis with hypothetical questions but you've brought up something I had not anticipated."

"Don't worry about it."

"Why shouldn't I?"

"What do Texans know about elections in New York forty years ago?"

"That's right. Thank you, Charley. Now—tell me straight out—what do you think of my plan?"

"Will it get you elected, you mean?"

"Yes. That's where I want your opinion."

"I think it will all the way, Walter. It may even be the coming thing in politics. It's so simple."

"That's wonderful."

"Mind if I throw in a little lecture? Sort of singing for my supper?"

"Please. Go right ahead."

"Walter, politicians may seem to continue on without much

111

reference to the people, but whatever they do is the will of the people."

"But—where does that affect my plan?"

"I just wanted to talk about how one idea can proliferate in politics. Let's say you run on a platform of warnings about a Communist takeover. Maybe in California a candidate is running on an issue of pensions for teenagers and in Ohio a man seeks office by offering free admission to race tracks. Well, people like me, the professional survivors in politics, would watch the people react to each issue, then measure the issue's usefulness against the plurality it produced for the candidate against other pluralities. The issues that get the best results are then moved along by people like me, to other candidates in following elections and, if these issues produce bigger and bigger pluralities all because of the accident of one man trying it out absolutely blind in Texas, a great national issue is produced."

"That is absolutely wonderful," he said exultantly. "I knew I could count on you to tell me the truth."

That was the moment when Walter foretold his own future. That was the isolated second when Walter and I, unconsciously, exchanged hats and styles. Suddenly it was as though I were marching along toward some kind of a demonstration in civics and Walter were sprinting straight toward corruption. Not that I knew it then. But we were both beginning the long journey along each other's divergent railway tracks, both of us lost.

Walter Slurrie, the 1947 anomaly, a Texas Republican, won his election. His plurality was the greatest in his state and in all other states where contests on new issues were run. I was on the phone talking to other political managers about it for almost a week. The professional consensus favoring Walter's issue was overwhelming, because it seemed to work so well and produce such golden results. With anti-Communism, Walter had built the boys a vote-getter, and they were all busy gearing up for the next election, in hundreds of local, state, and federal elections where Walter, with his flashing Red Crusade, was still the national star. "This little son-of-bitch may just have laid out the issue of the 50s for us," Pop said. "Are you sure this is the same long, blond drink-of-water with those busy eyes, the one who stayed with us and run out on Margaret?"

"The same one, Pop."

"The shitty lip-licker you went to law school with?"

112

"That's him. Walter Slurrie."

"I can't believe it. A shifty night court lawyer coming up with a great stunt like that. That priest musta thought of the whole thing. The boys are gonna make a lot of deals with this one, Charley, even if the Republicans are going to be carrying the ball this time."

Walter campaigned to establish in the prepackaged prejudices of Dallas voters that his opponent was subversively and dangerously Communistic, already acting as an advance agent of the Soviet government in the Congress. Further, twenty-six workers were paid to conduct a telephone canvass of individuals listed in the Dallas telephone directory to spread the word that Walter's opponent's twenty-year-old daughter was spreading gonorrhea throughout the city.

It is hard to imagine how anyone could be free enough from self-doubt to be able to run a campaign like that. Back-to-back the two charges ruined Walter's opponent's family. The AP carried a sidebar out of Heppner, Oregon, three years later that the daughter had killed herself. By that time Walter's opponent had already become a stumbling drunk and an outcast. But the campaign sent Walter to Washington as a crusader and gave all American constituencies the greatest fake issue to rally round since William Jennings Bryan and the Cross of Gold.

DATE: 10th August 1964
TIME: 3:10 P.M.
BASE REPORTING: Miami   DSP (Semley) Only

EDWARD CARDOZO (continued)

Wullair have a good year at Newport News. He live on the base. He read heavy books. When he get time off he go to El Paso to visit his mother. Also, he make himself a nice piece of money. I go up to see him about once every ten days. We meet in Washington. For the first time in his life he really want to move along. He used to be a lump. Now he is a fireball. He want to talk politics all the time. He also find out fish taste good, which make him happy because fish don't cost not very much.

Wullair's end for moving the contracts at Newport News is $51,226.28. He finish the work in November 1945. He is release from the Navy with the rank of Commander, which Harry get for him, and the Navy Cross, which took Nudey to get it. We meet for lunch that day at the Carlton in Washington, always Wullair's favorite if I get the check. All he want to talk about is how Dallas is gun to operate.

"I got a bronn envelope unner my chair," I tell him. "Inside is a full page ad which the Dallas Citizens' Committee run in both

115

newspapers and which Nudey pay for. The ad say the Committee gun to comb the whole state to find a Texas war veteran who is a lawyer, to be their man for Congress. The whole ad describe joo except the part which say the candidate got to be marry."

"Who would marry me?" Walter say indignantly. "Damn it, Kiddo. Something always comes up to spoil things. Can't Mr. Danzig get it into his head that there aren't any women in foxholes?"

"Dun worry abaht it."

"Everybody says that. How much time do I have before I meet the Committee?"

"About ten days."

"Ten *days?*"

"Joo remember li'l Betsy Ginzler? The pretty, red-headed Irish kid at the OPA?"

"My former secretary who quit me to go over to the Department of Agriculture?"

"Yeah."

"I didn't know she was Irish."

"Mostly Irish."

"Not that I object. There is a large Irish-American vote, although not particularly in Texas."

"The great part about Ginzler is that she can be German in Texas."

"Is she Catholic?"

"I think Lutheran. Walter, do you remember her?"

"Of course I remember her. She started this whole damned thing. She brought me to your buffet supper for the Haitian Ambassador."

"That's the one. She has got a crush on joo for five yirrs."

"*Ginzler?*"

"You never notice it?"

"No."

"Well, she crazy about joo."

"How do you know?"

"I was at Dom G's. She is there. We get talking. The firss thing she ask is about joo. A dozen questions. She is so proud of joo, tears come to her eyess."

"Why should she be proud?"

"I tell her joo going to run for Congress."

"For heaven's sake."

"She ask me if joo are marry. I say not yet, but esoon. She want

116

to know who joo marry. I tell her nobody exactly but that joo think the time has come to get marry. 'I wish I was the lucky girl,' she say."

"I am astounded."

"Wullair, listen. I have this hawnch if joo take her out to a nice dinner an ask her in a nice way, Ginzler will marry joo."

MRS. WALTER SLURRIE (continued)

You might have gotten the idea that there was nothing really loving about the way Walter and I happened to get married, but there was. I will never stop looking back on the night he took me out to dinner at the Carlton Hotel in Washington. The Carlton! *Walter!*

Even I wouldn't call Walter a handsome man. He has a fine torso but his arms and legs don't seem to fit it very well and they are all of different lengths, which is why he seems to move himself so awkwardly. His head seems to be on the wrong body altogether. It is too small. But his hair helps, in a way. It is so blond and nearly leonine if his barber can keep his mind on it. He has a really fine eyebrow line and a really distinguished set to his jaw. I suppose, taken one by one like that, it sounds as if I didn't love the way Walter looked. But the whole Walter was greater than the sum of his parts. He became Vice-President of the United States, didn't he?

Walter and I have joked a lot about that first dinner. We called it "The Courtship of Miles Standish," with Eddie playing the marriage broker's part unbeknownst to either of us.

I didn't have any idea I was going to get married until Eddie and I talked it over one night in bed at the Statler in Washington.

First he asked me where I was from. I told him: Winsted, Connecticut. (We lived right on Highland Lake.)

"Still have people there?"

"Well, a third cousin."

"You an orphan?"

"Well, I'm a grownup orphan."

"You like knocking around Washington?"

"Government work is romantic. At least in wartime. What is this, anyway, Eddie?"

"A frenna mine, you know him, is gun run for Congress from Dallas. And he'll win. Texas is a nice place—good climate, nice people—you'd like it."

"Why should I like it?"

"Because I have a very innaresting possibility for you to think about."

"Like what?" He was making me very nervous.

"Firss—you get a chance to get out of this rat race. Seconn—a thousand bucks for all the new clothes you want. Third—a diamond ring. Those I personally gorrontee."

"What do I have to do for that?"

"Remember Walter Slurrie, your old boss at the OPA?"

"If I have to I can remember him."

"Betsy, you gun be knock off you feet the way the Navy has change him. He is full Commander. The Navy Cross. He is still in uniform."

"Walter Slurrie? The Navy Cross?"

"Completely change man."

"I suppose he's all right. I never disliked him. And I never liked him. For me he was Prince Nowhere."

"Is now Commander Somewhere. Soon to be Congressman Somewhere."

"But it's so hard to believe."

"You could come back to this town on your own terms as the wife of a congressman."

"*Wife?*" It took me until then to realize what Eddie had been talking about.

"Wullair wan to morry you but he is too scare to ask you. An you know I am your frenn, that I wan the best for you. Listen, *ca-*

ritita, wha kind of a tonn is this for a single gorl? How many gorl you got to share the apartment with?"

"Seven."

"An still pretty lonesome, eh?"

"Eddie, I just don't think I could get used to the idea."

"You wan to think abott it or you wan to forget it?"

"I don't know what to say, Eddie. You have me all mixed up. Sure I'm sick of living the way I have to live, but there is no place else to go. If it wasn't for the sick benefits and the accumulated time and the pension I guess I'd have tried to get out of here a long time ago."

"Washington is a differenn place when you the wife of a congressman. Parties. No tabs. Hunnerd-dollar gift certificates to the big stores. Maybe a free credit card if Walter get assigned to a defense committee. Inside the White House once every year. Pictures in the papers. Free vacations in the Dominican Republic. Company planes. Free dog food. I tell you, Betsy, Washington today is like Hollywood in the 30s."

I could say it to him but I felt sad: "I guess you are telling me as direct as you can that my only choice is Walter. Is that right? Is that what you are saying?"

He covered my hand and nodded.

"Then I guess I'll have to take Walter," I said.

"Up to you, Betsy."

"But I mean does Walter consider this a proposal of marriage? Is that how a girl finds out that she's going to get married today?"

"Absolutely not! No! Wullair will court you. Is only that there is not much time *para la buscada* so he can work up slowly to asking joo. He got to get to Dallas. But you can be sure of this, if Wullair had any time at all, whatsoever, I wun be here to talk the whole thing over witchew because he would be doing the whole thing himself."

"I just don't think so, Eddie," I said.

Remember I *knew* Walter. I will bet he made himself *sick* worrying about what it would cost to take me to a restaurant like the Carlton. But he did it. That is a point very much in his favor because he knew we could have eaten at Dom G's on the cuff. It proves that Walter had a sense of occasion.

He looked very nice in his uniform. He was a little jowly for thirty-four but he looked healthy, a nice thing in a man. The

121

jowls were new but they balanced his unicorn nose. He was so relieved when he saw me that he must have remembered something much worse. I wore my new dress from Lansburgh's, out of the thousand dollars from Eddie. I still have it. It has wonderful colors and memories. I remember thinking maybe the Navy did change Walter, as Eddie said, because there was a sweetness about him. He seemed—well, he seemed helpless. He behaved nicely. He showed that he had respect for me, and in a different way he was like a small boy who had been forced to go to dancing class. He looked stiff and scared.

"Good evening, Miss Ginzler," he said.

I had to smile. "Walter, after two years at that crummy OPA together if you can't call me Betsy, who can?"

His voice was low and intense. "I want you to know that I am keenly aware that you seem to have been placed in a position which must seem to lack kindness. I want to hasten to assure you that only the unusual circumstances make it appear that way."

"It's all right. I don't mind."

"I know that you know that I know that you and Edward Cardozo have had some sort of preliminary conversation about this evening but I assure you that all of that was done without my knowledge or consent. No, no, please. You must believe that. I would never have allowed it to happen this way had I known."

"I don't know what I expected but I didn't expect you to be sweet."

"Let me explain a few things, Betsy. I—well, I've been overseas for a long time, alone in foxholes. As a result I just didn't know anyone who would marry me. I never did actually. Now I have this chance to make a life in politics but—well—it requires that I be a married man. Voters expect that, I am told."

The waiter came and fussed around with menus and saltcellars. After a while Walter said, "You were the only date I ever had all the years I was in Washington."

"Date?"

"When we went to the Cardozo party? In 1942?"

"Oh, *that* date."

Walter ordered two glasses of red wine for us. When he did that, knowing how he had weighed the additional cost, I realized what a serious business all this was for him. I said, "I feel too excited to eat."

His relief engulfed me.

"Just a mixed green salad, I think."

"Two green salads," Walter told the waiter quickly, "with lots of oil and vinegar, please."

"In that case we'd better cancel the wine."

"Yes," Walter told the waiter with great dignity. "Red wine only goes with hot food." The waiter left.

"Have you ever been to Dallas, Walter?"

"Not to Dallas, no."

"When must you be there?"

"Not later than a week from today. Betsy, may I say something?"

"Say it, certainly."

"There is no woman I would rather have by my side in the long climb ahead. I intend to become a United States senator. I ask you to be my wife and to share that with me."

We looked deeply into each other's eyes. He has such brooding eyes and I thought that long before Theodore H. White kept saying it.

"I will marry you, Walter," I told him.

TO: FIRST DEPUTY COMMISSIONER VIN-CENT J. MULSHINE

FROM: LIEUTENANT RICHARD GALLA-GHER, 17th HSQ

Last night I had separate calls from two-man teams with the SP and the FBI. They wanted to know if any "foreign power" aspects of the Slurrie murder had surfaced. I tell them not yet, but that is the only thing that hasn't surfaced. Both agencies told me that if anything came up that looked like a connection with "another government" that I am to notify them and only them, then I am to back away from it.

I told them I would share information with them if it would help them keep their jobs but that I wasn't backing away from anything. That made the FBI get mean and the SP more conciliatory. The SP said that surely I could see that I would be taking a lot of heat off myself if the word got out that Slurrie could have been hit by agents of a foreign government. I told them I wasn't particular who we nailed with the killing so long as it was the right killer and we had a case that would stand up in court. We let it stand there. It is possible that by now the PC has heard from the White House but I don't think the federal people are ready to stick their necks into this meat grinder yet.

We can't get to Horace Hind. The Las Vegas police say we should forget it. I sent Sgt. Fearons out and they handed him a list of people who had tried to get in to see Hind beginning with Lyndon Johnson, but Hind won't see anybody. The Chief at Vegas offered Fearons his opinion that it didn't figure that Hind would set up Slurrie's killing anyway. He never leaves that room so he'd have to tell somebody to tell somebody else, the Chief said, and he just wouldn't let anyone have it on him because he would be afraid of a shakedown. I told the press at noon today that Hind is obstructing justice but that isn't going to get us anything.

Ballistics says the murder weapon is a Japanese officer's model: Nambu 7mm. These were handguns made for their top brass. Some of these came into the country with GIs after the war. The grip slant makes for natural pointing and the gun is for quick shooting at close range. My own feeling is that it was used because it was the only gun the killer could lay his hands on. It throws about a .32 inch bullet weighing about 100 grams and its muzzle velocity is only about 860 feet a second. It has to have special ammunition (which to me rules out a professional contract killer because it would be too much bother and the bullets could be too easily traced), but Ballistics says a lot of amateur hobby shooters in this country know how to make their own ammunition for all kinds of guns. Fearons is now checking out all NY gun shops and has liaised with the FBI for a checkout of gunsmiths across the country. It could be that a familiar name may pop up on one of their customer lists.

We have the shoeprints and we have identified the gun. That is very encouraging.

These are the people close to Slurrie who may or may not relate to a Nambu 7mm: Coffey was in the Marines in the South Pacific. Slurrie himself was with the Pacific Fleet. (It is possible that this was his own gun, that he set up and paid for his own murder because of the way he let the killer position him in that slippery tub). Danzig has the connections (and so have the Soviet and Chinese governments) to come up with an offbeat weapon like this one. Good idea for Danzig because he knows it wouldn't be associated with a Mob hit, but when has he ever worried about that before? Horace Hind could have a collection of fifty Nambus. Betaut is very big with the SP, always has been. If he wanted a Nambu they could get one for him. The same reasoning goes for the SP itself, which Coffey told me had a motive for killing Slurrie. The Nambu would be a light and practical weapon for a woman to fire but so far we aren't coming up with any outside women in Slurrie's life but the woman could be a hooker gilled with speed, in the apartment on call, or her pimp, or both, who Slurrie let into the apartment. We can't rule out any homosexual involvement by Slurrie either, although we have nothing to go on there except possibly a man's picture found in his wallet.

Now – the motive Coffey supplied to give the SP a reason to want to kill Slurrie: revenge. We are checking this out with Betaut. Coffey says Slurrie was the single factor in getting the Director of Secret Police (DSP) fired in 1961 when Slurrie's actions caused the public humiliation of the SP and caused a serious threat to their future in Vietnam and at home, which was changed only by the assassination of the President.

This puts me in over my head. I hand it to you to get a decision about what I'm supposed to do about that lead. God knows the SP have had a lot of people knocked off for less reason so – with motives like that – why not Slurrie? A Japanese officer's handgun would be just their style.

Mrs. Slurrie admits that Cardozo is the father of the Slurrie kids. She was entirely forthcoming about it, said it was done with the full knowledge of her husband who she said, when I intimated that Cardozo was a murder suspect, was impotent. Cardozo got very Spanish about discussing this. He became very much the man of honor but the fact is Cardozo is nothing but a hoodlum. He has worked with Nudey Danzig all his life. This is from the Miami police who have a sheet on him.

127

As business partners, Slurrie and Cardozo had taken out $2,500,000 insurance policies on each other's lives in what Cardozo says was a straight business operation. Also, Cardozo says, they both wanted to be sure that Mrs. Slurrie and the children would be taken care of for the rest of their lives. When asked why the policies didn't then show Mrs. Slurrie and the children as beneficiaries, Cardozo said that the bulk of his estate and Walter Slurrie's (the Slurrie family are Cardozo's heirs, too) is in the businesses which Slurrie and Cardozo owned and operated, and the $2,500,000 insurance policy was to insure the continuance of the business.

If we can match Cardozo's shoes to those footprints and can connect him with the gun we'll have a helluva case.

Since not more than two pennies have to be involved to cause a murder, I have had to include Mrs. Walter Slurrie among the suspects. She and Cardozo make a natural suspect team.

The murder weapon has just been brought in. It was found in a city trash basket at 54th & Lexington. There are prints on it but they are in very bad condition. If the lab can get anything out of them it will take two days.

DATE: 10th August, 1964
TIME: 11:20 A.M.
BASE REPORTING: Dallas

MRS. WALTER SLURRIE (continued)

We were married in a simple ceremony two days after Walter proposed to me. Walter asked if I would object to having both a religious and a civil ceremony. While I am not a religious person I have always felt that there is something, you know, more sanctifying about a religious ceremony so that was fine with me. When I asked him what religion, I somehow expected a Baptist playback because Walter looked like a Baptist, or maybe it is only that all politicians have that look.

Walter said we would be married in a Conservationist ceremony because conservation was becoming a prime political issue—and because Nature stood for the pursuit of honesty and straight thinking. Personally, I don't think you could ask for more than that as a marriage intention. When I asked if the ritual was about the same as in other marriage ceremonies, Walter said, no, not really. I asked him if it was legal, like if we had children would they inherit without any problem? And—a fairly big thing in politics—would we really be married?

That was when he told me about the plan to have two ceremonies. "As you know, I am a lawyer," he explained once again. "Let me say this, and by all means correct me if you differ in any way. We will be married in a civil ceremony first, by a judge who is a friend of Dom G's. After that, a Conservationist clergyman will seal the marriage under religious rites so that when and as conservation becomes a large political issue we can have our wedding ceremony to prove our early interest."

"What kind of a ceremony is it, Walter?"

"The clergyman addresses the forces and beauty of nature, as I understand it, then we tap each other on each shoulder with oak branches—or twigs if we can't get branches, or seed packets if we can't get twigs—then over the heart . . ."

"Hard?"

"No, no. Lightly, lovingly. Then we drink an infusion of acorns which, I can assure you, at least the way Mother made it, is delicious. Then we pledge our lives to peace and honor and vow that we will make our marriage as strong as the trees of the forest."

"Walter, it's a beautiful ceremony."

Walter was able to find a Druid priest for our Conservationist ceremony, named F. Marx Heller, in the East Village, New York City. Father Heller's fee to perform the marriage was $55. Walter was shocked and tried to renegotiate the whole thing on the telephone. He said Father Heller told him that he hadn't put $192 into a Druid theology course so he could walk around with a basket of acorns. Walter said he would give him $10. It sounded as if Father Heller were trying to come through the phone to get at Walter. He yelled, "How many practicing Druid clergy do you think there are on the whole eastern seaboard? Worse, how many Druids? When they sold me the diploma they told me 600 but if we make a deal you will be the third set I joined together in nineteen months."

We decided to let the ceremony rest with the one the judge would perform, which was terrifically legal. Eddie Cardozo was our best man. He brought a photographer and *The Dallas Morning News* ran our wedding picture over the caption: TEXAS VET MAKES BID FOR SEAT. Seat? Where? We never seemed to sit down throughout the entire campaign. Walter never took his uniform off from start to finish.

Walter and I had happiness and balance in our marriage. I liked being the wife of an important man. Walter was also a great man, which made it all even that much more fulfilling. I liked his friends. Mr. Danzig had a terrific sense of humour and was always bringing me little things, pretending it was my birthday. I had to like Mr. Danzig. He thought I was a terrific cook.

After Walter finished his Red Crusade—I didn't go on tour with him because the moving demonstration of Americans' faith in America was almost too powerful for me—but I was up there on the platform for the really big rallies. In fact, I met Walter's mother for the first time at Soldiers Field, Chicago. They flew her in from El Paso in a huge Air Force helicopter and set her down on a high pad that was on a level with Walter's Freedom Altar— perhaps he had to run up a step or two—but he went to her with a microphone in his hand and I don't think the people of our great country have ever been so touched as when he knelt beside her and, placing his hand upon her head, he took a pledge to spend his life defending the United States of America from a Communist takeover. Over 90,000 people sobbed in that stadium and the sound filled the hearts and minds of TV viewers—live— from sea to shining sea.

When the Red Crusade was over, that is, when the barnstorming phase was over, I suppose we became one of Washington's most popular couples. Hostesses ranked us just below cabinet level. It was a sensation almost like suffocating because the telephone would not stop ringing. Walter wouldn't okay hiring a secretary, but he did allow Mr. Danzig to send me a telephone answering machine.

I love parties. Walter loves the lavish displays of free food and the chance to express his political opinions to so many different people, and we had some wonderful times. Walter can play the banjo by ear and really does liven up a party, and he is simply tremendous with card tricks. He had an even disposition because he seemed to be brooding all the time. He was very nice to our baby. He was unfailingly courteous to me. He was—well, emotionally Walter never seemed to change much. Biologically if not politically, he was neutral.

That is a nice quality in older people, but I happen to love sex. I have loved sex ever since I was fourteen years old. I could never get tired of sex. Not that Walter pretended to be too tired or said that he didn't have the time. I mean, he could have said that. Frankly, I even felt that I was entitled to that much consideration when we were first married even if insincere.

All the rules for our sex life were established by Walter on our

131

wedding night. What a night. First, to make it plain what I was there for, I didn't wear anything to bed. I just lay there and breathed loudly on him. I made sure that he understood we were there to fool around a little.

He just lay there.

His pajamas—Walter wears blue serge pajamas—were buttoned up to his neck and straight down, including his fly. He let me do anything to him but he didn't do anything to me. I was deeply hurt. Also, it was making me very, very edgy. I told him, straight out, that I could not understand what he thought people were supposed to do on their wedding night.

But, just the same, Walter was such a considerate man. He seemed to sense, rather than understand, what the occasion must have meant to me. He didn't put me off. Instead he explained. He started by saying, "Someday, I realize that now, I am going to have to see a psychiatrist about this. I can't right now, because if a thing like my being under psychiatric treatment ever came out, it could ruin me politically. But, someday, this will all be cleared up. I just know it."

"All what?"

"I have never told this to anyone," he said, "but you are entitled to know—as my wife."

"Yes."

"If anyone is entitled to know."

"I am entitled, Walter, as the wife."

"It is very hard for me to try to tell you this, Betsy."

"Walter, for Christ's sake, what is it?"

He spoke steadily but he couldn't look at me. "We all lived in a turd-colored house in Salopado, Texas. The store was downstairs. There was a storeroom and a big bedroom upstairs. Father was still with us when we were kids. I was the oldest after two of my brothers died. I was ten or eleven when Father left us." He tried to control his breathing.

"Father and Mother would have sex every night. It took them a long, long time every night. It turned them into noisy animals. They barked and bit each other." I felt him shudder.

"That happens to thousands of children, Walter," I tried to explain. "It really does."

"I know." Sweat shone on his face and forehead. "And I knew it was what God wanted. But I couldn't sleep while they did that, even if I understood that they had to do it."

"Is that why you can't—"

132

"Mother got sick," he went on. He hadn't heard me. "It was the only time she was ever sick until the accident. They put her into the hospital at Lubbock and she was gone about seven weeks. While she was away it was so quiet in their bedroom that it kept me awake. Father would sit downstairs in the kitchen. Just sit. He never read anything. It wasn't as though he were too tired to read because Father never did anything to get tired. He never helped with anything around the store. He just seemed to exist as a brute who lifted crates now and then, and made sex with Mother. Sex was Father's demon and, with Mother in the hospital, he could do nothing to get it off his mind."

"My God, Walter," I said in horror, "he didn't molest you? He didn't molest his own child?"

"I couldn't sleep for waiting for him to go to his bed. I heard the front door open, very quietly, then it closed again, just as softly. I couldn't stay still. I began to imagine things. I told myself that he had run away from us. I became convinced that his mental balance had gone because of a lack of sex and that he would set fire to the house with all of us in it. I made myself go down to look for him."

I held on to Walter's hand tightly.

"A lantern had been lighted in the shed. I crossed the yard and stood in the doorway. Father was standing on a wooden box."

"He was going to hang himself," I moaned.

Walter's voice trembled and tears ran down his cheeks. "He was standing on that box," he said. "His penis was inside our cow. He was moving his hips rapidly. He heard me at the door and turned. He saw me." Walter made a dry, sobbing sound. "He was covered with cowflop from his chest to his knees. I went back to the house. Father went away that night and never came back."

Walter closed his eyes and gripped his lower lip between his teeth and lay there motionless. I felt bound to him. I kissed him and stroked him and, after a while, he turned and kissed me on the forehead. "I want you to know," he said, "that I am sincerely not against fellatio, if you feel there would be anything satisfactory for you in that." He lay back, neutral again.

I did my best, so much so that on the day following my wedding night, I had to find a dentist because my jaws had immobilized with temporomandibular joint dysfunction.

The next two months were very hard on me. I finally had to talk my problem over with Eddie Cardozo, even though I felt disloyal to Walter by doing it. "This is a serious thing, Eddie," I told him. "You know how much I like sex but I am married to Walter and he is an important man so I am not about to go out and screw every Tom, Dick, and Harry. You know how I am, Eddie. You know me. I have to get it regularly or my skin goes. He absolutely will not do it to me, Eddie. What am I going to do?"

"You got a problem, baby."

"Eddie, I don't need you to tell me I have a problem. Tell me how to solve the problem."

"I am thinking."

"Eddie—you, yourself, are a terrific lover. By now everybody understands that you have to be around us a whole lot because you are like his campaign manager. Walter knows he is inflicting mental and physical anguish on me and he hates that. And you know something else? This is hard to believe considering, but Walter loves me."

"Why not? You are lovable, that's why. You are the most lovable woman I have ever met. *Hombre*! That Wullair is something else."

"That isn't all." I axed a sound out of my chest that I really had intended to be a laugh. "I love Walter. That's right. I love Walter. Now go figure that out."

"Yeah, hah?"

"And you can't understand it no matter how hard you try. There is no way you could know without having a sex change operation, God forbid. Because, in order to handle this terrible situation, I would have to be unfaithful to my husband. And that's just the beginning. It gets worse. Because he loves me, Walter would want me to be unfaithful to him." I sighed like a lunch whistle. "So—he's going to have to turn his back."

Eddie took a deep breath, then let it out slowly, let it all go out, puffing his cheeks.

"Remember when you first talked to me about marrying Walter?"

"*Si.*"

"We were in bed? You had just ravished me for the fourth time?"

"*Si.*"

"And you told me how a man couldn't get ahead in politics if he stayed a bachelor?"

"I remember."

"Well, if that's true—and it probably is—then it just isn't

134

enough for a man who wants to go a long way in politics just to have a wife. He's got to have a family. Voters have kids, so the voters have to think he is the same as they are."

"Yeah."

"But how can he have a family if he can't screw me?" I was pleading and I could see that Eddie understood me. "And he has to have a family."

"Okay," Eddie said, taking off his jacket, his eyes opaquing. "Let's give him a family, sweetheart."

I told Walter the good news when I was five months pregnant. I wasn't exactly sure how he would take it but I knew I had done the right thing, all around. He was thrilled.

"A baby," he said. "You are actually gravid. Well! Well, well, well. Why, this is about the best news anyone has ever brought me." He wept a little bit and held me close to him.

"Have I made you happy?" I whispered.

"Yes. Oh, yes, yes."

"I love you, Walter."

"I love you, Betsy." He sobbed. Not an acting sob. "I never thought anything as beautiful as this could happen to me."

DATE: 10th August 1964
TIME: 12:05 P.M.
BASE REPORTING: El Paso   DSP (Semley) Only

MRS. VICTORIA SLURRIE (continued)

It was a miracle of thrift that Walter had been able to save up that much money to spare us the disgrace of what could have followed that accident. And it was a miracle of generosity and love that he did this freely and voluntarily, without my knowledge, without any urging from anywhere but his own heart.

I am really not sure what happened to us that day in the car. Druidie was home from his Coast Guard Service. He borrowed a car from a girl he knew over at Grellou City & Combined Shopping Center, which her family owned. Druidie had taken her home from a dance at Concertina Land, but when he got her home he couldn't get back the eighteen miles to our place because it was the girl's car. So the girl let Druidie drive her car to our house—they had a lot of cars, he said—and that she would come by to pick it up on Saturday night when they were going to another dance.

Our panel truck was laid up and I had to get to the Cash & Carry and to the stale bread depot, so Druidie said we could take the

137

girl's car. I drove it because it was such a treat to have the chance to drive a brand-new Cadillac El Dorado after years behind the wheel of the panel truck. We were listening to the radio, talking, and really enjoying ourselves then, the next thing I knew, I woke up in the hospital. They told me Druidie was all right but he wasn't, of course, he was dead. My right shoulder, my right thigh bone, and my kidney were smashed, and other things, too.

I suppose I was unconscious for a long time. I do remember Walter sitting beside my bed at all hours, in his uniform. When I was able to talk and understand he told me about Druidie. And he told me he had sold the store and the house to Joe Eagle Claw and that he had found a nursing home for me in El Paso. He explained how that all had to be because he had to go back to the Navy, but that he was being transferred to Virginia.

I was sixty-three years old and a broken woman. Without Walter I would not have made it. The accident cost him a powerful amount of money. There was government insurance money from Druidie, but Walter wouldn't let that be touched. He said he wanted me to know that I had that money. He banked all of it for me, $10,000, in El Paso. He said I had to feel independent if there were any mean nurses at the home.

I knew how much everything cost Walter because I have been working with numbers all my life, trying to make them come out. Lawyers brought me papers to sign; there were a lot of papers. I kept my eye on the numbers and it worked out that everything must have cost Walter $67,000, including Druidie's funeral.

Walter always had a power of love in him and a very, very large dignity of vision. It was just that he couldn't show the love he felt the way other people can. I've been over everything a thousand times in my mind. Walter gave me most of what he made in Lubbock when he was a lawyer there, so he couldn't have had anything to save. I don't know what the OPA paid him but it was just a little government job in an expensive wartime city and he sent me $25 every week from that. But somehow he settled every last penny due on that accident. The lawyers told me it was all paid up in cash and that nobody could ever come back at me again about it.

What I fear when I try to go to sleep at night is that Walter may have gone so deeply into debt because of the accident that he couldn't find any way to get out and that, in the end, that was the reason he had to kill himself in that New York hotel.

I ask myself over and over where did he get so much money?

The house, the store, and the panel truck weren't worth a bushel basket filled with stones. And where would old Joe Eagle Claw get money to buy anything? Walter wasn't a gambling man because our religion is strict about keeping gambling out of the family. Still, $67,000! I had to decide that he must have gotten one of those sweepstakes tickets from somewhere and he must have won with it. God does provide in His mysterious ways.

It is an impossibility to tell whether Walter was glad or sad, he has that kind of face. His father looked like that, but then his father was a quitter. But there was never any difficulty in telling where Walter's heart was because it was bigger than God's barn, filled with loving kindness, with all the love that he was willing to share whenever the sharing was needed.

God has taken four of my boys to his bosom. I drove Father away from me with my feelings of guilt. I killed my son, Druidie, driving that sinfully elegant car, and now I search my soul with the cold wonderment of not knowing, but fearing that it is so, fearing that it was I who threw Walter so deeply into debt that he fell with the burden and killed himself to get free.

DATE: 11th August 1964
TIME: 9:21 A.M.
BASE REPORTING: Chicago   DSP (Semley) Only

FATHER FRANCIS DENFER

I point out to you that Walter Slurrie was an inverted personality, a self-examiner who accused himself ceaselessly in the hope of finding salvation through conversation. Deaths such as his only harden our hearts against such lightly carried hopes to gain eternal pity. Walter and I were very, very, very close aboard the *Matson*. I taught him everything he knew. But as soon as he was ashore and running toward what he saw only as immense self-aggrandizement, he quickly forgot everything we had done together.

Walter was not popular in the Navy and I befriended him. He lacked the personality needed to mix with so many hundreds of people at such close quarters. He was a morose and self-pitying man. I would conjecture that he was killed by a robber *of some kind.*

I shall miss him. He was not a Catholic but he was an unswerving believer in a crusading cause—the cause of American continuance—as we know it. The cause of civilization.

Did you know Walter was a card cheat? And considering the degree of his morbidity in constant self-examination, you might well wonder why this didn't bother him. He cheated so well. The other officers actually expected him to win at cards because he prepared them so skillfully and with such attention to psychological detail. I often watched him explain, in the wardroom aboard the *Matson,* how deeply interested he was in the *theory* of poker. When they wanted to discuss sex or baseball—oh, yes, they spoke of sex all the time, even in my presence—Walter would steer the conversation to poker and speak abstrusely of various combinations of cards and of the variety of psychological ploys demanded by the game. They were all overawed by his knowledge of poker, but when he cheated them he never used psychology or philosophy. He used polished, practiced manipulation. But they expected him to win. After all, didn't Buffalo Manning commandeer him as a bridge partner? They lost to him cheerfully. Most of them were such *silly* men. Walter took away money they would have spent foolishly ashore on one or another of their silly vices—something that, I must say in his favor, Walter would not think of doing.

I am not implying that one of these cheated officers killed Walter. Still, it is a possibility, isn't it? And men like that would naturally have resented his ascension in political life, wouldn't they? So much for your officer class. They can't bear to see one of their own kind get ahead.

I did nothing to interfere with Walter's cheating. I never even told him that I knew, even after we had become intimates. My mission among the officers was to provide mental and spiritual comfort, if I could, if they allowed me to, and not to create anguish. In fact, Walter's very coldness—and it really did have a sort of brutality to it—the way he planned his play, the skill of his execution, made him *extremely* interesting to me. His hard objectivity, that desperate ambition, as well as his utter glibness-beyond-conscience, suggested to me that he might be just the sort of apparatus I had been searching for since the Soviet beast had been spawned.

The war started for only one reason. It was structured to chain every nation of the free world to Communism. Even in my own service to my Church and my God, again and again, not only have I met Communists personally but my colleagues have kept me up-to-date on the extent of Communist infiltration. The greatest service and obeisance I could bring to Him, I realized, would be to find that Christian soldier whose zeal for the extirpation of Communism from the human mind could match my own, then cultivate him to grow into a mighty, unchallengeable force. I sought an ambitious, cold, cruel man who would not hesitate to exploit mass fear under a banner of national security. Only such men could protect the preciousness of democracy—and our holy Church—from the wanton anti-Christ who plotted in the East.

I cultivated Walter by bringing him what he loved most in this world: frankfurters, ketchup, boiled cabbage and store cheese served in my cabin by my own Chinese boy. Can you imagine placing such a grotesque price on the future of this planet— frankfurters and ketchup? Walter was a disturbingly vulgar man, even though I got to know him very well and to enjoy his company *very* much, but nonetheless he was a plebe who slept in his underwear. It was his very coarseness that enabled him to mingle as a leader among the *lumpen* of American national politics, wasn't it?

As we came to know and appreciate each other, I was able to lead the conversations toward politics in the postwar world, a subject that Walter Slurrie at that time held indifferently.

"One can have knowledge of the future, dear Walter," I said to him, "and it is held by scholars who do know that postwar politics will be different, so different that a man who would become an American leader will have less need of what you would think of as a knowledge of technical politics than at any time before. Technical knowledge will become fragmented among specialists in polling, public image construction, and theatrical makeup, to name a few examples. They need only money to operate effectively. The leader of tomorrow will need a charted course, but just as important, a deep interest in America. I assume that you love your country."

"I love America," he said to me with that spurious basso voice.

"If you love," and I put my hand on his thigh to emphasize my point, "and I am sure you do love America, if you were given the vision to see the great peril in which she will stand, then, as a young, intelligent man, can you promise that your interest in saving her would grow frantic?"

"What peril, Father Frank?"

"The peril of postwar Communism."

"Russia?"

143

"Yes."

"But Russia is our ally."

"A mockery," I warned him.

In the ensuing months we spoke of the relentless probability of either direct Russian attack or insidious infiltration upon American society and of the inevitability of the success of either tactic if Americans were not armed to repel the ideological assault. I was able, gradually, to lead Walter's interest on into deeper studies of these subjects. He had an intuitive grasp of what was basically beyond him, and he had an astonishing capacity for facts ingested through willful, enforced book study. He seemed to have no interest in women, diversions, the company of fellow officers, or even playing cards, which he abandoned entirely except when he was summoned to play bridge with Admiral Manning, one of those typical, scrappy American leaders who hated to lose. However, I have to think that some interest in women had to be Walter's because he certainly proved that by marrying after the war. I bring this up in passing because I have been wondering, and I have begun to feel that I ought to pass this along to you, whether perhaps Walter had formed some sort of *liaison manqué* of a sort that could have led to his murder by one of *them*. But, all that to one side, back to our discussion. I was able to procure many, many texts relating to world Communism to strengthen Walter's growing horror of what it stood for.

Walter's head was not easily turned. I tell you, when he caught the excitement of the message, he seemed to bolt himself into the chair and remain there with those high stacks of books, grinding them down, making his porridge out of them for hour upon hour. I have known him to remain in that trance of concentration for five hours.

I believe now that Walter had a natural talent for politics hidden beneath his deplorable personality. He was capable of anticipating the theories and the tactics needed in the politics of world struggle. He knew instinctively, as he was to demonstrate to all of us later, how to maneuver people to turn them toward his own goals.

By the time he had finished absorbing all of those books, he understood that I had handed him a weapon of extraordinary political ferocity. He saw how to control mass fear and how to turn it to work for him, to nourish it and to operate it with the greatest efficiency. He now knew how to cause abominable mirages to

144

loom up before the faces of the people, belching the smoke from his dry ice, emitting isinglass fires, while he would cry out shrill warnings, offer himself to fight the appalling illusion, and turn the people to his support of any cause because of the very fears he had been able to implode within them.

Walter became very excited over this great chance. We began to drink wine together. He became radiantly excited, boundlessly so.

Most of all, and I thank God for this, he saw that the threat of Communism to America could be the single, most enduring postwar issue.

Then his mother committed the accident that killed his brother. He was granted immediate leave, went off to Texas, and never came back to the fleet. Not that we didn't see each other after that. We did. He called me his little Rasputin and I like to think that I helped him on his way.

When the terrible news reached me that he had been murdered I faced black guilt. Had Walter not met me aboard the *Matson* he might have been safely back in Lubbock practicing law and following his life as a circus elephant follows the elephant ahead of him around the ring. I blame myself and absolve myself in a tortuous plait of reason. Walter was chosen as the vessel to carry the warning that has preserved our freedoms from the Russian knot of total domination. Only in a political sense am I going to repeat the words that were spoken of the Master and apply them to Walter: "He died that we might live"—under the privileges of democracy. Let us each strongly desire to know our murderer's face.

TO: WIFE OF ACTING COMMANDER, ABOVE CASE, PATRICIA GALLAGHER

FROM: LIEUTENANT RICHARD GALLA-GHER, 17th HSQ

This looks like it is going to be the third night in a row that I won't make it home since some creep blew holes in Slurrie. Not that there has been much chance for talking on the phone either. I hope you guys are still there and that the kids haven't been rocking the boat. I've had my picture in the paper so much in the past two days that Raymond must think I've been elected Mayor. It gets in the papers so much because there is so little else they can print on this case. Thank God they don't get this hysterical every time somebody gets himself knocked off.

It's been a pretty bad day for me. I spent over an hour with Richard T. Betaut, the man who almost but not quite made it to the White House (twice). He told me things about Slurrie and the Secret Police and the biggest operating hoodlum in this country, and all three of them together in Dallas on a certain day in November last year, that if I wasn't able to write this to you to get it off my chest, I don't think I could live with carrying it around with me. I can never tell you or anyone else what he told me and I am too ashamed to know it myself. Slurrie was garbage, enough said. I not only have to learn to live with what Betaut told me, I have to find whoever it was who killed Slurrie, doing the country a big favor when he did.

Mulshine and the Chief of Detectives, Joseph Maguire, and the PC all came down on me like sledgehammers about twice today. They are getting a little hysterical themselves. They must be catching hell from people way up there and out there. The media are merely rabid. They won't stop foaming at the mouth until they have an arrest to work over. Chief Maguire says they have never been this bad. I don't look anymore. I shout them down at noon every day then get the hell out of there.

I have been pretty rough on my own people. They dump on me from above so I do likewise on my lads, and they take it because they know that's the system, just the way I take it from the PC, Mulshine, and Maguire.

After what Betaut told me today I have to accept the distinct possibility that the SP killed Slurrie. I don't have the slightest idea how to prove a thing like that or who I would arrest if I could. I am going to try to make a case, then heave it right upstairs for the brass to decide how things like that can be done.

The cost of dragging the country through that kind of blood and pain to prove that one set of monsters killed another monster will keep a lid on this one even if I could prove anything, which I am 100 percent certain I could not.

You had to marry a queasy cop.

Let us pray devoutly that a hired hit man, working for the

148

boss hoodlum Danzig, knocked Slurrie off, so it can be shown in court that they were brothers under the counter.

By the law of averages I have to get home soon.

Maybe you'll do us all a favor and burn this letter. Better now that I have written it and I feel better, maybe I won't send it at all.

DATE: 11th August 1964
TIME: 11:52 A.M.
BASE REPORTING: New York

DSP(Semley) Only

CHARLES COFFEY (continued)

Along with fifty or sixty other congratulatory telegrams I sent one to Walter on Election Night 1948. He called me two days later to set up a meeting. I decided to meet him in Dallas, not in Washington, so I could get a feeling of how the voters felt about him after a campaign like that.

I checked into a suite at the old Stoneleigh out on Maple Avenue. We had a system of grading key hotels around the country by the effects they produce on the people we are working on. The effect of the Stoncleigh is old-fashioned, solid, steady, and reliable. If I had been in Dallas to see either of the two U.S. Senators I would have stayed at the Fairmount. Walter was proud to meet at the Stoneleigh, which he decided the Felsenburshes must own.

I got to Dallas a day ahead of the meeting. My reading of the local people was that they had decided to believe Walter about the Communists getting ready to take all the good things away from them, but not to believe that Walter had had anything to do with the gonorrhea story about his opponent's daughter. They felt that the war had shown that we couldn't trust people like the Russians because the Russian people weren't "free." I bought a poll to be taken when I got back and the percentage of people in Dallas who felt that Communism was their number one enemy was about the same as the percentage of Walter's plurality. It was a tailor-made issue, I could see that. We were going to have to run it up the flagpole in a few different parts of the country and see who saluted it.

Walter came into the suite with what might have looked like verve or enthusiasm on anyone else. At least he was smiling broadly. He was actually out of uniform only three years after the war was over. His thrusting jaws held up his dumpling jowls like bags of breadfruit and his widow's peak was like a plow. His wife must have insisted on going with him when he bought suits because this one almost fit him; a navy blue serge piece of protective coloration.

"How's your father, Charley?" was the first thing he asked, even though after greeting each other once Pop and Walter had never spoken to each other.

"Just fine. He sends his best, of course, Walter."

"And Dennis?"

"Dennis killed himself about a year ago."

"What?" He expelled the word as if the news had struck him forcibly. He sank into a chair.

"Yes. He jumped off the Manhattan Bridge in New York and landed on a French light cruiser—on top of two French sailors, actually, so they died too."

"But he was so young." Walter closed his eyes and leaned back in the chair, probably calculating whether or not he should weep in Dennis' honor. I headed him off.

"I certainly hope I am going to meet the bride tonight," I said. "That was marvelous and unexpected news."

"Oh, yes," he said. "Absolutely. Betsy insists that you come out to the house for dinner tonight."

"Great."

"I hear you went and got married yourself, Charley."

"Oh, I'm an old married man," I said, wondering how I could ever invite Walter home to dinner.

'Well, Charley," he said. "Just as I told you that night we had

152

dinner in Washington last year, I not only went into politics but I won. And I think I proved that the people of Texas were just waiting in ambush to vote Republican."

"You really set off a bomb down here, Walter."

"Oh, I'm going to beat the brains out of the media with this issue, Charley. I'm going to investigate them, and the radio and the movie business and stretch headlines out like miles of laundry. I'm going to drag people to Washington until I have the Communists on their knees, begging. Until the press and every other outlet of information in this country understands that Americans will not be poisoned by swarms of enemy propaganda."

I grinned at him. "You are such a hick, Walter. You look at America and you still see Salopado."

"Don't be so sure, Charley. It took a hick like me to find the real political issue in this country."

"The Communist issue or the gonorrhea issue?"

He looked baffled. "Gonorrhea?"

"Come on. The telephone campaign."

"What are you talking about?" He looked as if I were trying to set him up.

"All right. We'll pretend it's news to you that while you were on the platform or kissing babies, a telephone team of twenty-six people called every telephone subscriber in your election district and told them your opponent's daughter was spreading gonorrhea."

"Why would anyone do that?"

"They were saying, symbolically, that Communism is an infection like gonorrhea. Like father, like daughter is what they were saying. And, as you said, your gimmick worked."

"What can I say? If you believe I could do that, then you'll believe anything rotten you ever hear about me."

"Then I'll ask you, Walter. Did you have people hired to do that?"

"No."

"Did you know it was happening?"

"No."

"It's just a business. You were managing a business."

"I had nothing to do with anything like that and I would prosecute anyone in my campaign who did that in my name." His voice quivered. He was mad. He wasn't faking this. I don't think he was.

153

"Okay, Walter. I apologize. It did happen though."

"I am going to look into it," he said grimly.

"I am very sorry if I gave you any idea that I believed you had done it."

"Thank you, Charley. But it is something that has to be put right. It just serves the purpose of showing me, early on, how rotten politics can be."

"Explain it to yourself this way, Walter. Some friends of yours smeared the daughter, you smeared the father."

"What good is a man like that in Congress in times like these? I'm an expert on this issue. The people need protection from the inside. I can fight for them because I know what I'll be fighting—that fellow was just an amiable drunk, Charley. If the House were filled with replicas of him, the Russians would just overrun this country."

"What did you want to talk to me about?" I asked him coolly. I wasn't going to get into the nature of his gimmick and what a cold-hearted hustle it was. I had never known Walter to believe much in anything except frankfurters, and I knew he only believed in this issue just as far as he thought it could carry him. But there was a chemical change in level-headed people who would have turned their backs on such a lunatic idea if anyone spoke to them about it, which caused them to go just a little crazy when they read about it in the newspapers, heard it on the radio, and saw a carefully selected candidate take it seriously enough to make it the entire issue on which he would be elected or defeated: the same level-headed people registered TILT. The chemistry people like Walter counted on transformed them. They became irrational.

"May I speak frankly, Charley," he asked, using his spaniel look, which he knew proved his dedication.

"Why not?"

"In the short time I have been in politics I have heard—here and there—about the practical side of Felsenburshe sponsorship of American politicians."

"You mean the slush fund?"

"Ah, yes. I suppose we can call it that."

"I see that you are already on the pad with the Dallas Citizens' Committee for $18,000 a year."

"I don't know how you learned that. But it is substantially true. I have a lot of expenses."

"With your salary and mileage and office expenses plus the

154

Citizens' Committee you're doing all right for a freshman congressman."

"You know I deliver. You, above anyone else, know that I deliver."

"I could probably get you $7,000 a year."

"Charley! I am handing the Felsenburshes *the* issue of the 1950s. I am young and unknown. I never saw Dallas before. I ran as a Republican in deepest Democrat territory and I delivered 81.3 percent of the total vote. Nobody has done anything like that before."

He walked across the room through a door, across another room and into the kitchen. I watched him find a pot, fill it with water, then set it over a flame on the stove. "You want some coffee, Charley?" he asked. He rummaged around until he found some instant coffee and some cups. It was pretty awful stuff but we drank it.

"Match the $18,000," he said to me. "Just for this one term. If I stay right where I am I'll never be worth it. But if I go up into the Senate—and I have some pretty active plans for that—you and the Felsenburshes will have yourselves an important friend in Washington long before the insurance people or the aerospace people or the conglomerate people can try to put me on their pads."

"You just convinced me," I said. "Sign our paper and you get the eighteen."

His face got weary and sad. "I suppose you think I've come a long way," he said. "I suppose you are thinking that last year when we had dinner I wasn't talking this way."

"No. This is straight business, Walter."

"I had things explained to me. But when I sign your paper that won't make me a crook, any more than a lawyer could be called a crook when he takes on a retainer. Would it, Charley?"

I said, "When an airline takes a subsidy from a government or an opera house accepts a million from a private patron, does that make the airline or the opera house management crooks? What are they? One is a vital service that helps to keep the country going by transporting the mail. The other is a vital force that gives the country a part of its culture. You are one tile in the mosaic of our government, Walter, in a system that demands you compete for votes but does not give you the funds to finance that competition. You have to get money to continue. You are vital to the continuation of our society. That's why the Felsenburshes, functioning the way the Medici functioned in the Renaissance, try to support and subsidize as many dedicated public servants as they can. You are a part of the American continuance."

We sat facing each other, staring at each other.

"As you know," Walter answered, "I do not approve of vulgar language, Charley, but that is purely just a load of shit."

DATE: 11th August 1964
TIME: 8:47 A.M.
BASE REPORTING: Miami   **DSP (Semley) Only**

EDWARD CARDOZO (continued)

Wullair's finest hour is the Red Crusade. He was tremmenus an we make a very big score. He give the American pipple their firss field day with the Communist peril and the connree is rilly ready for the show we put on for them.

We are on the road for two years altogether, in and out. Wullair get back to Dallas every six weeks or so an the local committee always stage an event so he can report to his voters direct by radio and press. He is in his seat in the House maybe thirty-fi' percenn of the time, which is high attendance for anybody. Every time he always let the House know what is the issue.

In two years, Wullair appcar live in fronn of more than five million pipple and he get maybe ten times more pipple on the radio and the newspapers an magazines. He is very big in the newsreels. We only play big ballparks an arenas. We cover forty-six cities in the whole connree. Wullair is espeaking from *el corazon* under the biggess American flag that was ever sewn together. In a parade it goes for three whole blocks with hunnerds of beautiful girls holding it and the pipple throwing money into it from the sidewalks an the windows as it march past. We are good for $6,000 from that flag every time. *Que bandera!*

Wullair espeak to crowds of a hunnerd fifteen thousand at one time to warn them of the peril. He knock them out. They want to touch him. They try to cheer him an they cry. He is saving them from the Red Menace.

Wullair roll don the Main Estreet of every city on his red, white, and blue bandwagon with a brass band up there on a flat car. On the bandwagon are dozens of real an fake celebrities. Anybody can ride with Wullair for a thousand in cash an there is no tax on cash, amigo. A lot of people meet Ward Bond that way. We had all the big starss. We have the big industrial honchos, the top jocks from the Big Four sports. We get Nashville people an network leaders. We have the biggest Syndicate *capos* an lawyers—which always convince everybody because they are the most patriotic people in the country. There is millionaire poets, big cops, pastors of all the faiths, and Dick Betaut, twice the stannard bearer for the Republicans.

We fly in Wullair's mother on a stretcher to Soldiers Field in Chicago the night that 42,316 pipple, out of a total of 109,488 pipple, "Declare for Democracy" at up to fifty bucks a head in cash. This was Wullair's own gimmick. All that night there is never less than 3,000 pipple on their knizz at the Altar of Freedom. Oh, jess! They walk up on their knizz, like they are at the Virgin of Guadalupe, toward Wullair, who stann proud at the very top of the Altar with his Guard of Honor, the bodyguards who protect him from Commie assassins. It is very exciting. It ivven gets to Nudey.

Wullair is honor with everything plus money. He get rabbit feet, Shriner hats, a free lifetime trittmenn in chiropody, hunnerds of brassieres, Civil War battle flags, keys to cities an honor scrolls, a few thousand free feels and some mothers' kisses for this man who lay his life on the line for America. He get swords, cakes, torches, an honorary degrees. Everything pour out on Wullair from the heart of America. He get a genuine Cheyenne scalp which is autograph by General Custer. Wullair donate everything to the Smithsonian Institute an get a tax credit for $97,723.04.

The Red Crusade not only put Wullair in the Senate in 1951, but it make him more than his first million dollars.

I am in charge of the cash. We don like contribution by check. Nudey get the souvenir program printed in a nonunion shop but arrange to have a union label on every one. In two years, at dollar a copy, the souvenir program bring in $908,143.49 in cash. The record album of Wullair's espeeches ("I Give You Your Freedom!"—United Artists label, $6.95), with the liner copy by J. Edgar Hoover, get us $112,846.21 in cash. Four cities ahead the advance teams line up the local esponsors in every Red Crusade situation. They set up Red Defense posts in the supermarkets, tho laundromats, the barbers, an the bars. They organize Businessmens' Freedom Fighter Battalions on "pledge now, pay later" basis and we average maybe six days' pay from every Freedom Fighter. Everybody is sworn in at the ball parks while Wullair says the Prayer for Freedom over the loudspeakers then their names are put in Tho Goldun Book. We average out at $14.37 per name in that giant book, which has 318,739 names.

The pipple are not only save from Communism but they have a terrific time. They get top glamor, Vegas-quality entertainment, and the best color printing. No one is hurt. Nothing is change. An we pay very little taxes because almost everything come in cash.

Whoever shoot Wullair cost us one estupendo piece of money. Whether he was out of office or in office, Wullair churn out more money than anyone in history, Nudey say. I hope I can get my hans on the fahkeen bahstair who eshoot Wullair. There is never gun be two of Wullair. He is all-time champion.

DATE: 13th October 1963
TIME: 1:40 P.M.
BASE REPORTING: New York

DSP (Semley) Only

MRS. CHARLES COFFEY

When I found out about Charley, it began the change of everything in our lives. What had been decked out in vibrant colors, wherever we were or looked, turned to gray. Honesty became evasion. What had been warm from the moment we met turned to winter stone. Not just for me. Charley couldn't handle the guilt of having cheated me out of the truth for about sixteen years and he couldn't allow himself to take the blame for it either. I was stupid. I ask myself how I could have gone on believing that he was just another successful company lawyer when I should have known differently. But that wasn't how Charley's job worked for the Felsenburshes. He worked underground and behind the scenes. He was never connected with candidates or campaigns or issues as far as the public eye could see, and I was a lesser member of the public because I had refused to read or speak about anything political anyway.

161

It was ironic how Charley was betrayed. His own father, a political lobbygow for sixty years and a walking closet full of secrets, let the cat out of the bag.

Pop arrived early for dinner so he could have a chat with the children. They were on their way to a movie and, since they ate all the time anyway, weren't hungry at that moment. I stayed in the kitchen cooking one of the meals that had slowly turned Pop into an Italian. When the kids rushed off, Pop came in and sat at the table drinking some cold Soave. I loved Pop! He knew everything, or something about everything. It all had the flavor of having been made up on the spot for my delectation. It was mostly very exciting but very ancient gossip about dim, old days when all proportions were larger than life. Al Smith was Pop's centerpiece. The stories were hilarious.

But Pop had become old and forgetful. He had been losing millions of brain cells a day for a long time so he can't be blamed for forgetting that he wasn't supposed to tell me what he told me. Could Charley truly have believed that his real life could remain a secret forever?

I happened to say something foolish like, "How is Charley doing in the legal department, Pop?"

"What legal department?"

"At the Felsenburshes."

"Legal department? He's their political fixer."

Everything changed. My vision went distorted not within my eyes but in my soul, the way it happened to the little boy in "The Snow Queen." Pop told me something that should have been incomprehensible, it was so violent, but I understood it as if I had never believed my husband about anything he had ever told me. Charley had laid those three words—a political fixer—at my feet three dozen times when we were first married, when we were quarelling bitterly and when I should have accepted what he had to do because I was young then and I could bear it better. He had made it vividly clear that he was no lawyer, that there was only one trade he had with which to make a good living for all of us. But when he had pretended it was otherwise I had duped myself.

"What's the matter, Marie?" Pop said. "You look surprised." There were three or four beats of silence while we stared at each other. "Jesus," he said. "I forgot. I'm sorry, sweetheart."

"Still that's what Charley is, isn't he, Pop? A fixer."

"Ah, no, Marie. That was just a slang way of sayin' it. Charley runs the largest nongovernment political department in the

162

world. He operates for the Felsenburshes in thirty-one countries. They think he's a world beater, Dick Betaut tells me."

"Good *Christ!*"

"Marie—Marie—take a good look at it. The man is unique in what he does. Why, the Secretary of State himself couldn't do what Charley does. And why should he burden you with a lotta dirt."

"Dirt. You can't understand what I object to, can you, Pop?

He shrugged. "Well it *is* hard to figure out, Marie. Charley told me you're against everything he and me, my father and my grandfather did all their lives. I mean, it certainly seemed like a fine profession we had, to me. But you're entitled to see it your way, too, of course."

"I feel so much shame right now that I don't know how I see it."

"I can tell you because I know it, if I know anything, that politicians are just like other businessmen with common interests— funeral directors or shoe salesmen. Our business is to keep government moving, that's all. Charley is a good man. You know that."

"I wonder if we'll ever know what he's done to history. I've seen what other politicians have done. I stood among the dead they piled up. They have to take the blame because they could have stopped the war before it started by any means. We see hundreds of men die and Charley goes half-blind but when I weep for them he says I am neurotic, when what ho means is that anyone who loathes all politicians as much as I do must be insane for, he tells himself, am I not a politician?"

"I better be goin', Marie," Pop said. "Charley'll be home any minute. I'm not hungry anyway." He shuffled over and kissed me on the cheek, then he went out.

I could feel the apparition that Charley must always see standing behind me. I turned off the stove and took off my apron. I went out to the living room and made myself a drink, then looked out at the traffic in the rain while I waited for the sound of Charley's key and we set out, with system and purpose, to destroy each other.

Charley was late but he was in high spirits. He gave me a big kiss and said, "Where are the kids?"

"It's Friday night. I said they could go to the movies."

"I thought Pop would be here for dinner."

"He was here."

163

"Was here?"

"He decided to leave."

"How come?"

"Well, he made a slip and it embarrassed him. He forgot the deal you and he had, and he told me that you were the Felsenburshes' political fixer."

Charley made himself a drink. He said, "Well, I'm glad it's finally out in the open."

"Are you?"

"It has been pretty schizoid, you know."

"I think I could stand your having made a fool out of me, but this isn't just a husband-and-wife fib to make some newlywed adjustment. Do you know how long I thought you were a respectable, responsible lawyer? Sixteen years, Charley. Sixteen years. Every morning you leave with a smile and I think you are going off to draw up some leases or negotiate a contract or sit down with a labor union. For sixteen years I've picked you up at your office and everyone says, 'Good day, Mrs. Coffey. How are you, Mrs. Coffey?' and I thought I was in the law offices of the company. So it's been sixteen years of contempt. The worst kind of contempt because what is so blatant is that you felt you had to live this maudlin charade because, if you did not, poor Marie would freak out again. That's what you thought, Charley."

"Marie, please—at the very worst I am one of those American institutions called a lobbyist."

"Are you registered as a lobbyist?"

"No. Really. The work is slightly different."

"What do you do?"

"May we sit down while we talk?"

We sat down. I felt I was wearing the apparition that Charley saw as if it were a shawl around me. Charley said, "Marie, all the Felsenburshes are after is political stability. They do not want wars. Whatever power they have is used to prevent wars. To maintain political stability they have to seek out the available men of good will, men who have a stake in this country, to encourage them to run for public office." He came across the room and sat beside me. "We work inside and outside the system. You know what the Felsenburshes have done for the blacks and the poor. What I am doing is okay, Marie."

I threw my arms around him and began to cry. What good are justifications? Everything was different now. Everything had changed.

DATE: 10th August 1964
BASE REPORTING: Los Angeles

DSP (Semley) Only

N.B. *The following autobiographical text was transcribed from tape cassettes found in the Bel Air, California, house of Horace Riddle Hind. An audio copy has also been made. The original cassettes have been returned to the Hind bedroom in Bel Air.*

Horace Riddle Hind (continued)

I was concentrating on the California end of my operations when I sent for Walter Slurrie for the first time. When I am in God's own country the American West, where I am the fifth largest defense contractor in this country, I like to spend as much time as possible at my movie studio.

There is an interesting item in that connection. Although it is widely known that I have slept with the most glamorous and desirable women in the world, I can now say that I was astonished to learn that one of these was a female impersonator. I did not actually screw this person but came very, very close to it. I was shocked. I threw her out on her ass and hounded him out of the business. He later got work in Rome but she was heavily into some opium derivative and couldn't really keep score anymore.

165

My people, whom I have had keep an eye on him over the years, tell me she is now a saleslady at Bloomingdale's in New York. He has been photographed while working there. You would hardly recognize her. She was once a tremendous star. She was a fantastic beauty. Anyway, by now she is about sixty-eight years old, and that is bound to change the looks of a woman who uses narcotics.

I was carefully briefed on Walter Slurrie's entry into politics, and his campaign, in my home city, Dallas. My people know I have a great love for Dallas. Walter Slurrie ran a tight, professional campaign for Congress and he deserved to be elected. *We've got to stop Communism!* Perhaps Slurrie seemed to overemphasize Communistic elements in his opponent's record but *we've got to stop Communism.* I felt so strongly about this that I had my people hire a team of twenty-six telephoners to call everyone in that election district to tell them that Slurrie's opponent's daughter was spreading gonorrhea all over Dallas, because I knew that would make a strong analogy between that loathsome infection and the infection of Communism. It is my belief that this single political coup got Walter Slurrie elected to Congress. It put him into politics. Slurrie has been my man since before the beginning.

Some years ago in Hollywood a famous actress (and a very, very beautiful woman) gave me gonorrhea and I hounded her out of the business. She is now married to a Swedish financier. They live in Lagos, Nigeria. I have my people keep an eye on her.

Let me say that Walter Slurrie's opponent was not a Communist. I know nothing about his daughter's personal life. The man was an easygoing sort who belonged to the Dallas Country Club and was a member of the Colophon Society at S.M.U. My daddy once loaned him money and he repaid it right on the dot. However, I would say that he was mentally lax and probably would not have done a thing to stop Communism if he had known what to do, which Slurrie did know. Politics is politics and youth must be served. The business of politics is getting elected, and this country might not have known it but it was waiting for a leader to appear who would warn it against the Red menace, then prove the danger. Walter Slurrie had the courage to do that. I was relieved to know that a man of his ruthlessness would represent the people of our city, my parent company, and my Dallas real estate holdings in the House of Representatives, which for too long in our nation's history had been dominated by Eastern-ers.

However, I did not send for Slurrie at the time of his election. I had my people watch him and report to me. It would be some time before he could earn the seniority that could get him on a congressional committee which could be of any use to me .

Then—almost immediately—he began his historic Red Cru-sade. I love America. I can state that I had been growing frantic over the indifference of the controllers of our government to the Red menace. The Eastern oligarchs and their kept press simply did not wish to look at the obvious. But, as Walter Slurrie was warning us, Soviet Russia was determined to infiltrate our gov-ernment and other institutions of this country to bring about its overthrow unless every American was put on patriotic alert. Walter Slurrie was doing that singlehandedly for us.

He had nothing personal to gain from his Red Crusade. He gave up two years of his life without receiving one red cent in re-turn. He was not running for office, he had just been elected to one. He was a modern Paul Revere, a figure of comparison I have frequently used when thinking in this connection, to warn us that we had to arm America if we wanted to save her from Com-munism. Slurrie did not "hog the stage" on this. He called to his side on the many platforms of the land some of the finest men, women, clergy and movie stars of this nation. They were proud to serve.

I knew the Crusade would bring him to Los Angeles. When his advance men arrived, I told my people to mobilize the entire mo-tion picture and defense industries, the oil interests, the rag trade, and the citrus and avocado farmers. We produce the finest avocados in the world in California and I have eaten this deli-cious American fruit in 102 different forms, according to my rec-ords. I enjoy it best as a cracker spread, which I now manufacture as a gourmet item under the trademark name of *Crock O'Molay*.™· We distribute it in both the regular and the giant economy size. It is, so far, my only entry into the food industry. Try it.

I sent for Congressman Slurrie the day he reached Los An-geles. He would understand that I did this without arrogance as a prime defense contractor. We met in the Men's Room at the Tam O'Shanter Restaurant in Glendale (serving probably the best hamburger sandwich made of the finest beef served with crisp bacon on buttered toast anywhere in the world and I have no

167

financial or any other kind of interest in this enterprise or its product). I am known at this restaurant so my people were able to arrange for our exit to be made through a prepared opening in the outside wall of the Men's Room, which I had had constructed and which I frequently used to expedite meetings without fear of observation. We were passed directly into the rear of a panel truck (after introductions) in which we were driven to my car, a 1937 Chevrolet, parked on Hyperion Avenue. Cars for my personal use are examined for surveillance devices every two hours. One of my people was sitting in it to protect it from being bugged. He got out. We got in and I drove the car away.

"Where are we going, Mr. Hind?" Slurrie asked.

"We will drive in a seemingly aimless pattern," I told him. "There are many people who would like very much to record my conversations and I have no doubt that the Soviet Union would like to record yours."

"The Soviet Union?"

"I am a Dallas man, Congressman Slurrie. I have the perspective. I want to tell you that you have outgrown your Dallas backers, who incidentally are not all that you think they are."

"How do you mean?" he flashed loyally.

"I have had my people check them all out. Three of them have indirect affiliations with organized crime."

"Crime?"

"You know—the Mafia. But be that as it may. We all have to use the Mafia at some time or another. You are in the national arena now. You need a political friendship that can help you move into the Senate, where you can do some good for this country."

I had to stop at MacReady because it was the only telephone booth available in that area. I left the Congressman in the car and took dimes from my reinforced change pocket. People who have not studied engineering may not realize that if you carry eight to twelve dollars in dimes in your jacket pocket that they must be reinforced or they will tear. I dialed Lorraine Center. "Get me Ira Skutch," I told them.

"Ira? Horace. What did the doctor say?"

"Bad news, Mr. Hind. Those are fake tits."

"*Whaaaat?*"

"Yes sir. One of those $1,200 silicon jobs. Dr. Lesion again. Lesion told her those tits would fool you forever."

"Fool me? An engineer? Damn them! Get her out of that apart-

168

ment and hound her out of this town but keep a team on her."

I was so damned mad I slammed the phone down on the receiver. I took a wire cutter out of my pocket and severed the telephone cables. Goddam every telephone that sends through rotten news like that about a lovely girl whom I had sponsored and trusted. I was just hopping mad. I ran back to the car and got a can of kerosene out of the trunk. I threw it all around the base of the phone booth, then dropped a lighted match on it.

The little tart had been enjoying my hospitality for seven weeks, maybe more. If my people had not been on their toes and right on the spot to be tipped off by that informer, if they had not had the cash to pay him then and there, I might never have known the truth, because the girl's breasts seemed to me to be the most beautiful, naturally full, and perfect I had ever handled. The incident almost spoiled the meeting with Congressman Slurrie and would have if it were not for the fact that my country and my businesses come before all else. I got back behind the wheel of the Chevvy and we drove off. "Where were we, Congressman?"

"The Senate," he answered.

Slurrie had a unilateral dignity that reminded me, although there were no other physical resemblances, of the inner and outer stances of a cartoon character named Major Hoople, excepting that Slurrie is much taller and slimmer, of course. At first I thought he had extreme myopia, he walked so carefully and awkwardly. His voice was like a mighty movie-house organ but that was no West Texas accent he used. He spoke deliberately, giving over-attention to each delivered word. I wanted those qualities in my statesmen. I try to buy the best. Just to hear Slurrie and to watch him move himself with the determination of a figure on a south German town clock was to know you had value.

"Do you accept, Congressman?"

"It takes a lot of money, Mr. Hind."

I glared at him. Goddammit, he knew I was famous for lightning decisions and for backing my play once I had made my decision, big or little.

"What I am offering you," I told him harshly, "is an unaccountable personal expense allowance of $40,000 a year and a guarantee to assume the deficits of your campaign for the Senate, over an agreed budget which my people will have to control. Take it or leave it."

"You are proving what faith is, Mr. Hind," he said. Slurrie really has a glorious voice. It strikes the deepest chords of honesty and sincerity. To my surprise I detected moisture welling out of his eyes. That moved me, as my faith had moved him. "In the course of my Red Crusade," he told me, "I have met many American patriots from every walk of life, but meeting with you, listening to your faith under the threat of a very real but hopelessly ignored Communist peril, I have to rank you among the greatest of these."

"All right," I replied gruffly to cover up my emotion. "I will call you Walter and you may call me Horace. Yes, I am a patriot. I am also a scientist, an aviator, an inventor, and a businessman. But I am not any of these things for the money that might be gained from them. My daddy proved to me that money is the very last thing to look for. Money is a measure of the share I hold in America—greater than anyone else's share. I am a patriot, a scientist, an aviator, an inventor, and a businessman to protect my country and to keep her strong. Because of my faith—and my money—you will soon be standing on the floor of the U.S. Senate to protect—with me—Hind Electronics, Hind Oil Cargos, the Hind Foundation, Hind Aerospace, and SHOVE, as well as all my other interests in America. You will be my advocate to explain my Foundation to the goddam Internal Revenue, which has been persecuting me."

"That is a lot of service for $40,000," he had the nerve to say.

"All right! Show me what you can do! Pay off for me and the sky is the limit! Does $100,000 a year sound more like it? Two hundred? That kind of money doesn't *mean* anything to me, Walter. What has meaning is results. Excuse me."

I stopped the car on Highland to use their telephone at a cigar store. I dropped the dime and called Lorraine Center. "Patch in Jeremy Cox," I told them.

"Jeremy? Did the mother settle?"

"The lawyers are working on her, Mr. Hind. They're out at the Springs with her now."

"What does it look like?"

"The mother is holding out for $500,000, Mr. Hind."

"Five hundred *thousand?* That's immoral! You tell those lawyers that a week ago she was trying to lure me into her house—the house I pay the rent for—to get me to eat disgusting flapjacks. She was like a lovable movie mother! What the hell is happening to America?"

"Well, it's turned into a really grisly case, Mr. Hind."

"Grisly? I'll say it's grisly. Have those lawyers taken a hard look at that woman whom the so-called mother says is her daughter? She is at *least* twenty-five years old."

"The lawyers don't think so, Mr. Hind."

"But I know her intimately! You should hear the language she uses!"

"You see, the main thing is, Mr. Hind, that the mother has convinced the lawyers, with copies of the girl's birth certificate, school records, Girl Scout registration, and Pony Club papers that the girl is only fourteen years old."

"That is im*possible*. And even if it were true, do those lawyers realize that we are among the few societies in the world who do not admit that a woman is ripened and mature at fourteen? That girl *has to be* nineteen. You have no idea of the things she has learned to do with her body."

"Mr. Hind?"

"What?"

"They have pictures."

"Oh, *shit!*"

"And two wire recordings."

"I hate this. I hate it. All right! Tell the lawyers to settle for $100,00 and tell them to have everything signed, witnessed, and sealed by tonight. Then pack those two people back east as a condition of the settlement, and as soon as they get where they are going I want them framed on shoplifting charges."

"Yes, sir."

I was deeply disappointed in two human beings. The first time I had seen that girl with her old-fashioned mother was on a Madison Avenue bus in New York. The bus stopped for a light and I was in the car alongside. That was only five months ago. I had my people follow them home—a modest apartment dwelling—and get their names and telephone number so that the girl could be offered a career in pictures. And this was how they repaid me.

I am making this a part of my autobiography to warn men who will be reading this. Things—particularly women—are seldom what they seem. Perhaps my readers can profit from that.

I was so depressed by the incident that I felt like letting Slurrie just sit there for hours in that car. He was now my property and he would do what he was told and I had told him to wait there. But then I calmed down. For one thing I couldn't get out of the cigar store without being seen by him. The place had no back door, which was a fire violation, and my people have since reported that to the authorities and will follow up on it.

I got back into the car. We drove toward the Beverly Hills Hotel & Bungalows, where Slurrie was staying.

"We live in a great country, Walter," I told him. "The greatest in the world. But you and I are going to make it just a little bit greater."

SECRET POLICE
UNITED STATES OF AMERICA
SEMLEY, MARYLAND

DATE: 11th August 1964
TIME: 2:18 P.M.
BASE REPORTING: New York

DSP (Semley) Only

CHARLES COFFEY (continued)

I flew from New York to Cleveland, Walter's fourth rally city on his Red Crusade. He was giving the people a tremendous show and everyone loved the way he played on their emotions, mostly the masochistic. But the Red Crusade was already not only the biggest thing in the country. It had become the most surgingly popular political preoccupation. Churchill may ultimately get the credit for bringing that insane fear of Communism to America, with his speech at Fulton, Missouri, because this was a dignified, over-the-shoulder glance for the millions of people who make fools of themselves, but Walter Slurrie was the man who put it on the road and made it work.

We met in his hotel room at the Statler. The early success of the Crusade had made subtle differences in Walter. He smiled—or what passeth for smiling—more easily. He ate his frankfurters more slowly. He moved more deliberately, in a way that may

173

have helped him to feel like a statesman, and he wasn't as critical of other politicians. The most pronounced change was that he didn't flinch an inch when we got around to talking money. The last time he had done his best to fake reluctance. Now he was a man with a commodity to sell.

"I hope your people are following our progress with the Crusade, Charley," he said. "It is bigger than anybody ever thought it could be."

"Oh, yes. We've been with you all the way, Walter. Tremendous."

"Maybe you can see now what I meant when I talked about the Senate in two years."

"You are on your way, Walter."

"It's just the beginning, really. Two more cities to get our crews really oiled and operating, and you are going to see the media taken over like it hasn't happened since the war."

"Well, don't overload. You probably have a lot of cities to go."

"Oh, yes. Quite a few. We'll peak at about every fifth city. We'll have something newsworthy and we'll sustain the show."

"I know you will."

"Charley, some of my people were telling me that you have a special endowment fund that is a little different from, but in addition to, the slush."

"Yes, we have something like that."

"How does it work?"

"We call it the endowment fund, as you said. It keeps up with your cost-of-living index and the increased expenses a candidate has to face under special circumstances."

"Well," he said briskly, "I qualify for that. I doubt if many people are facing the increase in expenses that I have right now, . wouldn't you agree?"

"I had the idea that the Crusade was making a lot of money, Walter."

"It is an enormous moneymaker. But it is entirely a nonprofit operation. God, I couldn't take money for doing vital work like this, Charley. I'd hate myself. We have a paid professional staff, then all the rest of it goes into the nonprofit foundation to fight Communism."

"I see."

"I wouldn't have it any other way."

"Very commendable, Walter."

"What does the special endowment fund pay?"

174

"Eight thousand a quarter."

"Plus the slush."

"Oh, yes."

"Why by the quarter?"

"Well, naturally, endowment depends on performance. We expect—and we have a right to expect, I would say—a lot of service from a man who is getting both the slush and the endowment."

"And you should expect that, Charley. That's $50,000 a year. Tell me—do all key people on your pad get paid the same?"

"Well, let me answer you this way. The $8,000 a quarter is only for senators, just as there has to be yet a different one for freshman congressmen with no committee status."

"I understand. But with this Red Crusade, of course, I'm no longer an ordinary freshman congressman, and everything does point toward the very big chance that I'll soon be a senator."

"A junior senator."

"Thank you anyway, Charley," he said. "I think I'll wait and we can talk about the endowment plan another time. I wouldn't want today's rank to prejudice tomorrow's subsidies."

"Whenever you want to talk, Walter. We'll be ready."

I thought of buying votes from drunks with a two-dollar bill but the amounts were different and I was meeting a better-washed class of bum. I wondered if Walter could remember himself on Election Day in '35, one of the few honest moments of his life. Now it was a matter of letting Walter talk himself back aboard the Felsenburshe gravy train, because Walter was no boat rocker. This Red Crusade was all right as far as it went but he was going to milk it until there was the chance that it could get to be a habit instead of just entertainment, creating the opposite of stability. And thinking about the way Walter hated people, I realized that could be unconsciously what he was groping for. He wanted some chaos to fall back on, to pay off his childhood and his father and his memory of Salopado.

"Walter," I said to him, "I want to show you how much we believe in you. If you'll sign the insurance paper, and if at the end of a year or so of the Crusade, you'll agree to break in another man so we can move you up to bigger things, I'm going to recommend to the Felsenburshes that they give you the senior senator's endowment policy. How's that?"

"That is just great, Charley! And you know you can count on me."

I thought Walter had changed since 1935 but that I was the

same only more so. But I had changed. And knowing Walter had helped do it. I hated Walter and I hated myself, that was one change. I couldn't get the sound of Marie's arguments out of my mind, that was another. But the answer was the same now as it has always been. We had two kids going to school. We were paying off on the apartment and the house in Connecticut. I was useless as a lawyer. How could I make a living unless I pimped for whores like Walter Slurrie?

When Walter was elected to the Senate, neither Betaut nor I nor the Felsenburshes—nor, in good time, Walter—wanted it to appear that his sole political stance was protection of the United States from Soviet infiltration. That is what we said to convince Walter, at any rate. In reality we saw Walter as a good second man, a high-level dog robber, and every one of us knew he was too lightweight to be riding around the country on his red horse because that way he spelled out the chaos he was looking for. Finally he already had too strong a smell of power, and we intended to turn him into a professional second man and cut down on his negative appeal.

We hand-picked his successor in the red-baiting racket, a drunk in the Senate from Wisconsin who worshipped Walter. McCarthy was the only man I have ever heard say Walter was a handsome man. Walter drilled McCarthy like a cadet in a new army. He rehearsed him, then sent him out to West Virginia where the drunken son of a bitch made a botch of it, but still Walter worked with him, far into the night, and what a drunk and an almost teetotaler did far into the night in those hotel rooms I will never know. In the end McCarthy became Walter's thick club with which to smite his enemies and frighten his friends. Then, when it seemed as if there was no way out of the messes, Walter would step in as the mediator to win points from both sides as he settled everything.

Walter's new issue as a Senator was time-honored but no less effective. He was going to defy the presence of corruption in public office.

He rose to his feet in the Senate, wearing one of his old-time black body bags, and called out shame to both the National Chairman of the Democratic Party and the Chairman of Walter's own Republican Party, an act that permitted the media to marvel at his courage.

176

I pursue the insistence that both Mr. Ludy and Mr. Dunsworth must resign as Chairmen of the National Committees. . . . The basic issue is whether a high official within any political party should be in a position where he may profit financially from the influence he may be able to exert upon agencies of the government. . . . While Mr. Ludy did not become a paid public official until April 1949, he admits that he accepted fees totaling $1,250 from a military button manufacturer . . . and we must face the other fact that no matter how bitter a pill it may be for my own party to swallow—Mr. Dunsworth used his position to further a government loan to a business corporation of which he was general counsel. What I plead with this august body to consider is this: AN OPPORTUNITY FOR INFLUENCE DOES EXIST!

Walter was hailed from coast to coast by media and by voter for nailing corruption before it could possibly reach dangerous proportions. Within four days when there wasn't much else to write about, Walter was transformed into a sort of ombudsman. It was the hat trick. Twice Walter had ridden out and had slain dragons for his country regardless of what terrible risks there might be to himself. Jesus, was I glad that Marie refused to read the newspapers.

The Felsenburshes had Betaut organizing a pilgrimage by American political leaders to the shrine of General Kampferhaufe in Paris to sit at his feet and implore him to accept the nomination for the Presidency. Betaut, as always, did a sensational job. He not only organized appeals from the Republican Party, which was easy, but he even had Democrats lining up to plead with the General to take their nomination.

Mr. Nils decided that he wanted to get Walter there first, before the great pilgrimages started. "My God, fella," he said, "he has both anti-Communism and anti-corruption all wrapped up as his own private issues." He decided he had talked enough and told me he wanted me to work the thing out with Betaut. With Betaut these things were like setting up a score with a fellow mugger. He wanted Walter coached carefully on how to handle the General. "You've got to get him over and back without anyone knowing about it, Charley. That way, Slurrie can spring the news to the press gallery right from the floor of the Senate and we'll get maximum attention. Jesus, it can be a real feat of statesmanship."

I got Walter away almost immediately on May 4th, as an expenses-paid member of the Metric Conversion Delegation to an ILO conference in Geneva. Needless to say, we by-passed the ILO

177

meeting and flew on from Geneva to Paris. We stayed at a small hotel in the Rue du Bac, ate pretty well in the neighborhood, and waited to be summoned to the General's headquarters.

General David Arnold Dieter Kampferhaufe kept the senator waiting for two and a half days, but Walter knew what was being set up for him so he played it meek and mild and made about four elaborate apologies to both of us for the General each day. The call came in. A staff car with a five-star guidon was sent to the hotel for us. We were greeted at the General's headquarters warmly by Major-General Umberto Caen, Kampferhaufe's Chief of Staff.

"Sorry about the delay, Senator," Bertie Caen said. "We have had three days of icy crisis here. Europe could have gone up like a tinderbox."

"Thank God for Dad Kampferhaufe," Walter said.

"The General regrets this, gentlemen. But he will only be able to give you about five minutes."

"We've come over three thousand miles!" Walter protested.

"Blame the times we live in," Caen answered blithely. "Follow me, please."

Dad had stayed up too late the night before playing cutthroat bridge, then reading the new Cowboy Romances fresh in from Washington in the pouch. He had risen early to get in eighteen holes of golf before lunch. He had just awakened from his nap and was impatient to get back on the golf course. He and his partner, a Philadelphia golf professional who had accepted a spot commission as a Special Services colonel, would be playing the Duke of Windsor and Bob Hope that afternoon, and Dad didn't intend to be held up by any pissant junior Senator from Texas.

Bertie Caen and I were there as partisan witnesses to be able to deny anything that might be said or might happen, such as Dad overthrowing a table or flinging a lamp into the wall in moderate rage.

"Here for long, Senator?" Dad asked Walter. "Bertie, what the hell is this? Why aren't these pencils sharpened?" The General pointed a quivering finger at the pewter mug filled with lead pencils, his face going dark red.

No sweat," Caen said, rising easily and outplucking the two offending pencils from among the twenty-odd.

"How are the Felsenburshe boys?" Dad asked me.

"Never better, sir," I said. "Mr. Nils sends his greetings and asks you to try out this jade putter he sent along with me—if you ever get the chance."

"A *jade* putter?"

"The weight of the head is the big factor, General. And the balance is unbelievable. Mr. Nils says it will shave strokes off your game."

"Well Jesus Christ, that's goddam nice of Nils. Well! A jade putter. What won't they think of next?"

Walter must have been counting the minutes of his time, which were marching past. "I have flown six thousand miles from Texas," he said for openers.

"So have I," the General said. "I was born in Deaf Smith County."

"General Kampferhaufe," Walter rumbled, "in my own small way, I have been pushed into the role of American spokesman for anti-Communism and anti-corruption in the Senate—well, in the country at large, you could say. In that same enforced spokesman's role I have flown here to petition you—and I speak as a private citizen as well as a United States Senator—to urge you to seek the Presidency of the United States."

Dad slipped into his Noble Warrior/Wise Leader face, which on him looked like ten million gold doubloons. "I am on duty, sir," he answered. "I shall serve that duty."

"America and the free world need you," Walter said.

Showing restraint, Dad tolerated Walter's presence for the moment, even if it was keeping him from golf. That is, he didn't snarl or fling anything at us. He slid out the flat desk shelf from within his desk and read aloud from the card that General Caen had taped there.

"The decision must be taken by a greater Power than a simple soldier's will," he read, never looking up from the jumbo typeface. He stood suddenly. "Good to see you, Senator, Mr. Coffey. Give my best to the Felesenburshe boys and Dick Betaut. Godspeed, et cetera." He strode out of the room.

General Caen glanced at his wristwatch. "By George," he said, "he gave you seven minutes."

On May 14th, after Roll Call in the Senate, although there had been no indication that Walter's absence in Europe had been for any reason other than to stabilize Metric Conversion everywhere but the United States, and while the Upper House was getting

179

ready to debate proposed laws for the packing of rabbit flesh in cat food, Walter took the floor.

He was *particularly* sonorous. "May I, as so many fellow members of this learned debating society have done so many times throughout its distinguished existence, take advantage of the courtliness and courtesy of my esteemed colleague from Wyoming to ask if I may make an announcement of perhaps some interest to this assembly? I thank you, sir.

"I wanted to report, gentlemen, that I had a tremendous and—I hope—historical experience a week ago at the headquarters of General Kampferhaufe outside Paris, where I was profoundly impressed by the great work he is doing against the monumental odds the Communists set against him in that position of awesome trust which he holds. He indicated to me, in the course of our two-hour-and-fifty-minute exchange of views, that one of the greatest tasks that has fallen upon his broad shoulders is to convince our allies of the necessity of putting first things first."

As meaningless as Walter made it, his the-day-I-talked-with-Dad speech really got things moving for him. I had two of our communications people plant all variations on, and implications of, the story into all the important daily papers, the wire services, and the prime-time radio news slots and within three days fifty million people, according to polls we paid for, had linked Walter with General Kampferhaufe's candidacy. The way we were able to stage it, the public believed that Dad had importuned Walter to please come to his headquarters so that the General could ask his penetrating questions about the conduct of government, having marked Senator Slurrie's amazing youth, his courage as a Communist fighter and an implacable foe of corruption. The Felsenburshes wanted to be sure they owned both positions on the campaign ticket.

The senator, in turn, as the media explained it over and over again, had visited Dad's headquarters to learn at first hand of our European front-line defenses against the Communist bloc. The two men, everyone learned quickly, had shown enormous admiration and respect for each other. The Scripps-Howard *Daily News* interviewed Walter in Washington.

"I had never met Dad," Walter was reported as having said, "although he has always been one of my idols, so I warmed with the pleasure and honor of his personal invitation to visit him as soon as my own pressing work enabled me to get away to Europe. . . . General Kampferhaufe was still putting out the fires of the European and world crisis caused by Communist aggression . . . he insisted that I go to his home for dinner, a simple American home in the heart of France. . . Dad and I talked almost three hours and parted reluctantly, I to a dawn flight to Washington, he into secret maneuvers."

Walter's dramatic meeting got such extended coverage that it brought on a classic Kampferhaufe rage that required the cancellation of an entire half-day of golf. It was a rage so towering that Mr. Nils decided to have Governor Betaut and me fly to Paris to explain the American political facts of life to the General.

By June the night skies of Europe were alight with the planes of the pilgrims of the Republican Party crossing the north Atlantic to urge Gerenal Kampferhaufe to seek the Presidency. Walter had beaten all of them to the great prize by nineteen days. Under the continuing pressure, staged by Dick Betaut, the General declared that he was a "possible" candidate. General Caen told me, months later, that the General had even memorized the statement taped to his slide-out desk top, which Caen said was the clincher that the General was interested. Walter had been the first senior Republican aboard Dad's bandwagon.

DATE: 13th October 1963
TIME: 3:05 P.M.
BASE REPORTING: New York

DSP (Semley) Only

MRS. CHARLES COFFEY (CONTINUED)

For weeks after Pop made the mistake of telling me Charley's loathsome secrets, Charley and I lived together like half-strangers, under an uneasy truce. But if you love somebody you have to take him whole. Either I took the twins and went to California or I lived with my husband the way we had always been—in his bed, at his stove, in his life. Charley wanted it that way. He never stopped trying to get things back where they should be, so after a little time had softened the brutality of Pop's news, we got it together again. It wasn't the same as it had been, but every marriage knows it was a giant once.

Then one afternoon he telephoned to ask if he could bring his old college roommate home to dinner. I started to say "Of course," then I remembered who his old college roommate was. "Fuck him," I said to make everything crystal clear. "He's the worst of all of them."

"Marie, listen, Walter is my special charge and this is a tricky time for us. He keeps asking me why I haven't introduced him to my wife. He says I met his wife, why hasn't he met you? This has been going on for years, for crissake. Just this once, okay? We won't have a word to say about politics and I won't ever bother you with this again."

"All right. Bring him."

"Tomorrow night okay?"

"Yeah."

"Thanks, sweetheart."

We still lived on East 57th. We had made space for the twins and their inexorable growth by buying an apartment across the two-apartment entrance hall then breaking through at the rear where the two flats joined.

As Charley ushered Slurrie into the apartment an expression of disgust flickered over Slurrie's face. I don't think he was reacting to me. I think it was probably because of the cooking smells the pots and I were making. It was such an insensitive, stupid look that it made me think of the daughter of that man in Dallas years ago, so I really didn't need that flicker of disgust to keep me turned off him.

Slurrie looked like what you might expect from an outraged anti-gonorrhea politician. He had the faked personality that goes with constitutional psychopaths: they borrow every expression they have from dozens of other people they have seen reacting honestly. Slurrie was a flower without any smell; a pompous fake-out with a face like a manatee. We shook hands too heartily. Charley saw it.

Charley frowned, then wiped it off. Slurrie was "genuinely thrilled" to meet the "beautiful life partner of his old roommate." I told him I was all shook up to meet the old roommate of my new roommate. We all laughed like crows. Charley went to make us a drink.

"Nothing for me, Charley," Slurrie said.

"I know."

"Oh, perhaps just a small sweet vermouth."

"What's for dinner?"

"Some Italian stuff."

"I used to love guinea food in my early days in Washington," Slurrie said. "Have you ever been to Dom G's—well, it's called the Villa d'Este actually."

"I am a guinea," I said. "I can cook the stuff. So why go to a restaurant?"

"It was one of those legendary places," he explained. "It was supposed to be a Mafia joint."

"How romantic."

Charley brought us drinks. "Marie was a Navy nurse," he told Slurrie.

"Well! A Navy nurse. Then this is an all-Navy party tonight."

"Walter got the Navy Cross."

"How?"

"I was with Buffalo Manning's task force."

"I can't believe it."

"Good God, I don't want to talk about *that*."

"Walter is also a personal friend of General MacArthur's," Charley said, getting into the mood and enjoying himself.

"That figures."

"And a *personal* friend of Dad Kampferhaufe's."

"A great man," Slurrie said.

"Charley, did you pick up your hat at the blocker's?"

"Be ready tomorrow."

Slurrie sipped the guppy pee in slow, tiny little swallows. His hair was like brass filaments and he looked like he had just come in from Fire Island. Charley stood there, smarmy and superior, rocking on his heels and looking down on us as we sat across the room from each other. Charley was enjoying himself too much, so I said to Slurrie, "What about the Rosenbergs?"

"Excuse me?"

"What about the sentence they handed the Rosenbergs?"

He looked at me blankly. "They were paid Soviet agents." At least the fake affability was fading and Charley seemed a little more uptight. He coughed. Slurrie's eyes got like cold dishwater.

"But—a *death* sentence?"

"They stole our innermost secrets for the enemy."

"Do we have to *kill* them? We aren't at war."

"We are at war, my dear."

"Please don't call me 'my dear.'"

"They were spies."

"That really wasn't proved, my dear," I said.

"This is my own field, Marie. I know. I know more about this field than anyone in this country. The Rosenbergs would see this city bombed into the ocean and never bat an eye." He turned

185

away from me abruptly. "What sort of a fellow is Stassen, Charley?"

"We'll take that up tomorrow," Charley said, living up to his bargain. "We don't want to talk about politics while we're eating."

We got through dinner somehow. Slurrie was out of my house by half past nine that night. We did not shake hands vigorously when he left.

"Well," Charlie said with mock appreciation, "you sure know how to make a home where a fellow can bring his old friends."

"Sit down, Charley. And stow the sarcasm. You just shoveled garbage into our house. Do you agree with that?"

"By and large, yes."

"Another thing, my husband. While you and Slurrie are entirely different men you both have an air of doom about you when you are together."

"Ah, I married a gypsy. Look, Walter isn't as bad as you think, Marie. He may be the shallowest man we've ever had in American politics but, beyond bottomless greed, he isn't such a bad guy."

"Would you say he is normal?"

"How do you mean?"

"I mean where the rest of human life is concerned. You at least *look* normal, Charley. But you can't be. You are cheek by jowl with Slurrie, but you probably think you are superior to him. Listen to me please, Charley. By refusing to examine what you are doing to yourself and to me—and to the millions of other people who are affected—you are becoming less and less focused on what you have become. You have moved away from your center, your self-respect, and your control. And tomorrow you will be more aberrant than yesterday. You have become more dangerous to your loyalties, Charlie, than Slurrie is to his shallowness and greed."

TO: FIRST DEPUTY COMMISSIONER VIN-
CENT J. MULSHINE

FROM: LIEUTENANT RICHARD GALLA-
GHER, 17th HSQ

After the PC had a closed door meeting
with Richard Betaut he called me downtown. The PC didn't go into any details
with me about what Betaut had said to
him. He said he wanted to ask me why I
thought Betaut had told me, then told
him, what he had. I stated that it was about
as explosive a piece of information as I had
ever had handed to me after twenty-two
years on the force, that it seemed to me

Betaut must want to shake us up about whether we were going to build a case against the SP for the Slurrie murder.

The PC said it wouldn't be that easy if it could be done at all. He pointed out that the Pickering Commission had been meeting for over a year, going over tons of evidence on the assassination but that the SP hadn't come into it. He told me that if a case could be built, it would automatically become a political matter. He said it wasn't just a matter of the Republican State Committee and the Governor, who would involve the Mayor which would involve us, but his own opinion was that Betaut was somehow involved in all of it. Not maybe involved in the Slurrie killing – although nothing was impossible – but heavily involved with the SP.

So, the PC said, if Betaut is involved with them and the SP did organize the Slurrie murder, then we've got to decide whether we are strong enough with the case we built to take on the Felsenburshes, who are the factors behind Betaut, the Governor, the Mayor, the State Republican Committee – and probably the SP. They could roll right over us if we don't have a case that will convict.

So, he said to me, the reason I asked you to come down here is to say that if you can build such a case against the SP, I will okay a go-ahead because once the media gets their teeth into a situation like that, if we deliver, if we make it stick, nobody, not even the Felsenburshes, can touch us. What's your answer, he asks me.

I say I wouldn't begin to know how to build such a case. I ask him what would happen if it turns out that we can build a case against Betaut?

"The answer is the same," he says.

"Then what if it develops that we can build a total case against Danzig?"

The PC said that was a trick question in a way because Danzig is probably better connected than the SP. He can call in all the help the SP would be able to call in, plus he'd have the SP on his side. They can protect anybody forty ways. "Have we got a case against Danzig?" he asked.

I told him that we already had a good case against Danzig and against Betaut, because the way everything pointed it looked like Danzig and Betaut together organized the Slurrie hit. We are going to be able to make that case as soon as we

188

have pinned down who owns the shoes that left the bloody footprints. And who owned and ordered the special bullets for that Japanese gun. That is the only break we need in the whole case.

He tells me to wrap it up.

I ask him if I should write up this particular report to the First Deputy Commissioner.

He says he wants me to write it up just as if it were any other report, because he is pretty sure that, the way it was organized in the beginning, Betaut has been reading every one of the reports anyway.

SECRET POLICE
UNITED STATES OF AMERICA
SEMLEY, MARYLAND

DATE: 11th August 1964
TIME: 9:10 A.M.
BASE REPORTING: Miami   DSP (Semley) Only

EDWARD CARDOZO (continued)

I got to say that Wullair was a li'l nuts on the whole subject of money. No matter how much we make, Wullair want more. We never can talk about anything else when we alone. The Red Crusade was a great score. But we do better than that in Miami real estate. Then even better when Nudey fix it for us to get our own bank at Vizcaya Cove. But—*Madre de Dios!*—when Wullair is Vice-President is when we make the rilly sensational dills. Wullair would sell absolutely anything an make it look legit to himself. After that not only do he have so much money he don know what to do an which he cannot espend, him and Nudey make such a score out of Horace Hind that I deen think there was that much money in the world. But still Wullair nidd more.

I wash the money. I get the money back in this country when it is through the laundry. I put it in dummy companies so it keep growing and growing but Wullair keep saying, "Everybody else got money, why not us?"

He used to tell me that he use to think he got to get the power first before he can get at the real money. But after he has so much money he tell me that nobody got any power, that everybody workeen for somebody else an that they all ronneen aronn in circle shafting each other so he say the only thing worth getting together is more money than anybody else, except he knows that no matter how much you make there is always somebody who got more. Wullair kid himself but he don kid me. He thinks he invents a religion he minn it so much.

Wullair was once a very nice fella compared. But now he hates people. Everybody scare him so he hate them, an all he think of is to protect his money. An all the time he got to yell how poor he is because if the connree ever fine out how much he stole them, how much he take unner the bridge to keep the war going—*hombre,* they go in wherever he is an string him up by the neck.

But he was my frenn. When times is good, Wullair go bad. But when times is bad, he is hokay. An he's toff. Oh, jess. I remember one morning on the terrace at Vizcaya Cove with that gorgeous view of the bay an Wullair sitting there in the bright sun in violet and green silk pajamas, which some Koreans send to him with a gang of money for fixing up some textile imports for them. He is itting his usual Sunday brunch of frankfurters an bagels an ketchup an flashing his dingy teeth at me with the ketchup splashed all aronn his asshole-shape mouth like an old *barrio puta.*

He say, "I sincerely hope you don't mind, Kiddo, but I think nine million dollars is a considerable amount of money."

"Maybe you did before Boston," I tell him. "But you don think so anymore."

"I'd like to propose a new laundry system."

"What is wrong with the system we got? Everybody in the business uses it. And we use Nudey's own mover. Solly Potash. The best."

"Do we have to pay Mr. Danzig for that?"

"You know him. What do you think?"

"How much?"

"Three per cent."

He shake his head so sad that it could break his heart if he look in a mirror. "Three per on the millions and millions we have moved to Switzerland. And I suppose we have to pay their air fares too. We might just as well pay income taxes."

"Wullair, Nudey gorrontee the money get there."

"Well, we are no longer going to need a professional mover.

And we are no longer going to run the risk of leaving a paper trail."

Now, this is the time when Wullair is become a big Wall Stritt lawyer. His partners are experts at keeping money away from governments. "You got a new angle, Wullair?" I ask him.

"Yes."

"The Wall Stritt lawyers?"

"Yes. And Governor Betaut."

"Go ahead."

"First you will have to go to Switzerland personally."

"Wullair, we agree a long time ago that we don wan the Feds to have it on me that I leave the country."

"There is no risk. Mr. Danzig can get you a false passport. What we will be doing here is setting up barriers of protection between us and any politicians who think they could gain by exposing me. Or the media. Or the IRS. I have some of the best tax evasion people in the world in my firm. I am talking about lawyers who can almost think in Mr. Danzig's class. It works like clockwork. You fly to Zurich and have Herr Birmann at the Talacker Bank arrange for the incorporation of a Lichtenstein company for us. They can really craft those little companies. Now, by having a Swiss banker order the formation of the company, instead of having it done ourselves, we eliminate the danger of any contact with Lichtenstein. The Swiss bank will be the buffer between us and the IRS all the way: a numbered account, a Swiss banker, the Lichtenstein company. The IRS could never get through that maze."

"I hope not."

"I knew you'd like it. The Swiss banker is the only stockholder in the Lichtenstein company. The company can now open its own bank accounts in Switzerland to trade in gold, or go into the stock exchanges, or go into real estate. We can quintuple our money, Kiddo. Tax free."

"But how do we get the money to Lichtenstein?"

"You take it to the Bahamas—a foreign country—then one of Mr Danzig's banks there merely cables the transfer to Lichtenstein. No connection with us. No risk."

"But suppose the IRS subpoenas the secret trust agreement we got with the Swiss bank?"

"Kiddo, please. You are in the hands of experts. The trust agreement will be locked inside a box in Nigeria or Panama. In order to find out who owns our Lichtenstein company, the IRS would have to penetrate not only the Swiss and Lichtenstein legal secrecy—and remember, in both countries divulging any bank information is against the law—but after that they'd have to break the legal Nigerian or Panamanian secrecy as well."

Betsy look up from her knitting. "Isn't it something?" she say. "Here Walter and I have over a hundred million dollars saved up and we'll never be able to touch any of it without Walter going to jail. Just the same that kind of money gives you a wonderful feeling of security."

"Oh, you'll be able to get at it someday, dear," Walter say. "I have one of the best legal minds in Wall Street working on just that, right now."

There is a very big point here. The Lichtenstein bank account could have got Wullair killed. Maybe you don know those accounts. You don have to bring the right face or a passport or how you sign your name to get the money out of those accounts. You got to show the number and the name of the company at the bank where the company banks. That's all. So who could get the number, the name of the company, an the bank out of a fellow like Wullair? Who would Wullair tell that to? Who is Wullair's lawyer, one of the best legal minds in Wall Street? Who has to go over all the plans for the Lichtenstein company and okay them for Wullair? I tell you who Wullair's lawyer is an you not gun like it. Wullair's lawyer was Betaut.

DATE: 11th August 1964
TIME: 2:07 P.M.
BASE REPORTING: Miami   DSP (Semley) Only

ABNER "NUDEY" DANZIG (continued)

Waller lost for president in 1960. It was such a tight margin that Cook County, Illinois, cost him the whole thing. For the only time since I know him Waller blows up and refuses to take any advice. He stands up on the stage in front of a couple of hunnerd campaign workers in the ballroom at the Stoneleigh Hotel on Maple Avenue in Dallas, and tell them that he is getting together a fund to buy national television time to tell the people the truth about the campaign. Upstairs in the double suite later he tells everybody that he can prove that the White House was stolen from him. Kiddo called me from New York and right away I called Dick Betaut, who is in the Waldorf in New York.

The Secret Service tells Betaut that Waller went to bed at 3:25 A.M. and they won't wake him up for anybody. But they tell Betaut that he went to bed refusing to concede the election. Too late, it comes out that Waller took two Seconals. At 4:00 A.M. Betaut slams open the double doors to Waller's bedroom and goes in with Kiddo an Charley Coffey. They told the Secret Service to stay the hell outta there.

Betaut tells Waller to get up. Waller can't even hear him. Betaut throws a glassa water on Waller's face. Nothing. Betaut gets out of his clothes, even his shoes and socks, right down to his underpants. Believe me, Betaut is worth whatever Felsenburshe pays him. What moxie this guy has! He tells Charley to throw Waller inna shower. He tells Kiddo get two buckets of ice and a thermos of black coffee.

Waller's eyes are rolled up like winda shades. They drag him acrossa carpet like a silent movie drunk. They drop him inna shower. Betaut gets in with him and hold him under the cold water and slaps his face back and forth like it was some Rumanian dance until Waller's eyes are open an he is beginning to focus. After a while he can talk a little. They drag him out and rub him with friction towels until maybe his skin could come off. They drag him back to the bedroom, throw him inna chair, and Betaut rubs ice cubes in his armpits, over his stomach, and in his crotch, very hard. They make him drink coffee. When he is really focusing, Betaut walks over to his suit and finds a cigar. Kiddo holds the match for him.

Betaut stands there in his white silk underpants which are plastered to his legs and talks to Waller with his bass drum verce. "Can you understand me, Walter?" he asks.

"Yes."

"I want you to concede the election in writing. It is all typed. You will sign it."

"No," Waller says, loud.

Betaut sits with his face close to Waller's. "Do you know what confiscation is, counselor?" he asks Waller. "Well, sir, unless you concede in writing and forget your ideas about any broadcast, you are going to be indicted on charges of income tax evasion. Your bank accounts here and abroad will be made public, and the media and the Congress will demand that every cent of it be confiscated. The courts will so rule."

Waller stared at him in fright. He nods. Charley hands Betaut the papers and a pen. Waller signs five copies. They let him keep a copy.

Betaut gets dressed, taking his time. "I knew you would understand, Walter," he says. "You are a Party man. You've been under a strain in this long campaign. You're entitled to one slip.

Now get a good night's sleep and tomorrow Kiddo will take you to Florida to soak up some of that wonderful sunshine."

So Waller was out on his ass after twelve big years in politics. He had nothing but his money. I let him cook for a while, then I went over to see him at his house in Vizcaya Cove.

"Waller," I said to him, "It's time you got started up again."

"Mr. Danzig, I don't know where I can go from the top."

"You didn't make the top, remember? I talked it over with Betaut. He's gonna find you a solid, rundown Wall Street law firm. I'll buy it and he'll get them to put your name at the top and he'll explain they shouldn't expect you to be a lawyer for them because you are a politician, which could be very good for them, plus it could pay you like a quarter million a year and a piece."

He is gladda get it. He calls Horace Hind right away and gets three Hind companies as accounts. He tells Hind that although the voters will think he is practicing law he will actually be all over the country, setting up the nomination for '68. "After all," he says, very serious, "both parties have to share in the war in Asia. Sixty-eight has to be a Republican year."

Wall Street lawyers live behind every scene in big business. They are respectable because they are safe. They have forbidden themselves ever to say what happens between a lawyer and a client. No outsider can get inside their partnerships.

When Waller became head of the law firm, the Felsenburshes got him made a director of eleven companies and four mutual funds, combined loot: $9.2 billion. They get him made legal counsel for three of the biggest defense contractors. Then—surprise!—his law firm is retained by all these companies.

On his first day with the firm Walter tells the press, "I can say categorically that I have no contemplation of being a candidate for anything in 1964, '68 or '72. I have no political staff. I am not answering any political mail. I have no political base. I'm a New Yorker now. Anyone who thinks I could be a candidate for anything, in any year, is out of his mind."

Betaut got the Slurries a big apartment on Fifth Avenue in the same building where Nils Felsenburshe personally lived sometimes. Waller was very proud of that. "There is more money represented in that building," he said to Kiddo, "than anywhere in the world."

Betsy, the wife, said to him, "But we are sixteen floors under the Felsenburshes."

"We'll be invited up there, dear. You'll see."

She kissed him on the cheek. "That's what you always said about the Kampferhaufes," she said.

Charley Coffey turned Waller's legs to water by getting him made a member of the Knickerbocker Club, the Metropolitan Club, the Links Club, the Recess Club, and India House. Charley set up another press conference so the boys can get Waller's financial picture straight. Waller tells a big mix of the media that his assets are $509,000; liabilities $328,641. He tells them his assets are entirely in real estate: a house in Florida, one in Dallas, and the value of the apartment in New York. He said he had $9,213.23 in cash and that his personal property, including his wife's jewelry, was worth $3,057.19.

We never had a better liar in this country.

DATE: 11th August 1964
BASE REPORTING: Los Angeles

DSP (Semley) Only

N.B. *The following autobiographical text was transcribed from tape cassettes found in the Bel Air house of Horace Riddle Hind. An audio copy has also been made. The original cassettes have been returned to the Hind bedroom in Bel Air.*

Horace Riddle Hind (continued)

Statistically, or in any other way, my daddy would have to say that I have led a more interesting and fuller life than he did. I have emerged as a historically significant figure. That it is necessary that I spend $2,300,000 a year on my personal surveillance requirements and guards is proof enough of my accomplishment. Companies under my personal direction have produced $914,822,056.16 in net profits, a feat which my daddy could hardly have been able to claim as his own accomplishment no matter how hard he tried.

Let me say right here, in an area where my management executives are agile about maneuvering to take credit, that it was I who built Hind Aircraft from a shambles and transformed it into a great American electronics company, the No. 3 defense contractor in the United States, which of course means the world.

When I picked up my airline it was called Tri-State Transfers, Inc. It wasn't much more than a slapdash herd of puddle jumpers. I mean it flew regional mail and that was about it. I built that rickety little hopscotch game into Global Airlines, an international giant of the skies. And I did it creatively and with daring.

To say that I am an anti-Communist would be to state the case at minimum. Using Walter Bodmor Slurrie, a Vice-President of the United States (and an amount of money which I refuse to reveal here), I have fought Communism in the way which my daddy would have wanted it to be fought, to protect our holdings and keep them safe inside this wonderful country of ours, but I think the record will show that I went much further in this struggle than my daddy (who had certain frivolous elements in his character) would ever have done.

But I learned from Daddy. I owe him a great deal. He proved to me, by actual demonstration, that actresses have one weakness. They are helplessly wanton sexually. Daddy never bothered with other women, nonactresses, who were inclined to be frigid (which is the way a good woman should be), but somehow he stumbled upon this secret of dominating the opposite sex to an extent to which he never dominated Mom.

Daddy was a thoroughly masculine presence in every way. But he would no more think of suggesting sexual relations with a good woman than he would of desecrating our flag. His needs brought him solutions. He could do anything he wanted to do to actresses, who were all of them helplessly wanton victims of their urges and desires.

Nonetheless and notwithstanding, in this field as well I have outachieved Daddy. He would go on periodical sex benders, then he would go back to his work, refreshed. My own overwhelmingly masculine need was no less (and possibly a great deal more) than Daddy's, but I am a disciplined engineer. My work, and the expansion of everything Daddy left me in trust, is the most important thing in my life. Others extol me in the fields of aviation, advertising, film production, electronics, oil shipment, and other tasks to which I have set my hand. They are correct in their evaluations for I am a deeply responsible person. But I had my masculine needs just the same. Instead of slaking those needs, willy-nilly, as Daddy had done, I approached the problem as a trained engineer. I set the greater part of my 318 surveillance people and guards to locating and guarding beautiful actresses throughout the world for me to relieve my self upon sexually and, in the course of that act, bring them enormous pleasure.

While it is true that most of these women, as the files at my Lorraine Center show, were not actresses *per se* when we found them, the nature of my interests as the owner of a large motion picture studio enabled me to offer them careers as actresses. However, the women who accepted these offers, who were deeply attracted to the profession of acting, by the very act of signing acting contracts which legally transformed them into actresses, were therefore all wanton, sexually urgent women.

We have detailed case histories of 914 of these women, whom I brought to California from various parts of the world, but that file does not represent my total consumption (although it is far beyond Daddy's consumption of women) because there were many, many unrecorded sexual encounters with other actresses whom my people discovered in taxi-dance establishments, four different times in Mexican brothels (although I am almost certain that one of these instances brought in the same woman twice), at the doctrinaire Hollywood soda fountains—or even as teachers of music and calisthenics to our young, I am amazed to state. Although my people, through conversations with these women, were able to apply the test that I had developed to determine whether or not they lusted to become actresses, I did not sign these particular women to contracts but retained their sexual services for short periods in apartments or motels which we rented for these purposes.

It has happened to me that these various actresses—and I now speak of your star actresses known to every nation of the world— have betrayed me, or kept open telephone lines to friends in Europe from Los Angeles for ten months at a time, twenty-four hours a day before my people discovered it. They have transmitted certain venereal diseases to me, something which I personally hate, until I had to insist on a weekly medical checkup on each woman as an explicit part of the contract. They have stolen from me and attempted to blackmail me. I have been witness to every low and foul thing of which a woman is capable, all of which went to prove explicitly that Daddy was right when he warned me against women.

The strain of it gave me severe piles. Someday, among the

hundreds of thousands who will read this autobiography, there will be readers who, too, are afflicted with piles. This was my approach to the ailment as a simple engineer.

Adolf Hitler had piles.

Hitler treated his piles in Sitz baths of Apollonaris water, which was also the regulation issue beverage to his SS people. A Sitz bath, I am told by my people, is one where you just spread your jowls and sit (Sitz) down in the water. Apollonaris water brought Hitler great relief. I could not secure Apollonaris because all their plants had been destroyed by Allied overkill, although I pleaded with General Arnold to order our bombers to by-pass these factories. (If Walter Slurrie had been in office during World War II you may be sure this would not have happened. He would have come back to me with a written report on official stationery plus aerial photographs showing that although utter destruction of enemy property had taken place all around the Apollonaris water factory, it still stood, intact and unharmed.)

I now use Poland water for my piles, the finest bottled water in the world. It is a Maine product, I believe. At *great* expense during the war I had secured one case of Apollonaris water (by dint of paying one of my German-speaking people to enlist in the SS) because, as a scientist, I insist upon fair testing. I had the comparative tests run by two laboratories each in a different part of the country. The results showed that our American water, Poland water, was superior. This suggests that, had Hitler won the war, his first move might have been to expropriate the Poland water factories in Maine—I believe they are in Maine—to reassure his piles. (There is no one with whom I can check this because the entire contents of this autobiography shall remain secret until 250 years after my death.)

I take five enemas a day with Poland water. That which proceeds from these enemas is a vital part of me and is therefore stored in Mason jars under a date labeling system after the feces have been returned from their daily laboratory analysis, I fill the Mason jars with my urine as well for each twenty-four-hour period. When it becomes necessary to have my hair cut for reasons of vision and hygiene, the cut hairs are sealed in heavy plastic envelopes which are appropriately dated and marked. Why? That might be a very good question here.

I do not actually believe in voodoo, but I do a considerable amount of magazine reading in my search for women whom we might turn into actresses. I have read what the witch doctors of

202

the voodoo religion are capable of achieving with bits and pieces of a person's own body. I am also aware of certain progress which is being made in the process called cloning and would be appalled to think of replicas of myself walking into my factories and studios and taking over all authority.

My curiosity drew me to Haiti when I was much younger. I knew President-for-Life Duvalier. (He also suffered from piles and I shared the information my people had gleaned from those closest to Hitler and I am happy to say that this brought the President-for-Life considerable relief.) Duvalier was a superior nigger. He could actually speak French. In the course of our evening together (I had had our State Department introduce us), when he closed me in a bedroom with two uncontrolled members of the opposite sex from the black aristocracy of Haiti, it developed that their mother had been an actress.

The next day the President-for-Life explained that he was the Supreme Pontiff of the voodoo religion. Naturally, but courteously, I scoffed at voodooism, while not seeking to offend him. This moved him to tell me what could happen to me if he or his juju people could obtain a lock of my hair or a sample of my feces. When I heard what I heard I vowed that nothing like that would ever happen to me and was careful not to have a bowel movement while in his country. My training as an engineer does not permit me to take chances, therefore I store away, under lock and key, all organic emanations from my body for, and this is an enigma, I am a man with enemies.

This year, 1959, has been a hardship for me. The man whom I readily appointed to be my substitute father, a financial genius, had suddenly behaved abominably and has, since I threw him out, told the press the rotten lie that whatever I put my personal hand to is soon to be found deep in chaos. He will never get back inside even if he crawls to me on his hands and knees. More than that, just because it is my own judgment that the time for the use of jet engines in commercial aircraft is not yet at hand—at least eight years away—a handful of token stockholders in my airline have been stirred up by banks and insurance companies trying to steal my company. You may be sure that he who laughs last, laughs best. I have decided that the way out of my endless problems is to renounce people. They are unreliable. They are the cause of the troubles of the world and I do not confine that statement to troubles they have caused me alone.

I have been made ill by this intention-to-piracy by these banks and insurance companies—each one of them out of the East. My masculinity is intact but I cannot stir up any interest within myself for actresses. I still allow my people to locate and house these women against the day when I will have conquered my enemies and am able to turn again to my needs. Until then I will rest behind locked doors, well within a world which I control without interference from people and where they cannot approach me. I prefer to sit in the dark because I am studying motion picture production techniques by running and rerunning a competitor's movie, one which I admire, *The Kissing Bandit.* Being a creative man this tends to clear my mind and allow me to rest my body while I explore various food and feeding systems and principles which I have been developing for many years. I have my four interests which keep me ongoing: *The Kissing Bandit,* my science-comic book collection (extensive), food, and the protection of my organic emanations.

DATE: 11th August 1964
TIME: 4:35 P.M.
BASE REPORTING: New York

DSP (Semley) Only

CHARLES COFFEY (continued)

Harold Stassen reluctantly agreed that if the Felsenburshes felt that Senator Walter Slurrie had a political future, then he would abide by that. At his Strategy Conference in New Jersey on the day after Walter had come to dinner at our house, Stassen followed our scenario by openly offering to trade Walter the Vice-Presidential nomination on the Stassen ticket in return for the support of the Texas delegation to the convention. Walter stood up at the meeting, which was well covered by the press, and said, "Thank you, Governor, but I have far less control over the Texas delegation than you, yourself."

Late in June '52, Walter made the keynote address to the Convention of the Young Pioneers of the Republican Federation (COYPRUF), a national body. He spoke via leased telephone lines from Washington to Mesilla, New Mexico, where the Party leader, Calvin Coolidge, had wintered in 1930. There was a bad default in the transmission, which was unfortunate because this speech was Walter's own keynote for his own campaign for the Vice-Presidency. His voice just crackled over the line, not loudly enough for the words to be understood. But even though the speech was never heard by the COYPRUF delegates, the media reported it as if it had been. This was the Slurrie credo which Walter nailed to the cathedral door of Democracy:

> We have to work, we have to fight, we have to stand for something. We must attack inflation. But we shall not allow that emergency to be used to socialize any basic American institution. The American tragedy is that the other party has refused to recognize the fifth column in this country and to take effective action to clean subversives out of government.
> I plead with them to study these facts: Today there are only 540,000,000 people who can be counted as standing on our side. But there are 800,000,000 people who can be counted as standing on the Communist side. And there are 600,000,000 people swaying in indecision. In other words, six years ago the odds of people in the world were nine-to-one in our favor. today those odds are five-to-three against us. We have lost 720,000,000 people to Communism in six years.

That had to happen at a time when Marie was doing her best to show token interest in politics by reading the newspapers. She looked at the summaries of Walter's speech over breakfast and said to me, "Charley, for haven's sake, how can you work with this pickpocket?"

On the afternoon after his Mad Hatter speech I took Walter to meet Dick Betaut for the first time. Titular head of the Republican Party with the voice of a killer whale, Betaut was as towering a political figure as Walter had ever met. He was as much in awe of Betaut as everyone else had been throughout Betaut's life including his parents, his kindergarten teacher, and the man who made his elevator shoes.

I brought Walter to Betaut's apartment at the Waldorf Towers. He gave us a drink (which Walter accepted without demur) and a big, brown cigar each. "Walter," he boomed, "I am going to talk to you about your chances of getting the second spot on the ticket. If you get it, it will be because I got it for you. Always remember that."

"I could never forget that, Governor," Walter said. "It is beyond my dreams of serving America."

Walter had no background for men like Betaut and I felt pity for him. Walter was petty and mean, he wasn't tough or resilient. Cynicism isn't enough in politics. It took Betaut's long reach and sure grasp, and the eyes in the back of his head. Betaut had been a choir-singing country boy once, the same kind of hick Walter would always be. But Betaut had outgrown those limitations and Walter would never know how to extend his boundaries. Betaut was complex, dangerous, and resourceful. Walter was still the small boy who pulled wings off houseflies, as shallow as a whore's kiss. But the definitive difference between them was that Walter was pure in everything, a one-of-a-kind model. His could not be compared to the purities in which Betaut abounded. Betaut was a pure scoundrel with purer self-confidence and purest reasons for excelling. Where Betaut moved steadily into the battle to test himself against his peers, Walter sought out inferiors and weaklings so that his lack of faith and timorous morality could not be fairly tested. Walter had transformed himself into the lies he spoke so easily, and at last he almost believed that the fetid, oozing money stains upon his psyche were the wounds of brave battle.

"You're a good man, Walter," Betaut said. "We are pleased with your handling of important Secret Police matters in the Senate. You haven't forgotten that those of the SP are our pivots all over the world. They must remain strong, and we are moving to redouble that strength. When Dad goes into the Oval Office, John Garnicht Marxuach will be his Secretary of State and his brother, James D. Marxuach, will become head of the SP. A new era will begin. The Marxuach boys will bring spiritual comfort to this country. They are the best and final product of a long line of Baptist missionaries in Asia, for whom the Pacific Ocean is their own pond. Your colleague, if you are chosen to be Vice-President, will be the elemental James D., an intellect with a purpose, who cries out to multiply the meanings of our covert activities!"

"It will be a privilege to work with him," Walter breathed.

"Yes. Now, inasmuch as Vice-Presidents don't have much to do beyond being the President's janitor, what you are being considered for here, Walter, is the chance to become significant by taking over as the SP's undercover Action Officer in the White House."

Walter looked as if he wanted to speak but wasn't up to it in the face of history. I hoped he would not misjudge Betaut and suddenly begin to weep.

"Dad isn't going to rock any boats for the Marxuach boys, Walter," Betaut rumbled. "Dad's long-term Army policy is that he doesn't have to object to what he doesn't know about. He'll go along with what we have to do to build the SP by staying out of our way. The undercover Action Officer is the man who is going to make or break this plan."

"Governor Betaut, I—"

"I can make you the catcher inside the White House for the SP. The law states that the SP must refer all actions and plans back to the President and the National Security Council. We'll keep Dad busy out at Burning Tree and at the bridge table. If I make you Vice-President you'll be his natural deputy. You would catch for James D. Marxuach and throw everything back to him, all approved. Is that clear enough, Walter?"

"Oh, yes sir."

"All right then. We've settled that. Now you get out there yelling up and down the country about the Reds and corruption in government, and Charley and I will take care of the rest."

DATE: 11th August 1964
TIME: 10:57 A.M.
BASE REPORTING: Austin   DSP (Semley) Only

CLAUDE ALBRITTON

I was Governor of the State of Texas with seventy-three pledged delegates to the Chicago convention. I had a lot of smart people around me, and there wasn't one of them who didn't know I had a seventy percent chance of getting the nomination in '52. The front runner was Mal Foote, Senator from Michigan. Second to him was Dad Kampferhaufe, the big war hero of Berkeley Square, a natural politician and the favorite of all the Eastern big money. Now it was as clear as the writing on a child's birthday cake—just counting up and figuring out the disputed delegates who were or were not to be seated at the convention, then counting in the seventy-three delegates who were pledged to me—that Foote and Dad might be thrown into a deadlock, and when that happened the convention would have to turn to me as the compromise candidate.

I would have been President of the United States from 1952 until 1960 if it hadn't been for that Texas Judas, that unspeakable traitor inside our own camp, Walter Slurrie.

So he's dead, is he? Well, please just lead me out to his grave here in Dallas and let me loosen up my trousers so I can dampen him down good the way I should have done when he was alive. I have never known a man by contact, sight, or reputation, from Simon Girty to Benedict Arnold, who was more plain dishonest and more deserving of being shot than Walter Slurrie. They won't have too much trouble finding who shot him if they have the time to weed the killer out from among the thousands whose lives Slurrie ruined with his cowardly, fake, useless Communist charges. There are a power of broken people in this country who got thrown away with the bathwater because Slurrie pointed at them and called them Commie traitors just to get a few sticks of newspaper type.

Let me say this so there is no mistaking my convictions where Slurrie is concerned. If I hadn't had a bad cold all last week, which kept me to my bed, I would gladly have been the fellow who walked him into the bathroom in New York, sat him on that velvet chair like a fairy queen, and pumped him full of bullets. He was a carrion eater, skulking outside the tents of the Felsenburshes and the Betauts, waiting for scraps of their garbage. Whoever murdered him was a moral person.

Slurrie was just as irrevocably pledged to me as anyone else in the Texas delegation so he knew damned well he couldn't come out openly for Dad. Betaut was running Dad's campaign for the Felsenburshes, and it sure figured that Betaut damned well told Slurrie that if he wanted the second slot on the ticket he had to outmaneuver me, organize all the contested seats among the Southern delegations so he could stampede the South at the convention and swing the Texas delegation right behind Dad.

The diseased little varmint began by stirring up cabals against me *inside* the Texas delegation, but his sensitized antenna soon told him that it would be a mistake to take a direct approach like that because the word could get back to his good friend and colleague the Governor of Texas—namely me—and I might just nail him to the floor. So instead the slimy crook set up a meeting with me, pointed openly to his answer to Harold Stassen a month ago that (a) he wasn't interested in the second slot and (b) he had less control of the Texas delegation than anyone, and negotiated his total, assured, and guaranteed support for my candidacy in the event of a deadlock between Senator Foote and Kampferhaufe on the condition that—which he said was only recognition of his pride-of-place as the Party's U.S. Senator in Texas—he be allowed to select members of the Texas delegation. Well, I mean, all seventy-three had to be pledged to me so how could I lose on a proposition like that? And there was no way to threaten my seventy-three votes out of seventh-three anyway, even if I did know Slurrie was scheming out a way to destroy me.

What I should have felt and seen while I was throwing him those guarantees was that the man's word was worthless, that he wore his honor like a dried scab. The central meaning of Slurrie came over loud and clear via a Dallas radio broadcast the night before he left for the Chicago convention to take his seat as a member of the Resolutions Committee (which Charley Coffey personally set for him).

This is what Slurrie had the nerve to broadcast from Dallas:

It is the patriotic duty of the Republican convention to select the strongest nominee to whip the other party. Senator Foote and General Kampferhaufe will emerge with about five hundred delegates each. If they deadlock then our own Governor Claude Albritton, my good friend, is the sure-fire standby candidate. But there are seventy contested Southern seats at stake here that could decide this nomination. The Texas delegation, therefore, with its seventy-three votes and its benign Southern influence can actually hold the key to who is nominated and who is turned away. *We must have the winner. We must name the strongest candidate who can uncontestably whip the opposition.* We must *never* forget—if the convention does *not* turn to Governor Albritton, then it will become the duty of the Texas delegation to throw our votes to the unbeatable candidate who will be chosen.

Now that was the most contemptible double-cross since Hitler invaded Russia. He was out to prevent deadlock by throwing all the Southern weight to Kampferhaufe before the goddam deadlock could happen. What he had broadcast was that he was out to turn my own delegation, pledged to me, away from me and into Kampferhaufe's arms. When Slurrie got to Chicago he politicked day and night, never going near the Resolutions Committee. He told *everybody* there just wasn't going to be any deadlock. And he repeatedly told everybody, out and out, that I didn't have a chance. Then the little sumbitch chartered a plane and flew from Chicago to St. Louis—with Felsenburshe paying the bills—and boarded our delegation's special train to the convention.

He spread his pernicious convention gossip all over that train. He told my people that if I didn't release the delegation that the

State of Texas wouldn't get one goddam cent out of Washington after Dad was swept in. He kept yelling at them that they had to dump me.

Let me say that tempers ran pretty high. Old friends became enemies. Slurrie split that delegation wide open. Scott Miller threw a glassful of ice cubes at Slurrie, which struck the bosom of one of my heaviest campaign contributors, a beautiful and rich little lady named Miss Julia Sweeney, and we lost her allegiance.

You might have read that Slurrie got off the train before Chicago to avoid newsmen. That was a lot of bushwah. I personally threw that spoiler off the train by the scruff of his neck and the seat of his pants at the first suburban stop. "You treacherous sidewinder," I yelled after him as the train got moving again. "Change your name to Judas."

He betrayed me every step of the way. He sat on the Resolutions Committee and weasled in the "fair play" plank, then he caucused our delegation and wrested the microphone out of my man's hand. He shouted over the din through the loudspeakers,

> My conscience tells me that any candidate who is nominated would have far more difficulty winning for the Republican Party in November with those contested Foote delegates than the right way.
>
> So we must *all of us* call on Governor Albritton to release us, to allow us to vote our consciences. If we are going to be forced by Claude Albritton to feel that we are automatically bound just to go along the way that selfish aspirants in this convention dictate there would be no reason for us to come to this convention at all.

I lost my temper. I couldn't stand it then and I can hardly stand it now. I threw a wooden chair at the rostrum, missed Slurrie, but broke the eyeglasses of Dr. Richard Hitt, one of our prominent evangelists. Delegates who were once my friends called out for my expulsion. The Texas delegation voted 57 to 8 in favor of casting the state's unit vote for the "fair play" resolution and the drift toward Dad Kampferhaufe became a stampede.

DATE: 11th August 1964
TIME: 9:05 A.M.
BASE REPORTING: Dallas   DSP (Semley) Only

MRS. WALTER SLURRIE (Continued)

When I think of Walter murdered, all alone in that hotel bath-tub, I feel loathing for the people who were privileged to know him well when he was alive and didn't appreciate him. I refer particularly to Dad Kampferhaufe, who carried on as if Walter were toxic or something. Maudie, Dad's wife, tried to help me with this, which was really our only big problem as a married couple. Maudie said she could just feel the pressure I was under from Walter to get us invited upstairs in the White House for din-ner, even drinks, but Dad wouldn't have any of it. During the two full terms that Walter was our Vice-President he never saw any part of the White House above the ground floor and he didn't see that part very often.

He was never invited inside a building at Camp David. In fact, Dad never let him get off the helicopter pad. Dad would be stand-ing there when he landed, tell Walter what he wanted to tell him about getting some dirty job done, then send him back to Wash-ington. Needless to say, we never saw the inside of Dad's hallowed farmhouse at Valley Forge, which the insurance, airline, and chemical companies had bought for him and which the agricultural lobby and the oil industries stocked.

I would get so mad at Walter. He had this concept that he called " the law of contracts," which had probably been drilled into him at that crazy Coomber Law School. As far as Walter was concerned (and he knew better because I know Charley Coffey, Governor Betaut, and Mr. Danzig had told him differently), Dad and no one else had passed the word to the convention to nominate Walter for the second spot, even if Dad had been taking a nap at the time.

Walter leveled with me only once on this. "The people love Dad," he told me. "He is their handsome healthy father. Now believe me, Betsy, only a politician can measure the backup protection that love brings to the people Dad endorses. That's why I'll take anything from him. It doesn't matter if it makes me look bad temporarily. If I can break him down and get him to put his arm around me once a week in public, why, I can be the next President. We've got to swallow the humiliation and think of the future."

"You can't always live in the future, Walter. The present is where things are decided."

"I am not so sure about that, Betsy."

"About what?"

"Well, decisions were made in the past, which forms the present."

"You klutz," I yelled at him, "when the decisions were made it was the present and what you are calling it now was the future."

Walter knew it had been Dad who had personally tried to dump him from the ticket with the hilarious excuse that any running mate of his needed to be "as clean as a hound's tooth" because that rotten *New York Post* had decided they had the right to publish everything about Walter's slush fund from the Dallas Citizens' Committee, which was the smallest slush fund we had, for heaven's sake.

Walter, who usually resented everything, played it as though it were Dad's natural right to make so much trouble for him, then to try to throw him away. Walter had to cry overtime in public for the TV people and the still photographers. He was superb. I wish I knew how he did it. Overall, I've got to say that the whole thing worked out very well for us because Walter's TV turn, praising my "four-dollar Republican shoes" and "my kids' pet raccoon, Chessie," made Walter into "a touching, emotional figure" according to the press.

Having to make that ridiculous speech at all caused us a lot of unnecessary personal inconvenience, all on a whim of Dad's because the networks and the Republican National Committee got so much mail about that imaginary pet raccoon there was nothing to do but to send me streaking to New York in a fighter-bomber from Andrews to find a raccoon in an animal supply house that one of the New York Mafia families, through Mr. Danzig, had kindly located for us. I got the thing back in time for Walter to produce it at the big press conference. It got the ticket a tremendous amount of really sympathetic attention, but the damned thing peed all over Walter and over practically everything we had (including a Sunday leg of lamb). But we couldn't get rid of it because Walter's speech had imprinted it on the American Memory. We put up with Chessie for two years before Walter felt he could safely poison it. Then we took the little corpse—and Edward Dennis and little Franklin, our boys, two mobile TV units, thirty-one still photographers, four radio back packs, and fifty-three writers—and buried it in Arlington Cemetary. Walter wept a river for the cameras on three separate takes. We were sorry we had to put Chessie down but it wasn't as though she were gone. We could smell her everywhere in the Washington apartment for almost a year.

What I think Walter really felt grateful to Dad about, in spite of the constant humiliations, was the reflection of Dad's respectability, which shone on Walter like the sun and gave Walter such a clear shot at making so many fantastic money deals on the side. When we were first married Walter didn't talk about his business deals to me, but Eddie kept me filled in so thoroughly, in case anything happened to him, that I would find myself asking Walter questions about this and that and, after a while, all three of us talked over the deals together.

Dad despised Walter, I have to say it. But Walter told me he could understand how Dad felt and even why.

"A lot of people despise me," he explained to me. "It's some trick of my face, I think. My nose is the wrong shape and my hair does look as if I use peroxide on it. Naturally I am called upon by Dad to do many things that are despicable. I mean, if you were to compare being Vice-President of the United States with what a ski instructor does for a living or a drum majorette, there would be a heavy moral imbalance. But the truth is, Betsy, we both

215

know people who kill for a living. Dad made a great thing out of that, for instance, for the greater part of his life. We know doctors who push narcotics. We entertain usurers in our own home, and we know our share of bribers and men and women by the dozens here in Washington who sell the information they get at our dinner parties to newspaper columnists and foreign governments. But the fact is, all those people are likeable people and, by some accident of cast or conformation, I happen to be despicable, so people despise me."

"We don't! And you not only deserve to be loved but you deserve to succeed, you work so hard. If only they knew you. You have so much pluck, Walter. You have more character in your little finger than ten personality kids like Dad Kampferhaufe."

"Hey, just a minute here! You mustn't think I mind people not liking me," he said. "Great Scotch, as analysis shows, if people begin to like you they demand that you spend more time with them when you should be using that time to reach your goals."

"I love it when you think out loud like that, Walter."

"I am certain that one of the bases for people disliking me is my eye tic. My eyes dart from side to side, people tell me. And I have this wetting-the-lips thing that drives Dad so wild. They must make me look like some kind of cartoon crook. But if Dad had had a father who day after day liked to creep up behind him, then, with both of his huge, hard cupped hands, clap those hands on Dad's ears until they rang for days, then let me say that Dad, or anyone else, would be stuck forever with my kind of eye tic and this continual nervous wetting of the lips."

Our second son, Franklin, was born on September 15, 1955. Maudie Kampferhaufe sent a silver spoon to the hospital and arranged with Dad's staff to send him a "welcome to the world" letter on White House stationery, mentioning Walter, and signed by the facsimile signature machine they used to sign the General's name.

I was brought back from the delivery room, and when the media people organized by Charley Coffey for Walter had left, Walter said, "I hope they didn't tire you, dear."

"No. Having. The baby. That tires."

"What a day to be born!" he said. "Did you know that September 15th is the traditional day for men to put their straw hats aside? Not that anyone wears them anymore. It's called Felt Hat Day."

216

I didn't answer. What could I say?

"It is also the birthday of William Howard Taft. Perhaps we should call the baby William Howard Slurrie."

"Or Felt Hat Slurrie."

We had named the first baby Edward (after Eddie) Dennis (after some dead friend of Walter's) Slurrie. In Walter's effects, which the New York Police Department just sent me, was a picture in his wallet of a young man. Across the bottom of it was written, "With best memories, Dennis." That's all I'll ever know about Edward's middle name.

"I'd like to name this one after my father, Walter."

"What was his name?"

"Gustave Ginzler."

"Gus Slurrie," Walter mused. "G.G. Slurrie."

"Oh, all right!"

"What did your father do?"

"He was a wholesale butcher."

"Where?"

"Winsted, Connecticut."

"You grew up in Connecticut?"

"Walter, we've been married six years. Can you wait until I get my strength back for this information?"

"Gustave Slurrie is a fine name. There are millions of German voters."

I lay there, regrouping. After ten minutes of quiet I said, "I kind of like Franklin Marx Slurrie."

"Marx? *Marx*? They'd crucify me."

"Not that Marx, silly. After Groucho Marx. My God, haven't I ever done my Groucho Marx takeoff for you?"

"No. But I'd love to see it. No, no. Not now, dear." He grabbed my ankle under the blankets as if I were trying to get up. "The Felsenburshes would definitely crucify me if we called the baby Franklin. Franklin means FDR—or am I wrong again?"

"Not FDR! The fat guy with the square glasses and the kite."

"Aaaah." He fumbled with his strange nose. "Charley told me last night that Dad is going to try to dump me from the ticket next year."

"What is the matter with that man?"

"Charley said that Dad had told Nils Felsenburshe that he doesn't consider me a statesman, that I hadn't grown or matured in office, that I had no roots, that I was too political, and that I wasn't presidential timber."

"Oh, that son of a *bitch*! What is Charley going to do?"

"He says it's going to be all right. Mr. Nils will spend the weekend at Dad's farm at Valley Forge on the first Saturday in July, which is close enough to the convention, and he will reason with Dad, who lusts for a prize herd of 600 Angus cattle, Charley says. Dad also wants about seven miles of high fencing, two new tractors, a combine hay baler, and a new paint job for the main house. You know Dad. Well, Mr. Nils is going to take care of that and, just to keep a lock on him, add 550 Plymouth Rock pullets and an automatic feeder for the pigs. They are all pretty sure that will keep me on the ticket."

I fell asleep.

I woke up forty minutes later when Eddie kissed my lips softly. "Hi, Mom," he said.

"Oh, Eddie! You were swell to come."

"He's my kid, ain't it?"

"Still, a lot of people wouldn't have bothered. We are going to call your son Franklin Marx Slurrie."

"Very nice."

"How's little Edward?"

"Not so li'l."

"Is he eating nicely?"

"About a dozen franks an ketchup in two days."

"God, the way he copies Walter. Oh, well. Get him some more. Life is so full for all of us that we might as well fill up Edward, too."

DATE: 11th August 1964
TIME: 5:53 P.M.
BASE REPORTING: Miami   DSP (Semley) Only

ABNER "NUDEY" DANZIG (continued)

Waller says Betaut has power. Betaut knows the Felsenburshes got it. Who do the Felsenburshes blame? I been tryna figure
out power all my life since I am sixteen years old and working
for a car mechanic to learn how to soup-up cars so we could out-
run the cops. When I was eighteen I was in a loose partnership
with Charley Lucania and Frank Castiglia. I brought Benny Siegel in with me. He was fourteen years old and he had the most
moxie of any of us. Even then they expected me to do the thinking. We did stick-ups, loft robberies, shakedowns and contract
hits. I hadda fight evvybody because I was a shrimp. You can't
make it only on brains when you want the power. Twenty-nine
years later Charley Lucky tells a newspaperman, "That little guy,
Danzig, is the toughest little guy, pound for pound, I ever knew
in my whole life, and that takes in Fat Albert Anastasia or any of
them Brooklyn hoodlums or anybody else I can think of."

I stayed fast on my feet, which the Sicilians think is the whole
magillah, but if you want the power you gotta use the mind, you

219

gotta think, which people hate to do. We got rich on Danzig's Law. I said to Charley Lucky, "If you got what people want very bad, but don't need, and you sell it to them, you can shovel in the dough. We gotta supply the demand. We got to get good whiskey, then sell it at high prices to all them dummies who don't have the brains not to drink it."

Prohibition boosted me out of strong-arm stuff and into the booze business. I put Benny and me into insured transportation of booze for other mobs. It was the first inside protection racket. We took contracts for hits in eleven states about eight years before Albert ran Murder Inc. I organized the labor rackets and put Lepke in. I brought in the numbers. The Sicilians made so much money that they had to take up time with meets trying to figure out what to do with it, until I told them, "Banks lend money already, why shouldn't we?" That's how we got into sharking.

By 1925, the take from booze alone was over twelve million a year. By 1935, when Prohibition was out, the take was seventy million a year in the middle of a big Depression from gambling, sharking, numbers, labor, protection, broads and dope. By 1963, after I am able to prove to evvybody that we got to run our operations the way General Motors organizes, we took in three billion eight *net*, no taxes. You can't beat a business like that.

Since 1932 I been insisting that we put away twenty percent of every dollar we make to buy local police and judges acrossa country. Then we bought political organizations and state politicians. Then we moved into the U.S. Senate, the House, and the Court of Appeals until a couple of days ago, when we had Walter Slurrie and a clean shot at the White House going for us.

It was worth every cent it cost us. We now have such a business going in dope that our good friends in Washington had to get us an extension of the war in southeast Asia.

So what is power? It certainly didn't help Waller very much, if he had any. I'm an old man now and power is beginning to look to me like just a lotta vaseline for mirror fuckers. Whatever else it is, power is a habit, because if you don't use the power you got, right away you don't have any.

Look at Charley Lucky. They never made a bigger rackets guy. But Betaut sent him up for fifty years. Charley had the real power, evvybody thought, but Betaut put him away so Betaut musta had the power. What power? How much? He couldn't get himself elected President. So who's got it? Betaut knows. Maybe I

220

know. Find out who owns the President of the United States and you are beginning to catch on who has really got it.

When I thought I had the power, I really ended up finding out how even a sensible Joosh fella can kid himself. I delivered New York State and a couple more to Betaut in both of his campaigns. So whoever it is who is watching us knows I can deliver. Later, that's where Waller Slurrie comes in. He worked for me in the House. He worked for me in the Senate. So when Betaut comes to me in '51 to deliver at least New York State for Kampfcrhaufe, I tell him he can have anything he wants if they will line up the second slot for Waller. Betaut passes the word up to the Felsen-burshes and they okay it.

I am telling you we would have made him President, the first Mob President, in '68 if that creep hadn't done that number on him. Now lemme tell you what I am driving at. What is the power? Money is the power. Whoever hit Waller or had him hit had to be involved with a tremendous amount of money. I happen to know that Waller stole almost twenny million dollars in his seventeen years in politics. Only three people knew where Waller's money was and how to get at it if Waller was out of the way. Those people, who I am telling you from a long life of experience with that kind of money are, the people who had to be the ones who killed Waller: one, his wife, an otherwise nice lady and a good cook, two, Kiddo Cardozo, who was Waller's partner but no matter how you slice him just another hood, and three, Betaut, who is Waller's lawyer and a very, very big operator from away back. I say it is either the wife and Kiddo in combination or it's Betaut on his own. Remember what I told you about power. The people who own Betaut can give him a helluva lot of protection.

TO: FIRST DEPUTY COMMISSIONER VINCENT J. MULSHINE

FROM: LIEUTENANT RICHARD GALLAGHER, 17th HSQ.

    Richard Betaut and Edward Cardozo have been confirmed by witnesses (Morton Stone, a house officer at the Waldorf, and Hilda Hess, cashier) to have been "speaking together" in the Lower Level passageway/arcade near the barber shop, approximately outside the Men's Room on the evening of the day Walter Slurrie was murdered in the Waldorf Towers.

    Sergeant Fearons is in Miami and,

with the cooperation of the Miami police, is questioning Edward Cardozo about this.

I called Governor Betaut and told him we wanted to talk to him. He asked me how much time I would need which is a little different approach to the usual police questioning. I said that would depend on his answers. He got a little testy. He asked just what it was I wanted to talk to him about. When I told him he was a possible suspect in the Slurrie case he laughed at me. I amused him. I amused him so much that he said it would be okay for me to come to his office and that he would make time for me. There was no question about his coming uptown to the precinct house but I knew that before I started. I went to Betaut's office in Broad Street, taking Detective Paul Weldon with me.

The firm name is Betaut, Masters, Fulton & Chapman. The offices are a lot like the Frank E. Campbell Funeral Home crossed with the World Bank. This is a law office with two receptionists who do nothing. I told one of them who we wanted and she said go right in, corner office four doors down on the right. We went right in. We took off our hats.

Betaut had been a DA for so long that he didn't need any preliminaries except that he told us to have cigars. They were Filipino cigars. If we had been clients we would have got Cuban. After that he asked us to sit down. Then he sat behind his dust-free desk and grinned at me. "So I'm a possible suspect. I'll be a son-of-a-bitch. That is really about as screwed-up as police work can get."

I didn't answer him. I sat, comfortable, and stared at him. I looked right into those shoebutton eyes until he stopped grinning. "What have you got?" he asked me.

"Walter Slurrie was murdered at approximately seven peeyem on the night of August 9th."

"The whole world knows that."

"Edward Cardozo, who is Slurrie's only business partner and who is, therefore, knowledgeable about all his assets, had a meeting with you, in the Lower Arcade of the Waldorf, where Slurrie was murdered shortly thereafter. You are Walter Slurrie's lawyer so you also have knowledge of his assets. Both you and Edward Cardozo had the accessible time and the motive of material gain for murdering Slurrie. You were carrying the key to your own apartment where Slurrie was murdered. That's what I have, Governor."

224

He made a steeple with his fingers. He tapped the finger-tips together for about fifteen seconds. "Let's have a drink," he said.

"If I was ever on duty, I am on duty now, Governor, and Detective Weldon doesn't drink."

"That was just a joke about screwed-up police work, Lieutenant."

"Didn't I laugh?"

"Just the same. Let's go through the motions of having a drink so I can think about this for a minute before we go any further."

"I'll have a Coke," I told him.

He got up and walked across the room. It's a big room, about thirty by thirty, and it is decorated like a country house. He pushed a stud in the wall at the left side of the room and the whole thing rolled up like an awning and gave us a regulation bar just like it was onstage at the Roxy. "We'll talk over here," he said. Weldon stayed where he was. I got up, crossed the room, and sat on a bar stool. He stood behind the bar and made two drinks. He had a Seven Up. "No ice cream?" I asked him.

He looked up at me slowly. Betaut is a threatening man by habit but now inclination had taken over, his eyes were – well, they were what people call killer's eyes. "You have the facts right," he said.

"Make a statement, please, Governor."

"On the late afternoon of the day Walter Slurrie was murdered in my apartment at the Waldorf Towers at approximately 7 P.M., I left the hotel with Dr. Huggems at approximately five-fifteen. My car was waiting for us in the Waldorf garage. It drove us directly to the Yale Club in Vanderbilt Avenue."

"We checked that out," I told him.

"While we were waiting for a drink in the bar, or maybe we had already been served, I don't remember, Dr. Huggems told me he wanted to run for the Senate. He said he had spoken about that desire to Mr. Nils Felsenburshe, my client, and that Mr. Felsenburshe had suggested that he talk to me about it. It's not a bad idea, you know. Dr. Huggems is an authority on absolutely everything except domestic affairs."

"How long did that take?"

"Well, we began to talk on the way over actually. We weren't in the bar more than a few minutes when I remembered

225

that I had a very sensitive and confidential memorandum about one of the New York senators in my safe back at the hotel so I decided to go and fetch it."

"You decided not to send for it? Slurrie was there. He could have gotten it to you at the Yale Club."

"The reasons are obvious. It is a sensitive document. The safe is locked."

"What did you do?"

"My car took me to the Waldorf and as I left the garage on the lower level I had to pee. I realize that the New York Police Department must think that the sight of the Waldorf is a diuretic to me but I have this tendency toward gout and high blood pressure and the doctors give me these pills to keep me peeing."

"Hotel doctor?"

"Dr. Norman Lesion. East 54th Street."

"Go ahead."

"I ducked into the Men's Room in the Lower Arcade and when I came out there was Cardozo. We know each other but we are hardly friends – I probably would have had him arrested in the thirties – and certainly we had no mutual interests beyond different tacks on Walter Slurrie. We spoke just long enough for whoever your informer was to see us together. I went directly upstairs from the Lower Level in the garage elevator – no witnesses – got my papers from the safe in my study and went straight back to the Yale Club. The entire transaction could not have taken more than twenty minutes."

"Did you see Slurrie?"

"No."

"Why?"

"Well, I suppose he was in his bedroom, which is the second door down the hall, or showering, or something like that. I had left him only a few minutes before so there was no reason to look for him. We were all talked out at the moment."

"Did anyone see you leave, Governor?"

"No, actually. You see – well, I was in another empty elevator down to the garage level. My car was waiting where I had told it to wait and the plates I have on it make it unlikely that anyone would suggest that it shouldn't be waiting there. I got into the car and was whisked back to the Yale Club."

"What is your driver's name?"

"Bryson – 469 East 127th Street. And Cardozo will confirm my story. Do you have a man on Cardozo?"

It was my turn to grin at him. I grinned and I held on to it and I didn't say anything to him. His face got red.

"Let's hope, for your sake," I said, "that the police work doesn't continue to be as screwed-up as you think it is, Governor. Because we are doing pretty good." I got up. "If you know what I mean." I got out of there.

Fearons' teletype from the Miami police department was on my desk when I got back. Almost word-for-word – in exactly the way lawyers have of coaching witnesses – it said precisely what Betaut had told me and I didn't believe one goddam word of any of it.

DATE: 13th October 1963
TIME: 4:10 P.M.
BASE REPORTING: New York

DSP (Semley) Only

MRS. CHARLES COFFEY (continued)

I sat there with a warm bottle of gin, waiting for my husband to get back from the convention where they had nominated one man who had made his life out of war and killing, and as his second, a dough-faced crook who would climb a greased, electrified rope to get at money. I had been there alone with the gin for three days. The kids were spending the summer with my mother in California.

I didn't feel like a woman anymore. Charley and I lived together like half strangers. We pretended it was a truce but there was no peace to negotiate. He had gone further and further into the unspeakable and now spent as much time as he could away from me. When he was there I ignored his criminal activities with politicians and he tolerated what he was sure was my insanity. If any love was left—on his part or on mine—I don't know where it could have been hidden. To me he was one of the hyena pack. To

229

him I was sick and unsafe. I didn't want to breathe when Charley was home with me. Now I waited for him just to hear him explain why *he* wasn't sick and unsafe. He and Betaut had just finished putting the figure of death, Kampferhaufe, within reach of the White House for their masters. Figures of death were what had come to have meaning to the world.

Until I sat down with the warm bottle of gin I still went through the routine movements for Charley. Until he produced the bitter farce starring those two brutalized men in Chicago, I kept house for Charley: cooking, shopping, and housecleaning. That was about all he wanted from me and yet again more than I wanted to give. I slept across the entrance hall in the children's side of the apartment.

Charley let himself in late in the afternoon. He wore a blue striped tie and a Panama hat. He not only looked exhausted, he looked guilty.

"What the hell is that?" he said in greeting from the entrance to our living room.

"You mean the gin?"

"For Christ's sake, Marie. Do you drink alone now?"

"What does it look like, kingmaker?"

"You can lay off your particular brand of invective, Marie. I have had a very rough two weeks."

He sat down wearily. He still had his hat on.

"How are things in the black market in morals, sweetie? How many men did you ruin during the week? Or would you rather tell me again how your family has always been in politics?" I poured a gin for myself. He watched my hand shaking. He got up and walked over to the bar. He filled a tall glass with ice, then, ostentatiously, poured plain ginger ale over it.

"Tell me," he said, "are you against government? Somehow I never asked you that."

"You know what I'm against. That's why you look like a hired murderer. You are covered with guilt from it, Charley. You can't look at me."

"I am sick and tired of you, Marie."

"I know. Charley, what kind of a country will this be in ten years because of the men you lifted to the throne this week?"

"Will you let up for just a little while?"

"No."

"Marie, Kampferhaufe has a lifetime of experience with authority and leadership. He has moral judgment."

230

"How about Slurrie, sweetie?"

"Vice-presidents don't have anything to do with keeping this country running."

"Not until they become Presidents. And you know that's what you want. Slurrie is your man, Betaut handles Kampferhaufe but the Felsenburshes gave Slurrie to you. You want him in the White House because that will justify your life."

"This pain you are shuffling around this afternoon has nothing to do with reality. You think you are a force and that you are right when all you are doing is standing in blood on a Pacific beach at a quarter to seven in the morning and the dead are piling up at your feet. That's when you stopped thinking, Marie. You left right, which is reason, back there. Nothing can take you back there to wipe everything clean of blood. I can't scrub away the guilt you carry with you, larger and larger, heavier and heavier, all because you weren't killed with the rest of them on that morning. I can't untie the knot in your mind, which is so tight now that it has you screaming inside your skull that only politicians and your husband make the wars that kill young men."

I began to cry. He came to me and put his arms around me. He kissed me over and over again but he didn't speak. I wish we could have been frozen there in each other's arms forever.

"Charley—*please*—quit politics."

"If I stop treading water I'll drown."

"Practice law. Ask the Felsenburshes for a museum job. Ask them for work in some resort hotel."

"They don't need me there."

"Think of something, Charley!"

"I am tired."

"We are running out of chances. It may never be this near again."

"Marie, if I handle Slurrie right, if I deliver for the Felsenburshes—after the election is out of the way there will be nothing they won't do for me. I know them. I'll go to them then and we'll get what we want."

I disengaged myself from his arms. "In the sweet bye-and-bye," I said, as I walked away from him toward my part of the house to lock myself in the bathroom.

231

DATE: 11th August 1964
TIME: 10:45 A.M.
BASE REPORTING: Miami   DSP (Semley) Only

EDWARD CARDOZO (continued)

Lass year, say ten months ago, the boy, Edward Dennis Slurrie, get meningitis. Is very bad. An he is an imporrant boy to us. Betsy don sleep for two days an nights then finally she fall asleep in the nex bed to him in his room at the house in Vizcaya Cove. Wullair an me, we sit jus outside. We sit in the boy's study room with the light on, where we can hear anything that happen inside the other room. Wullair flew in from London. I flew in from New York. The doctor say the crisis come soon so we wait so Betsy can sleep.

Wullair cries a lot. It is real. He say to me looking in my eyes how Edward could not be more like his own son. Is the first time he ever say this. Edward is twelve years old. Is the first time we ever come close to talking about it.

"He is strong, Wullair," I tell him. "He will make it."

He say. "I am grateful to you for being Edward's father. It saved all of us. It saved Betsy for me. It saved the marriage. Most of all it gave us two fine boys."

I deen answer.

"I was taught that only work counted," he say. "My mother said if I worked and worked life would be solved for me. And it isn't fair, really, that it doesn't work that way, because the way I see it, it's the only thing that makes any sense. I mean, it eliminates luck. It equalizes other peoples' advantages of birth and beauty. Why, look how far I got by applying so much hard work to that little book *Magic Tricks With Cards*, Kiddo. The work I put in there would equalize me with any Felsenburshe at a card table, do you see what I mean?"

"Work is something to do for some pipple, I suppose. I dunno. I was a Mexican for too long, maybe."

"No, no. I don't believe that anymore. I would have been exactly where I am today regardless of whether I believed in work or not, providing I met Nudey Danzig and you when I did."

"A long time ago, Wullair."

"Anyway, now I fianlly have the courage to thank you for those two wonderful boys."

"Listen—I know what you minn but joss the same less knock it off. You know, for Betsy sake?"

"But if it weren't for you—"

"Wullair, look. You are the one with the guts. You unnerstood how much she nidded to have kids. You didn't make trouble. You didn't get *macho*. You didn't yell for a divorce. Not for the rizzins of politics but because you love her an I appreciate that. The boys are as much your boys as my boys—maybe more. They love you. They are proud of you. You are *gran caballero, muy macho y muy charro*, Wullair."

"How did I get into a position like this, with all the power and all this money? I was never meant for it. But then again, maybe I was."

"It is right that you are what you are."

He laugh in a funny way. "What I am, most of the time, is what I'd rather not be. I don't fit in anywhere unless I can work. I can only prove that I love people with money and I don't give much of that away. I wish I wasn't the way I am. I don't want to be anything else either, so that reduces what I hope for to about zero. I guess I'd like to have *reasons* for doing things instead of just the wet fear that I won't get ahead. I'll forget I said these things tomorrow because I'll make myself forget. In fact, I want to forget it right now."

"No, Wullair. Tomorrow and ten years from now you will re-

234

member only that you sat here when your son was in danger and you were honest. You think outside youself tonight, not only of youself. Loving the boy make you bigger, Wullair. You will remember that you gave something when you were honest an that is good."

He make a desperate, short sound, not a sigh but a sound like he was pushing the terrible weight of life away from him. He say, "I don't deserve to feel good if it takes reasons like this. I would give and give—anything else—if I had anything to give but I stand here drowning in a shallow pan of water, which is about the depth of all the feeling I have. What the hell, Kiddo. Isn't that doctor due back here by now?"

DATE: 11th August 1964
BASE REPORTING: Los Angeles

DSP (Semley) Only

N.B. *The following autobiographical text was transcribed from tape cassettes found in the Bel Air, California, house of Horace Riddle Hind. An audio copy has also been made. The original cassettes have been returned to the Hind bedroom at Bel Air.*

HORACE RIDDLE HIND (continued)

No one could say that I had not made my airline into a heroic international asset before the Eastern banks and insurance companies stole it from me.

As the world knows I certainly made a success of my movie company, nonetheless a powerful alliance of stockholders, suborned to action by the Eastern elements, claimed falsely that I had not.

After making sizable profits, year after year, building one of the great defense contracting units of this country (which means the world), the Secretary of the Air Force, acting as messenger for the Eastern powers of this country said—to my face—that the U.S. government would not give my company one more defense order unless I divorced myself from its operations. They took my aircraft company away from me, a prime electronics industrial power, and made me sign it over to my Foundation, where other people got the credit for having made it so successful.

I don't care about the money. My lawyer, the former Vice-President of the United States, Walter Bodmor Slurrie, got me a large tax credit for that transfer. I didn't want any more money. I only wanted history to record truthfully that I had accomplished more with my life than my daddy had with his, at everything each of us had tried—but my enemies prevented that.

Frustration can consume people, hence my need to maintain a round-the-clock medical staff of doctors who hold narcotics licenses to keep me calm and serene despite plots and machinations against me in the East and to keep my metabolism balanced with injections of vitamins and minerals. It was this frustration and the health threats that it posed for me which brought about what the media in their blind ignorance have called my "withdrawal" into what they insist are "dark, smelly rooms."

My room does not smell. Blankets are nailed to cover the windows because light hurts my eyes. I am bathed daily. Although my hair has grown long, my people wash it twice weekly, to which I consent as a courtesy to others even though it means a loss of body particles. There is a saying—in the Russian language, I believe—that "we all make mistakes." The single mistake I may have made was in believing what I read in some business magazine about a new breed of professional managers who were supposed to be like scientists when it came to turning profits for the companies in their charge. I hired three of these "scientists" for my aircraft company, and right from the start they opposed every decision I made to keep my company ongoing, then had the brass to tell me that I did not understand the complexities of running a large, modern company. I said if a man owned his own company and the hired hands were able to tell him he didn't know how to control it, then what was happening to America?

They wanted a revolving credit of $45,000,000 and—just to give them a hard time—I damned well told them that all they could have was $35,000,000, so those lickspittle traitors went straight to Washington and complained to the Air Force, a good client of mine. They complained about how I was handling my own company, to give you one example of how Communism is taking hold in American life. I could have asked them: who had

238

spotted and exploited Walter Bodmor Slurrie when he was only a freshman Congressman? Who had retained Slurrie to get himself route approvals that had been denied to the same swollen-headed type of scientist-manager for the St. Louis-Miami route? Who had retained Walter Slurrie at a fat but eminently worthwhile fee to go in there and get the government to reverse a ten-year-old decision against letting me lend $5,000,000 to my own airline from my own aircraft company? Who? I'll tell you who. I did it, that is who did it. Not any scientist textbook manager.

I paid Walter Slurrie $603,00 to make the government recompute mail transport credits to my airline, thus turning the airline's debt into a multimillion-dollar refund. I had made Slurrie Vice-President of the United States by then and I am here to testify that every red cent of the two and a half million dollars I had to pay out to him was worth it, right down to his ability to get me SEC approval of a stock transfer fund, which had been turned down seven times previously. *Or,* the reversal of that bad IRS judgment on my Foundation. *Or* the dropping of the anti-trust action against SHOVE.

I am the managers' manager. The professionals learn from me. And when that Commie-leaning Air Force Secretary made me transfer my aircraft company to my Foundation I told him—to his face—"If the American government would destroy a great business like my aircraft company on the unfounded charges of a few disgruntled employees, then that government is sponsoring socialism, if not Communism."

But everything seemed to go wrong. I cannot understand it. Everything is in trouble no matter what feats of management I perform. It was sickening to give my companies so much of my personal attention only to have pieces of them crumble and break off in my hands.

When the Eastern banks and insurance companies stole my airline from me on the pretext that I had missed the boat on jet engines, the Eastern courts of law ruled that I had cost my own airline $45,870,435.93 and—all at once—all the predators moved in on me. It was damaging to me. It had been bad enough that I had had to sign over my aircraft company at a time when it *happened* to be making $700,000,000 a year in defense contracts. I had been forced to sell my movie company for a ridiculous $7,000,000 profit and that saddened me in an inconsolable way because I was perfect for the movie business, and my ads, which I wrote and designed entirely by myself only with the help of an airbrush artist, an art director, and a production man, were the talk of the film industry.

At a time when my companies were making more money than Daddy's ever made, I was no longer to have any control over them. They were all being "scientifically" managed by a lot of socialist fanatics.

Then the Eastern courts dropped that shocking default judgment on me and the Eastern bankers and insurance companies took away my airline. I was the most famous aviator in history, next to Charles A. Lindbergh (and I had flown a lot further and faster and higher than Lindbergh), yet I was told by the Supreme Court that I was not *competent* to manage my own airline.

All I got in return for a lifetime of work was $546,549,771.19, and they arranged the entire thing so that it was given maximum exposure by the kept Eastern press so that everyone expected me to pay every cent of the taxes due, as if I were some ribbon counter clerk, when I knew damned well that Walter Slurrie could have come to some kind of a benevolent arrangement for me with the Internal Revenue Service if I hadn't been forced out into the open. In the end, all I ever realized from an airline sale which I desperately did not want was $486,000,000.

It broke my spirt.

DATE: 11th August 1964
TIME: 6:10 P.M.
BASE REPORTING: Miami   DSP (Semley) Only

ABNER "NUDEY" DANZIG (continued)

Betsy Slurrie invited me over to their house on Vizcaya Cove for some bean soup on a Sunday. I sat with Waller out on the terrace looking at that gorgeous view. Waller has no small talk, and not much big talk either. This time, so he won't have to try to think of something to say, he hands me a file of clippings about how Horace Hind just got himself almost a haffa billion net for selling his airline. I read the file twice because I am getting an idea. The IRS was being a big pain in the ass about the skim from Vegas. We had the Bahamas and the Caribbean going for us, but it would be bad business to let those pricks take over in Vegas and cost us about two million free dollars a month. When I say Us I don't mean Waller. Waller has nothing to do with Vegas.

Pablo, Waller's man, brings in the soup. Very good. We don't talk because Waller can't think of anything to say and I'm thinking.

"Waller," I said to him, "this is terrific what you just handed me. You are gonna sell Vegas to Horace Hind for the four eighty-six million."

He comes all awake. The numbers are already inside his pants. "How?" he asks me.

"Think about it."

"Mr. Danzig, I'm no casino operator. I just don't know about things like that."

"Waller—*think!*"

"Well, legally he has to reinvest the money right away or take a terrible tax beating. Also, knowing Horace, I would say the larceny in the Vegas operation would appeal to him if the figures were right. He loves tinsel and glitter and cheap women."

"Who doesn't? How do you think I make a living?"

"He doesn't have control of many things anymore—oh, a few breweries and SHOVE—so he might love playing around with a complicated toy like a city full of gambling halls and prostitutes."

"How would you sell him?"

"What—ah—would my part of the deal be, Mr. Danzig?"

"A finder's fee."

"How much of a fee?"

"Waller, fuhcrissake, when did you ever get it in the can from me? We gotta get the deal first or there ain't gonna be any finder's fee. Pick up the phone and call Hind, Waller."

He went inside to get his big, black book of private phone numbers, which he had the White House switchboard make up for him when he was Vice-President. He called Hind in California, got Hind's message center, then they put him through to Hind in Boston.

"Boston," Waller says to me, covering the mouthpiece and waving to me to get on the other phone. All of a sudden he turns on the quadruple sincerity, so much so that Hind must be reaching to protect his wallet 1,600 miles away.

"Horace," he says to the phone, "we have had a pretty fine lawyer-client relationship over the past seventeen years."

Hind's high-pitched, squeaky voice says, "I agree, but without attribution."

"Attribution?"

"I may not be quoted on that." His voice was pale and farther away than just miles.

"I have always honored that, Horace."

"What are we getting at, anyway?"

242

"Horace, I am your lawyer. You have been dragging almost a half billion dollars in cash around the country. Now that isn't safe. Also, we've got to talk about protecting it from the IRS."

"It is a difficult decision, Walter."

"That's what you have a lawyer for."

"Nobody is getting this money, Walter."

"Horace—this is *me*—your own choice to be the next President of your country."

"God bless you, Walter." Hind's voice was a whisper.

"I know you through and through because I care about you. You are the most creative financial mind of this century. In that I even include your father. And I say that it is simply not possible that you would expose a half billion dollars of your money to *further and deeper* tax incursions by the IRS. Or even permit it to lie fallow, unable to earn increment."

"I don't feel good, that's why. I feel very, very rotten, Walter, and my doctors just don't seem to know what to do about it."

"I say that right now you are crafting investment plans that will knock the American business community right on its ass."

"Walter—" Hind sounded as if he weren't getting any air.

"Horace, I am pleading with you. Don't finalize your decision for one more day until I can talk to you. What I have to say is too big for the phone. And remember, Lorraine Center is recording everything we say, Horace."

"Oh, damn them! How soon can you get here?"

It was half past eleven in the morning. "Four o'clock this afternoon?" Walter said.

"All right."

"Where are you in Boston, Horace?"

"The Back Bay Hotel."

"What name?"

"B. J. Bennett."

"Good. Okay. Please leave word at the desk—and with your people—that you expect me."

Hind began to cough. Sometime later during the coughing he hung up.

"Jesus, he sounds terrible," Waller said. "And we were taking chances because Lorraine Center in California tapes every incoming and outgoing call, and they think of it as their own interests that they are protecting."

He got on the phone and called the SP Duty Officer in Washington to order a fighter-bomber to be standing by at Miami Air-

243

port to fly him to Boston. "You better come with me," he said to me.

"I'll go to Boston. I'll wait in a hotel room, but I don't talk to Hind unless there's a deal."

"There'll be a deal."

"Just the same, Waller, I want my own witness in your meeting with Hind."

"You don't trust me?"

"Are you kidding?"

"I realize there is nothing personal in that reply. Who is the witness to be? Harry?"

"I'll take Charley Coffey. Call Betaut and get him for me."

Waller looks in his big black book and dials. Betaut doesn't ask any questions when Waller tells him he needs Coffey to witness an important deal with Horace Hind. Waller gives him the hotel and the Bennett alias. He tells Betaut to ask Charley to meet him in the lobby at five minutes to four.

We got to the Back Bay Hotel at about a quarter to four. Coffey was waiting near the desk. He didn't see me. I told Waller I'd be waiting in my suite.

DATE: 11th August 1964
TIME: 5:50 P.M.
BASE REPORTING: New York

                    DSP (Semley) Only

CHARLES COFFEY (continued)

The room clerk at the Back Bay stood at attention when he saw Walter. After eight years as U.S. Vice-President, Walter knew how to crowd situations like this by playing them against type. He was all affability and easygoing goodwill asking for B. J. Bennett as if he were asking for a hometown neighbor, which for all I knew he was doing. The clerk handed the key to the farthest left elevator in the bank and asked him to press the button for the ninth floor. "The White House is sure waiting for *you* in '68, Mr. Vice-President," he said. "And we're rooting for you."

"Thank you, son, "Walter said gravely, and we headed for the farthest left car.

"Who is B. J. Bennett?" I asked as we went across the lobby.

"It just isn't something I can talk about here," he told me.

At the ninth floor two nasty cases were there to meet us. They greeted the former Vice-President and looked at me with professional hatred. The squat one held a Doberman pinscher on a short lead. The dog made disgusting sounds as if its throat were clogged with blood. Behind them a kid who had to be a mental defective sat tensely in a chair with a sawed-off shotgun across his lap.

"Jes' walk slow," the squat man said, "an this ole dog ain't gonna bother you."

They walked us slow to a partition that was a baffle in front of a locked door so nobody could come running out fast. The tall man unlocked it. The squat guy, the dog, and the guard stayed outside. We went in. The door locked behind us. The tall man herded us down a short hall to a door with a red light burning above it. The tall man said softly through a wall speaker, "Vice-President Slurrie is here, sir." A buzzer sounded. The door unlatched and we went into the gloom. Walter locked the door behind us.

A painfully thin, very long, and enormously old man with long white hair was stretched out on a black Naugahyde Barcalounger. He looked as bad as anyone I had ever seen, including a recent photo of Rameses II in *The Times*.

"Horace," Walter said, "may I introduce Mr. Charles Coffey? Charley, please meet Mr. Horace Hind."

I couldn't believe it. Jesus, it was like running into Superman in a shower and finding out he wore false teeth and a truss.

A movie was running itself out in a projector at Hind's right elbow, showing itself on a small movie screen (on a line with his bare feet with their great, horny yellow toe talons), and casting an eerie light in the darkened room. Walter leaned over Hind and turned the projector off.

"Just for the duration of the meeting, Horace," Walter said.

Hind didn't open his eyes. Two filled hypodermic syringes had fallen to the floor beside the chair. What in God's name did Betaut and Walter want me to witness?

"Horace?" Walter was saying clearly. "Horace?" There was no answer. Walter smiled to me indulgently. "I am used to his eccentricities." He turned back to Hind. "I don't think you are looking all that good, Horace." It was if an undertaker had said it to a body that had just fallen 103 floors to a pavement, but Walter was forthright about it, in a way he had taught himself because it could sometimes convince of his honesty. "I am going to insist on sending you one of those Sears electric, in-place bikes. You need more exercise."

246

Hind didn't answer.

Walter moved a chair from across the room to a place where he could speak directly into Hind's hearing aid, using the hearing aid as if it were a microphone in a floor show.

"Horace," he said beguilingly, "you can buy Las Vegas, Nevada. All the key action. Round-the-clock gambling, beautiful showgirls, hundreds of actresses—action, power, glamor, Horace."

Hind didn't answer.

"You would not only control a tremendous hourly cash flow, but politically you would be buying the State of Nevada because you would own all the big casinos that call the tune in that state. You would be the only American who owned his own state of the union. Your daddy never dreamed of a thing like that."

Hind opened his eyes dazedly, as if galaxies had been exploding inside his head. "Vegas?" he murmured. "My own state?" There was a long, long silence but Walter waited. "I would be a fascinating man," Hind whispered, then his head fell off the Barcalounger and hung there limply.

Walter looked at me as if I were the Hind family doctor. I went in and tried for Hind's pulse. There wasn't any. "I think he's dead," I told Walter.

First Walter went to the door to make sure it was locked, then he walked back to Hind, burrowing in his own pocket and coming up with a small pocket mirror. I realized then that all down the years Walter had seemed dignified because he was vain. It was wild that a man with a face like that should carry a pocket mirror to haunt himself with. Walter held the mirror to Hind's lips and nostrils for what seemed a full three minutes.

"No vapor," he said. "Horace is dead, all right."

"Walter, what the hell am I here for?"

"I have to think." He sat down. He summoned up his expression signifying deep thought. It was my feeling that he was trying to figure out how he could make money out of this.

Walter was fifty-one years old. Time had carved two perfect jowls with the dough of his face. His mouth was pursed in a permanent pucker formed by all the asses he had kissed to get ahead. His eyes were muddy, shifty, and alert.

"Holy *shit!*" he said suddenly as he leapt across the room, going directly to two large suitcases. He laid them flat and opened each one. I goggled.

Thousand-dollar bills in banded bundles of a hundred thousand dollars each, stacked tight bundle upon bundle on top of each other. Nobody outside the Bureau of Printing & Engraving had ever seen anything like this. The effect of it on Walter was to drop him, literally, where he stood. He fell vertically to his butt upon the floor. He didn't know he had fallen because he was giving all of his consciousness to the contents of those suitcases. He forgot completely that I was there. His hand snaked out, flicked one after another into the two suitcases and removed a parcel of money from each with such swiftness that it amounted to sleight-of-hand as he concealed the flat packages in his clothing.

"Are you going to declare that, Walter?" I asked him.

"Declare it? To the I.R.S.? Are you crazy?"

"There must be somebody else in this deal who is going to count it."

He thought, then he nodded. Very slowly he put the money back. "Anyway," he said, "there's plenty there for everybody." He shut the cases to cut down on the torture. "A half billion dollars," he said. Then he went to the two telephones on the table beside the body. He picked up a green one, listened, then hung up again. "Lorraine Center," he said. He tried the other phone. It must have been the direct hotel extension. Then he baffled me still further by asking for Nudey Danzig.

"Mr. Danzig," he said, "allow ten minutes for me to tell the desk you are expected and to straighten out the reception arrangements up here. Then go to the desk, ask for B. J. Bennett, and come up to the ninth floor." He hung up.

He went to the door, unlocked it, opened it, and standing quite straight he assumed the role of the Vice-President of the United States before my eyes and marched out into the corridor. I sat down beside what was left of Hind and turned on the switch of the projector. Walter had forgotten that. The movie began again. The soundtrack was loud enough to be heard through the partly opened door.

Walter was outside about four minutes. When he got back, he stood in the doorway giving orders. "And please try for Russian dressing on the turkey sandwiches," he said, "and—ah—three Regal Colas, please."

He came back into the room, locking the door. He walked across the room and stood over Hind.

"My old friend," he said, producing beautiful middle-belly tones, "we made a lot of money together, he and I. We walked where other men can never go and I never found him wanting."

"How are you going to get these suitcases out of here, Walter? Because I know that is all you are thinking about."

"I'll need a little help on that."

"You can't have much time. His people in Hollywood must be scared witless that you are in the room with the money. They are bound to send an expeditionary force, Walter."

"I thought of that," he said dreamily.

"Getting past that dog and that shotgun can't be the easiest thing in the world."

"Mr. Danzig will know how to get the suitcases out and how to handle everything else."

"You'd better start remembering that it's Hind's money. You'd better stop thinking about how you're going to get the cases out. If it's all the same to you, get me out instead."

The buzzer sounded. Walter crossed to the door, unlocked it, then opened it, standing at one side to bar any view of the body. "Ah, Mr. Danzig," he said. "Come in. Please. Mr. Hind has been waiting for you."

He drew Danzig into the room, shut the door, and locked it.

Danzig stood staring at the body.

"That guy looks dead," he commented.

"He is dead," Walter said.

"Dead? Then what the hell did you get me in here for, schmuck?"

Walter held up one finger like a stage magician. He crossed the room, knelt, then opened one suitcase after the other. Danzig walked closer to get a better view.

"Is that it?" he asked. "It looks like very good queer."

Startled by the possibility, Walter passed him a packet. Danzig examined the money. He studied it, fingered it, and held it up to the light. "It's good," he pronounced. He handed the packet to Walter. "Close them and lock them."

"With what?"

Danzig jerked his head. "He's gotta have the key."

Walter looked at me.

"Not me," I said.

He shrugged, walked to the body, and went through Hind's pocket, lifting him as easily as if he had been a piece of rope. There was nothing in the pockets except four cellophane packets of white powder and one key. Walter took the key to the suitcases and locked them. Danzig held out his hand and Walter put the key on it. We were standing, forming a triangle.

"First," Danzig said, "thank you for coming to Boston, Charley. I appreciate it very much and I'm gonna send your wife some flowers, but I'm not gonna need a witness anymore so you can go back to New York."

"I don't think we should have all this going in and out," Walter said.

"Let Charley out," Danzig said impatiently. "And make sure he gets through to the elevator with his ass still in his pants."

DATE: 11th August 1964
TIME: 6:57 P.M.
BASE REPORTING: Miami   DSP (Semley) Only

ABNER "NUDEY" DANZIG (continued)

It could be that every time I saw Waller I saw a different Waller. We all knew about him and money, but those two suitcases filled with that kind of cash made him look a little crazy. He didn't give a shit what had to be done or what chances he took. This was a fella who had a lifetime of some pretty careful moving behind him. This was the two-time Vice-President of the United States.

That day, in the room with that stiff, he was absolutely Benny Siegel come back to life. Anything that got in his way had to be just taken out. I put out my hand and touched him. He didn't even feel it. He didn't feel anything but getting that money so I knew I had to either bring him down nice and easy or I'd have to kill him. He would have killed me if he could figure out a way to get the money through that room and past that shotgun outside, if he could just figure out how to get the money to Florida so Kiddo could start to wash it. But that's where his education let him down. He didn't have any experience at killing anybody and he didn't have the head to figure out the rest of it.

His greed was exhausting him, burning him up. "What are we going to do?" he croaked.

"Waller, siddown. You hear me?"

He sat down on the bed. I sat in a chair. "Now we got to put everything into the right size box, if you get what I mean. Everything is relative to something else, you get what I mean?"

"No. Listen, Mr. Danzig—Hind's people are on their way from California and when they get here they are going to come right into this room."

"This is more important. I got to make you see what is going for us here."

"What do you mean?" He wasn't breathing so good either.

"Waller—lissena me. The money in those suitcases is *nothing*."

"Nothing?"

I lean across at him. I stare at him for maybe a haffa minute before I talk. "Hind—this stiff, here—has two billion dollars. Maybe more. He owns companies, oil, breweries, buildings, bank accounts, factories, stocks, bonds, mines, lines of credit and contracts that are like nobody else's in the country except the Felsenburshes'. So—I am asking you this and I want you to think about it carefully before you answer—whatta you so shook up about a haffa billion dollars when I know how we can milk him for the rest of it?"

Waller begins to breathe as if he is getting laid. "How?" he says and I am afraid his eyes are gonna fall out.

"You don't know how?"

"No."

"You are sure you don't know how."

"I am certain."

"Then you need me."

"I know that, Mr. Danzig."

"That's why all my life everybody else gets the finder's fee and I keep the rest."

"I don't follow."

"I mean we'll get the split settled first, then *after* I'll show you how."

"What is the split?"

"You get the finder's fee."

"No. I nursed Hind for twenty years. I was how we got in here.

252

I was how you knew about the money. You couldn't have gotten near the money without me."

"Whatta you have in mind, Waller?"

"We will have to be full partners on this."

"Waller, lissena me. So I'll be glad to be partners with you on every cent if you can figure out how to get outta here. And how are you gonna milk him for the rest of it? Does knowing Hind for twenty years help you get the rest of it?"

He is getting calmer. I am talking him down, like a horse. He says, "What kind of a finder's fee?"

"The same. It's always the same. Two percent. You know, it ain't as if all the rest is net to me. You get a flat guarantee. You don't have to wait for your end. No tryna cut you down because so much is involved here."

"Only two percent?"

"Only? *only?* That's nine million, seven hunnerd and twenny thousand dollars—only on what is in the suitcases, fuhcrissake. And the rest of it—when I get the rest of it, Waller, you get two percent of a billion anna haff. That is worth thirty million dollars to you which is a pretty good score for a lawyer who doesn't have to do anything else but know Hind for twenty years. You still wanna try to fuck me around, Waller? Are you gonna tell me that thirty-nine million, seven hunnerd and twenny thousand dollars is a lousy legal fee for making a trip to Boston?"

The killing fever finally went out of him. He got grateful again, like the Waller I always knew.

"You're right, Mr. Danzig. The sight of the money must have unbalanced me for a moment. Thirty-nine million is eminently fair."

"So long as we understand each other. Now we gotta get to work here. First we sell him Vegas so the money is legally ours. You draw the papers tonight. I'll get them signed. I'll have all the details and valuations from our side ready and waiting. Deeds, mortgages, everything."

"Get them signed, you said?"

"Don't worry about it. Do we have to have that fucking movie on?"

"Oh, yes. While it's on, he's alive to the people outside."

"This is the scam, Waller. Everything the Syndicate owns in Vegas goes into dummy companies that Hind will own and we get this cash for the transfer. So the Mob is now outta Vegas. It becomes a healthy American playground with a few thousand hookers for the cleancut American businessman. For his haffa billion, Hind gets eleven casinos and hotels. His companies—but we operate them in a special way I have in mind."

"How?"

"How many men outside there now?"

"Three guards, a waiter, a doctor, a driver, and a supervisor. But the doctor is always drunk in his room. I would guess there are at least two people on the way here from Lorraine Center."

"Nine plus one dog. We'll give the California people four hours to get here."

"Then what?"

"By then I'll have some people here to take them all out."

"*Kill* them?"

"You got a better idea?"

"No."

"That's the easiest part. Still we gotta move fast. These people outside gotta go first. Then I gotta get a Sicilian embalmer up here to work over Hind so he'll last for a week or so even in a traveling freezer."

"You have your own *embalmer,* Mr. Danzig?"

"When he's ready we'll take him outta the hotel down the service elevator on a stretcher, then we slide him in the icebox inside the ambulance. Then we fly him to Nevada to someplace where we can pick up a train charter. Some out-of-the-way station."

"Why?"

"Why? We need him in Vegas, don't we, to operate eleven hotels and casinos he just bought? And I want a crowd to see him taken off the train in Vegas and driven in a ambulance through downtown. He always travels on a stretcher anyway. We'll do it early in the morning. Now we call the SP."

"The *SP?* Secret *Police?*"

"You don't remember what I tell you, Waller. Remember? Everywhere, in every country, in all history, all secret police need independent money for their really secret operations and they can never get enough. Those kind of people can't be dependent on governments for support, they could go outta business. So the SP will be our partners on this."

"What do we need them for?"

"They'll build us a Horace Hind double. Plastic surgery on a tall, skinny guy. Sooner or later his Lorraine Center people are gonna get a court order to look at him. We'll be able to stall them for a year or two but when they go into the room in Vegas they got to believe what they'll see. And don't worry about it. The SP surgeons could make even you look good."

"But his *voice,* Mr. Danzig. His *handwriting.*" He was getting scared for his money.

"Waller, lissena me. You think I'd do anything to keep you from being the next President of the United States? The country needs you, and I personally got a very big bet rolling on that. You know it. So fuhcrissake just listen and lemme work this thing out."

"I'm sorry, Mr. Danzig."

Waller is always polite. You gotta like him for that.

"Voice and handwriting are routine shit for the SP. They do it evvy day. What takes handling is finding the right outside man in Vegas who runs the whole thing for us, who thinks he is running it for Hind because he ain't never gonna see Hind. And I mean he aint gonna see the double, either. He just gets Hind memos and the voice on the phone maybe fifteen times a day. The SP will have somebody. They got two guys for evvything. Charley Coffey, for instance, would be great for the spot."

"Never," Waller says. "You should meet his wife."

"Still, if he ever gets sick of working for the Felsenburshes he can pick himself up three, four hunnerd thousand dollars a year for just sitting in the sun in Vegas."

"This is all very tricky stuff," Waller says as if he knew what was happening.

"For this kind of money, Waller, anything can be done. But I am wishing I didn't have Benny Siegel taken out. I could use three of him right now."

DATE: 11th August 1964
TIME: 11:17 A.M.
BASE REPORTING: New York

DSP (Semley) Only

JUSTICE MARTIN J. COFFEY

Sure, I'm glad you came around. You're government people and sponsored by Governor Betaut, so how can I go wrong? Anything you want, you got it.

Well, Slurrie was a little pissmire but the son of a bitch woulda been President in '68, no two ways about it, so getting himself knocked off like that was real death for a politician, if you know what I mean. Slurrie came a long way. I knew him when he was a law student. Over seventeen years he took all that guff and catspawed so many deals for God knows how many masters, then just as he gets in sight of the big money some bastard rings the doorbell and shoots him to death in a bathtub. He was a cheap crook and a weak sister but I can almost count the hearts that are broken today, the people who held him together and kept him on the track all these years, like my son, Charley, and Dick Betaut.

257

Now they're gonna have to pull reserves outta the woodwork and start all over again on the long, slow process of building them up for the campaign in '68. It's going to cost the Party an extra $20,000,000 because somebody blew Slurrie away.

I was running through my mind who coulda done it or had it done. We all have our theories. I personally think that, after all these years of sucking hind tit and pretending he wanted the White House, then always losing out just before every nomination convention so that the public could kid itself that his money couldn't buy him everything, that maybe Nils Felsenburshe finally did get bitten by the presidential bug.

Let me tell you that if that bug had bitten him, it wouldn't mean a damned thing that he already had millions invested in Slurrie as his own, controlled, sure-thing presidential candidate. Power is temperamental. Power has to eat when it's hungry.

Nils is getting along. He's had so much power for so long that he could even be getting a little nuts. At his age, after purposely losing, having trained teams to help him lose, at all the conventions in a row, conventions he controlled like his own fingers, after working as hard as that man worked to prove that, alas, it was hopeless for a man as rich as him to win it—because public opinion had the power to stop it—Jesus, if a man like that was *finally* bitten by the presidential bug, he'd have to have Slurrie killed because after all the hard work his people had done the Party was finally convinced that Slurrie was their candidate.

If you were Nils Felsenburshe and you decided that you wanted to be President, what would you do? Well, depending on how nuts you had become, you'd have Betaut talk to Nudey Danzig or to the SP about putting out a contract on Slurrie. You'd have a number done on Slurrie just the way it was done, in Betaut's own apartment, because the whole focus would be on the political loss to the Party and how they'd have to move fast to replace Slurrie with the very best.

Maybe Nils did and maybe he didn't. However it was, I can't help feeling that this country was very lucky Slurrie was killed because he was a weakling, a liar, and a man who despised people and the Constitution. To people who feed off the crumbs of power that drop off the tables of the owners—people like me, professional politicians—Slurrie did everything technically right, but he did everything morally wrong. Now—understand— these are personal observations. Money is our own culture so it's

258

got to be served. Power tries to remain benevolent but money has its limits and power does not. I'll be curious to see if Felsenburshe gets the nomination this August. He has the power to get it. The power is there. He'll lose it if he doesn't use it.

TO: DEPUTY FIRST COMMISSIONER, VINCENT J. MULSHINE

FROM: LIEUTENANT RICHARD GALLAGHER, 17th HSQ

George Fearons brought in George Palmer, one of the house officers at the Waldorf, at 4:45 P.M. yesterday afternoon. Palmer said he had been bothered by a "hunch" for almost two days but that he wasn't able to take it any further. His hunch was that one of the bellmen, Ugo Galvino, had been supplying women to Walter Slurrie. He said he was sure, without being able to prove anything, that

Galvino had sent a woman up to the Betaut apartment at 5:20 PM to 5:35 PM on the day Slurrie was murdered.

The Medical Examiner places the time of Slurrie's murder at about 7:40 PM to 7:55 PM.

Palmer and Fearons were in my office. I asked him how he still had the hunch without being sure.

He said, "Because we aren't that kind of a hotel. What I want to say to you is that I have this certain feeling in my mind but I am not going to sit here and tell you that our employees hustle women for the guests because they don't."

"What you are saying," Fearons told him, "is that you think Galvino might have something to tell us."

Palmer nodded.

"What time is he on?" I asked.

"He's on now. I'll get him down to the locker room," Palmer said. "You can take him there."

Fearons brought Galvino in; Male-White-43. I asked him if he had known Walter Slurrie. He says yes he has known him as staying in the hotel every now and then for about eight years.

I asked him if he ever did any special services for Slurrie. He says no, just checking him in or answering fronts. I asked him if he ever talked to Slurrie. He says yes about the weather, things like that.

"Galvino," I said to him, "you've been reading the papers for the past two days just like everybody else. When you go home you look at television so you know what kind of interest there is in this case. Am I right? You know that?"

"Yeah," he said. "I guess I know that. Sure. Certainly."

"Then you got to know that nothing I am going to say to you is routine. You know what I mean. Everything I say to you about this case is important. You understand that, Ugo?"

"Yeah. Okay." .

"Can we talk and get straight answers or is the sergeant here and another detective going to take you out in the woods on Long Island and talk to you?"

"We can talk, lieutenant. I am sorry. Ask me."

"Do I need to ask you, Ugo?"

"In about 1955, the first time I answer a front and it is Slurrie, I take his bags up to the suite he had and he asks me if I know any very special kind of broads. If anybody else asks me a question like that, I tell them they are in the wrong hotel, and also I don't need to ask him what he means because with that kind of question it means he wants a kinky broad. But Slurrie was Vice-President of the United States and if he can't get what he wants out of the Secret Service then he absolutely must mean he wants a special kind of broad. I mean – I never voted for Slurrie so it didn't mean anything to me but when a Vice-President of the United States can bring himself to ask a bellhop a question like that, you got to have respect for what it cost him, so I said, yeah, I could probably find out something like that. He hands me fifty dollars. He says that is for me. He says what he wants is a woman who is maybe fifty five-sixty years old. He wants her to be tall and skinny with grey hair and eyeglasses although, he says to me, if I can't find a genuine article, she can wear a wig. Can I do that? I say, well, I will ask around. He says he knows it might take a little time but that he has a big dinner, the Cardinal's dinner in the ball room that night, so maybe I can set it up for him, in his suite, at ten o'clock the next morning. He tells me it will look better at ten in the morning, anyway, if a woman comes to his suite.

"Well, I get the woman. I never seen her before. I don't know no whores, believe me, but I got a friend who knows who to call no matter what you need. I tell him to tell her to meet me at a counter joint on Lexington at half past nine the next morning. I am sitting in a booth and this nice like-old lady comes over and sits down. She says, 'I am Mary Sue Fuller. Sal Mangulo told me to contact you. What kind of a job is it?'

"I tell her I don't know except it has to be kinky. I give her the key to the suite and tell her he wants her to let herself in then go and find him and that she has to be there at ten o'clock the next morning. 'Do I return the key to him or to you?' she asks. I tell her to leave it with Slurrie.

"The Vice-President never came to New York very much until he moved here. When he lived out of town he might come in four-five times a year. He would always locate me and tell me to come up to his suite then hand me the fifty without saying anything then he would hand me the key. I would call my friend who knows who to call then I would meet her a half an hour before and give her the key."

"You ever ask her what went on in there?" Fearons said.

"Well, actually yeah. I did. You know – "

"Well what did they do in there that was so special?"

"She beat the shit out of him Galvino said. Then she helped him get dressed and went home."

"What did he pay her?"

"Two hundred bucks."

"How long did the thing go on?"

"Nine years."

"What happened the day of the murder?"

"Slurrie came down to the lobby. He called me over, in a alcove. He said he wanted Mrs. Fuller – that's what he called her I swear to God – to sit near the elevators, then after Betaut came down and went out, he wanted her to go up to Betaut's apartment and use the key for the second bedroom of the suite. It opens off the corridor. He said that would be about five o'clock in the afternoon, maybe five-fifteen."

"What time was this?"

"This was about one twenty in the afternoon, maybe a quarter to two. He just checked in."

"How do we find Fuller?"

"Lieutenant – Jesus. I don't think anybody is going to find her. After what happened she is probably on a bus to Florida."

"Just tell us where we can talk to your friend who knows how to find her."

"Please. I can't. I can't do that, lieutenant."

"Whoever your friend is, whatever he can do to you, that is nothing to what is going to happen to you on Long Island tonight."

"This is not only a Mob guy, lieutenant, but it is Mike Partanna. And not only that – holy shit – Mike Partanna is my brother-in-law."

We drove to Brooklyn with Galvino and talked to Partanna. Partanna played it very patriotic. He tells us that Walter Slurrie is one of the greatest men this country ever produced and that if anybody he knows can tell anything about who hit this man then we are going to see one hundred per cent cooperation like we have never seen. Galvino asks Partanna if he is in trouble.

"Shut up," Partanna tells him.

Partanna called someone named Sal Mangulo and told him

to get over there. Mangulo was there in under ten minutes. He tells Mangulo to take us to a woman named Mary Fuller. Mangulo says certainly but he doesn't know where any of the broads live. He says he can call her but that's all he's got.

Fearons took the number from him and went out of the room to call downtown for a street address on the number. Fuller lived on Riverside Drive at 111th Street. We asked Galvino if he wanted a ride back to town. He said no, that his brother-in-law might want to talk to him.

Fearons drove me through some of the most beautiful traffic the city has ever produced and we got to the woman's apartment at five minutes to five in the afternoon. She answered the door and she looked like what Slurrie had asked Galvino for nine years ago, only much older. I told her who we were and that she would have to come downtown with us. She said she couldn't go with us because she was cooking dinner for her son and her daughter-in-law who would be home in about forty minutes. I told her that if she wanted them to know about Walter Slurrie before she talked to us then we'd stay there. "Otherwise," I said, "get your hat." She came downtown with us.

She is a widow. She has three sons and lives with one of them. She keeps house for her son and his wife because they both have good jobs at IBM. She has been turning novelty tricks ever since the third son was born because her husband lost interest in her, she said. I told her we would go into all that when we had to. Slurrie had been murdered. She was the last person to be alone with him at the approximate time of his death. I said we wanted a statement from her and Fearons read her her rights.

She said, "I have known Walter Slurrie since 1955. I liked him and he liked me. I had nothing to do with his death in any way and I was shocked when the news of his murder reached me. We had our own kind of harmony, Mr. Slurrie and I. My business is punishing people and Mr. Slurrie needed to be punished. There was nothing personal about it. Two hours is a long time for a relationship like that, lieutenant. Ours went on for nine years. When I got him dressed again I told him that, for the first time, I had to hurry away to get home to get cold cuts on the table and Mr. Slurrie insisted on telephoning the desk downstairs in the Towers to have them put me in a taxicab. I went straight downstairs. It couldn't have taken two minutes. While I was at the Towers desk he called down again to ask if they had been able to get a cab for me. He was alive. Very much alive."

It checks out.

DATE: 11th August 1964
TIME: 4:05 P.M.
BASE REPORTING: Miami

DSP (Semley) Only

EDWARD CARDOZO (continued)

Everything I got come from Nudey Danzig. My father bring me here from Mexico because there is a lot of Espanish-speaking people here. We had nothing. We deen itt much. Then Harry Danzig get my father a job in a bookie office. When I quit school Harry give me a numbers pickup route on the Beach, then he get me my own territory working the laundromats in North Miami. After that come the Used Tires, the punchboards, Wullair, the big Vizcaya Cove development, the supermarket, the bank, and Betsy.

Betsy is the important thing Nudey get for me. She is the *mas linda* thing in my life. When they kill Wullair, they hit her hard. Nobody but me an the kids know how much she grieve for Wullair. That cut me bad because I don wan her to have pain. That is more imporrant to me than whether I turn out to be grateful to Nudey Danzig. I think all the time about what Wullair dead do to

267

Betsy so I wan to know who kill him. I feel it for me, too. Wullair was my partner. I hurt like six ways because somebody hit Wullair an I think I am entitle to pay back whoever done it.

So I say this to you an you do whatever you wan with it. Nudey have Wullair taken out. Wullair was deep in Nudey for a tremendous piece of money from what they take out of Horace Hind. There is so much money that Wullair tell me that he think Nudey give him a bad screwing on the deal. Wullair work himself over until he get his nerves way up, then he go to Nudey an tell him he is entitle to be a partner or he is gun blow a whistle. I am at the meet. Nudey get so mad it scare the cheat outta me, but Wullair don know what Nudey do when he get this way so he don get scare. Two weeks ago Wullair go to see Nudey again and he write his funeral because he give Nudey a date—August 9 is the date—for Nudey to make him a partner in the Hind money or, he says, he has figured out a way to get the news that Hind is dead to the cops.

Nudey is like ice. He stay izzy-going but he is ice. I see this before when Guillermo Peña, the Cuban, tell him that he is through paying Nudey money for something Nudey did for him a long time ago. Nudey smile at him and shake his hand. They say goodbye, and that night they find Peña cut in half on the beach eight miles north of Boca Raton.

He say to Wullair, "You know, in legit bidniz, they pay money out so they pay less taxes. But I don pay taxes. So evvy cent I pay out to you is a dead loss to me, you unnastan', Waller? You get two percent of the gross here. You think I keep the other ninety-eight percent? Schmuck! I got to pay out to forty people who help me keep it *after* it is cut up with the SP. The SP take thirty-three percent, Waller. Then I gotta pay a share to the Syndicate which it runs about eighteen percent so that cops and judges and state governors and DAs and bail people are always standing by. I got Keifetz, who is running Vegas he thinks for Hind at four hunnerd thousand a year. I got the deposits into the Swiss bank account of the creep who had his face made over to be Horace Hind for us, which it is an even million bucks a year. My end of the whole fucking thing—the entire thing—is maybe eleven percent at the very top. So believe me, Waller, your two percent looks very big to me. You are making me see that maybe I really need that two percent for everything I put into this deal."

Wullair say, "Well, Mr. Danzig, I know what I am getting for my two percent so that I can only say that your nine extra points over and beyond my share comes to an absolutely tremendous amount of money no matter how much you put into setting this thing up."

"You got to remember how long I been in this bidniz, Waller. A hunnerd guys I started out with are all dead because they didn't know how to think, and the ones who knew how didn't think about the right things. Now, for the last time, this is what I wanna say to you. You got to keep saying to yourself that there isn't a whistle in this country big enough to blow on me in this Hind thing because I did all my thinking and there is nothing anybody can do to me because I've got Hind's money, plus my money, and all the clout that goes with those. So look at it this way, the minute you try to blow the whistle, even if nobody can hear it, the payments stop—you never get another cent and my end goes up to thirteen percent of a lot of money."

By this time Wullair already knows that Nudey is gun have him taken out. He begin to apologize. He say he want to forget the whole thing. Nudey don't talk to him, he just look at him. Wullair begin to cry. But it is fake. He tell Nudey how much Nudey done for him, how Nudey actually made him but Nudey wun talk, he just look. Then, to give you jus a li'l idea of how scare Wullair is, he tell Nudey that he want to give back one percent of his two percent because now that he see what Nudey had to do to make the dill possible he don think Nudey is getting enough of a piece.

"Well, what the hell," Nudey say to him. "You still have the original nine million for that afternoon's work. Be sure nobody takes that away, Waller."

That was the 5th of August in North Miami.

I know Nudey since I am a kid. He is Nudey. But he is also a man who give Wullair his place in the world and get him mos of his money. Nudey is the kind of guy who could decide he was gun take it all back, every cent. Nudey and Betaut are so close, like brothers since the early 1930s when Betaut was the big gang-buster and Nudey wan to get rid of Charley Lucky. When he give Lucky to Betaut it almos make Betaut President. They do business for each other on different sides of the stritt for thirty years. Nudey know Betaut is Wullair's lawyer. Nudey can figure that Betaut know where all Wullair's money is hid an how to get it. So I think Nudey put it to Betaut. He tell Betaut the time has come to cut up Wullair's money. He say he gun take care of Wullair and as soon as Wullair is taken out Betaut got to go straight for the money. Nudey took Wullair out, then he take all of the money Wullair has hoarded away from him after he is dead. That is Nudey's kind of revenge. He is *todo mentalidad.*

Of course, it could work the other way aronn, but I don't think so. Betaut could get the idea to have Wullair taken out so he could go for Wullair's money. If that was the way, he would go to his old frenn Nudey Danzig to set it up for him. Nudey is gun have Wullair hit anyhow, but he know it is better to put it on Betaut, in case anything go wrong, because Betaut got all the Felsenburshe muscle.

So I know who kill Wullair. Now I tell you. Now we both know. *Que pasa mas?* What can we do about it?

CHARLES COFFEY (continued)

Two days after the Presidential assassination in Dallas, the new President issued National Security Memorandum No. 273, which reversed the dead President's order of the withdrawal of troops and materiel from Vietnam. It inaugurated a period of concentrated buildup, leading to conventional warfare with heavy American troop allotments and installations. Within five months all Special Forces under the direct command of the SP became a reinforced, independent military headquarters with power to act in Cambodia, Laos, and Vietnam, and in northern Thailand in coooperation with Thai forces, that region where opium was the great cash crop and Number Four heroin was processed for export to North America.

Marie didn't make the connection, thank God, between the assassination and the acceleration of the war any more than any other voter did. But the murder of the President messed up Marie's mind. She didn't believe any of the hurricane of cover-up stories, each one heading off in another tangential direction, until the people were ready to believe anything the Pickering Commission (of which James D. Marxuach, ex-head of the SP, was a prime member) chose to tell them.

Marie was obsessed with her idea that I had something to do with the murder. She believed that, no matter how indirectly, the Felsenburshes had ordered it, and that Walter Slurrie had organized its execution. To Marie, Walter was everything that was sick, corrupt, and decaying in American politics. She connected him to me like a Siamese twin.

I will never know now how far Walter had been included in planning for the assassination but I was there as an eye and ear witness the night Betaut and Danzig forced him to undertake the vital follow-up on it. From that moment on, neither Walter nor I any longer had the alibi of "That's politics" with which we had justified ourselves for so long. If what I was witness to that night was politics then we had gone back to the Dark Ages. I think, now, that is where Walter and I belonged, just as Marie belonged a thousand years in the future. Pop and Betaut and the Felsenburshes are there with me and Walter. The difference, although not subtle, is that the others don't know they are there. It is "Politics as usual." They think of themselves as being "pragmatic," but now they know what the assassination has taught us about despair.

From the time the news hit the 66th floor at Felsenburshe City, I was either on telephones to people all over the country and Europe and Japan or running in and out of Nils Felsenburshe's office. The day finally ended at 7:50 P.M. with secretaries still weeping and a few executives openly drunk.

I hadn't spoken to Marie because I couldn't bring myself to call her. I was reaching for my hat to go home when Betaut called and told me I would have to get over to his place at the Waldorf immediately. I asked my secretary to call Marie and tell her I would be home just as soon as the Betaut meeting was over, but I dreaded the time, very soon, when I was going to have to face Marie at the end of a day when the President had been murdered.

I got to the Waldorf at 8:20 P.M. Betaut, Danzig, and Slurrie were waiting. Betaut was as direct as a cannon. "Please absorb this, everyone," he said. "I was a founder of the SP. I considered them to be the supreme patriots of our nation. However, they have now made an irrevocable error because of all the past misunderstandings about the Bay of Pigs, which led to the dismissal of James D. Marxuach, and because they were about to lose their command of the war in southeast Asia—they assassinated the President. There are no pros and cons to discuss. That is now history. Very well! Included in their plan was a person who is known in the parlance as a fall guy. He is now under arrest in Dallas but the police can't keep him bottled up very much longer. If he is interviewed by the press and television it will become clear that he had no knowledge whatever about the events of the day. Mr. Danzig is familiar with the two riflemen who actually carried out the assignment. One has left the country. The other is in Dallas. Mr. Danzig feels that the second rifleman can be persuaded to eliminate this fall guy for an appropriate fee and certain guarantees at his trial.

"I am not going to go into what is at stake here. The reasons are formidable and compelling. Therefore, because of his high former rank, his association with Dad Kampferhaufe and the Red Crusade, I have decided that Walter will need to fly to Dallas immediately to persuade this man to do this important job."

"Me?" Walter said instantly. "Oh, no. I refuse to have anything to do with this."

"You'll do it," Nudey said.

"I am not going to Dallas tonight. I will not talk to that murderer. I am not going to do it."

Mr. Danzig, who had been sitting relaxed, now got to his feet. "Waller, excepting Kiddo, we are maybe all the friends you got in the world. I am here because I got my own interests in this thing. The Governor and Charley are here to protect the Felsenburshes. Get up, Waller. I wanna talk to you."

Walter didn't move. "Keep away from me, Mr. Danzig," he said with a shaking voice. I realized that Walter was afraid of Danzig. Looking at the short, slender, white-haired man as he moved toward Walter, I suddenly wondered why I had never been afraid of him, too. Danzig pulled Walter out of the chair by the front of his shirt and shook him. He stared into Walter with those cold eyes and said, "If you keep saying you won't do it, you can either say so flat, just once more, in which case I am gonna throw you outta the fucking window, or you can just say you don't wanna do it and get the shit kicked outta you until you say you'll do it."

"I don't want to do it, Mr. Danzig. They went too far today. It is wrong. What you are asking is wrong. I don't want to do it."

Danzig's hands moved so fast that he hit Walter heavily three times before Walter went down. Walter made sharp, grunting sounds but he didn't cry out, complain, or try to defend himself. I like to tell myself that I started forward to separate them but I didn't get very far. My excuse is that Betaut got an iron grip on my forearm and held me.

Danzig lifted Walter to his feet again, then, quite deliberately, he hit Walter four times directly in the stomach, his own elbows very close to his sides, moving out like pistons and snapping into Walter. Walter moaned pitiably each time he was hit, then he fell slowly sideways, holding his stomach with his arms. As soon as he hit the floor, Danzig began to kick him viciously, with all his power, up and down the rib cage. It happened, all of it, in a few seconds.

Danzig knelt on one side of Walter's body and Betaut knelt on the other. Danzig said, "Waller, are you taking this because you decided inside your head that you got to be punished for evvything?"

"What did you bring me into this for?" I shouted at Betaut.

He looked over his shoulder at me and said, "Shut up."

In a daze I stared at them. There was much, much more at stake than the SP to these three men. Betaut would have thrown the SP to the wolves if they were caught red-handed in the assassination. They were all just a lot of political appointees to Betaut, and there were more where those came from. Whatever it was that could frighten these two figures of ice and that poor, greed-transformed man was a tremendous force bearing down on them. Without knowing what it was I feared their fear.

Walter was in an agony of trying to breathe. As he stared up silently at Danzig as the old man talked to him about his demand to be punished, there was no expression on his face, only silent tears pouring out of his ruined eyes, not from the pain and humiliation of being who he was and yet being beaten and kicked, but from other, older pains.

"You gonna do it, Waller?" Danzig asked.

Walter nodded.

Danzig and Betaut stood up. "Order a fast plane," Danzig said to Betaut. "I'll get some tape from the john and fix up Walter so he can travel."

I walked out of the apartment and out of the hotel. Betaut yelled after me but I didn't hear what he was saying.

* * *

I got home before eleven o'clock. I let myself in, confused and sick and almost destroyed in my mind. Marie was drunk in front of the television set, which was retelling the assassination. All she had on was a pair of lace panties. There was an empty bottle of booze on the floor and an open bottle on the low table in front of her. I sat down in the first chair I came to.

She was a mess. Her makeup was out-of-register, her hair just sat askew on her head, and her eyes were red and bleary. I wasn't sure she knew I was in the room until she looked at me sadly and said, "I screwed the delivery boy from Gristede's."

I got up. "I'll make some coffee."

"What brought you home, Charley? Where did you get the guts to come home?"

"I live here."

"Did the Felsenburshes have him killed?"

"I don't know."

"You know."

"Come on. Into the tub. You stink."

"Booze and sweat and sperm, Charley. That's all you smell."

I slapped her and she whipped around in the chair like a loose body in a car accident. The chair went over, taking her with it. I leaned down to grip her arms and began to drag her toward the bath, while she sobbed and cursed me. I hauled her from the living room through the bedroom to the bathroom. I dumped her on the floor, then turned on the cold water in the tub. She stayed on the floor. She lay there, face down.

"Who had him killed?"

"Some freak. You know more about it than I do."

"You are going to hell for this."

"We'll talk about it tomorrow."

"No!" She rolled over and propped herself against the wall. "I don't want any more lies from you. I am scared. Two days ago I thought it was anger but after that hideous murder in which I *know* you had some part, I have to get away from you."

I knelt and touched her but she struck my arm. "I had nothing to do with it, Marie. Nothing." I could have said that four hours ago but now I was an accessory after the fact and I wasn't standing in the office of the Attorney-General telling what I knew, I was arguing with a stinking drunk.

"Did you resign today?"

"No."

"Are you going to resign tomorrow?"

"Marie, for the first time I really understand what you've been saying to me all these years. If I could have gotten out today, I would have. But this, of all days, wasn't the day."

"You can't quit. Your friends might kill you, too. Worse, they are going to let you live and you'll have to go on doing what you do for them."

I picked her up and rolled her into the cold water tub. She didn't gasp or flinch or try to get out. She lay there face down in the icy cold. Every time I turned her over she would go back with her face under the water. I took her by her long, beautiful, black hair and half lifted her out of the tub. Her eyes were open and staring at me with hatred. "I screwed the delivery boy from Gristede's, Charley," she said. "That's how much I value you."

DATE: 12th August 1964
TIME: 12:07 P.M.
BASE REPORTING: Dallas   DSP (Semley) Only

MRS. WALTER SLURRIE (continued)

I like Dallas. No, better, I love Dallas. The house is very small but I like that. The places for the kids and the dogs and the bikes and the kitchen were nicely planned. The shopping is terrific, the people are nice, and Highland Park is quiet and clean.

Dallas was Walter's political base and Walter was always in politics even when it looked as though he were out. The bad part about the house in Dallas was that Eddie couldn't be around a lot the way he was in Florida. The neighborhood kids—well, there is one red-headed kid I know, anyway, who peeks in everybody's windows, and if Eddie were around that could cause a lot of talk, if you know what I mean. That wouldn't be good for Walter, so I prefer the place in Florida.

Florida is Eddie's place, first and foremost. He and Walter developed our entire Vizcaya Cove area there. They made about six million bucks out of it. Eddie is also the leading banker in our area. And because he is Walter's best friend and partner, everybody sees it as natural that he is around the house a lot, so when

277

we are in Florida, the family is together a lot more and that's the way I like it.

I like Washington. I have nothing against Washington. We have a lot of status there but it's a tiresome place. You always have to watch your step because there are so many political trade paper people around, like *The Washington Post*, a trade paper Walter hated. It's a pain in the ass to try to go shopping with a couple of Secret Service men attracting the kind of people who want you to sign their shopping bags. We had a nice apartment in Washington that Walter won in some deal but from now on, because we won't be in politics anymore, I am very happy not to be living in Washington.

New York has terrific shopping and, while Walter was a Wall Street lawyer (that made him laugh the loudest), I was between Secret Service men. I don't mean one on each side of me but, with Walter out of the office for the moment, I could go shopping in peace and comfort.

We had a gorgeous apartment in New York. Walter always poor-mouthed the press about how he was struggling to pay for it, but it was just an apartment on loan from the Felsenburshes for as long as we were useful to them. It was big and comfortable. Central Park and New Jersey and the 59th Street skyline stretched out under us. In fact, we could see almost everything except the Felsenburshes. I swear to God, Walter and I never clapped eyes on those people in our lives. They watched us all the time but we couldn't see them.

Visits in Washington were strictly out for Eddie because of the political trade papers. But nobody in New York cared who we were. So Eddie flew up to New York to see me and the kids as often as he could, which was sometimes twice a week. We would all go out to lunch or dinner together the way a family should and the apartment was big enough for him to stay over whenever he wanted to. Also, the hotel suite he always takes is big enough for the occasional matinee. I loved New York.

Eddie has matured so well for a guy who never went to high school. He is very handsome. I love short, dark men. He has such beautiful teeth and such a marvelous disposition. Franklin, our younger boy, even tries to talk like him. Eddie is good with kids. He takes them to the movies and ballgames and he helps them with homework. I was the luckiest woman in this country. Then somebody killed Walter.

I loved Walter and Eddie. They loved me. And yet they were

278

wonderful friends to each other. I mean I *loved* them. Eddie gives me my whole sense of belonging to a family. Walter gave me his kindness and unselfishness and a large place in the world. Just being married to Walter made me into somebody. He was a great man. He was the greatest man in American history since World War II.

Anyway, we were in New York and Walter was a big lawyer who was on the road most of the time so he could get the professional politicians ready to grab at the idea that he had to be the next President. One morning I was shopping at Bloomingdale's and, to my pleasure, I spotted Marie Coffey, the wife of Walter's college roommate. We had only met once, at a Navy Day reception aboard the *Matson*, Walter's old ship. The Coffeys were there because they were both Navy. Marie and I got along great. We really had a good time together. Walter and Charley got involved with Buffalo Manning and the brass, but Marie and I just sat out there in the music, drank rum grog, and talked about our kids. Marie was a dazzlingly pretty, dark woman with a sensational figure and very good shoes. It turned out that she was a schoolteacher. In Harlem, for heaven's sake. Can you imagine such a thing?

"Harlem?" I asked her. "Isn't it dangerous getting to work?"

"I never had any trouble. And I never knew anyone who did."

"Walter is scared stiff of blacks."

"Maybe he never met one," Marie said. "Harlem is a stimulating place. The people care about life. They want to be sure they've lived when the time comes to get around to dying."

I hadn't known black people felt that way. Walter says they are a bunch of freeloaders but I didn't mention that to Marie because she was proud that she taught school in Harlem.

So I went over to her at Bloomingdale's. "Hey," I said, "why aren't you at school?" Then I really saw her. Jesus, she looked terrible. "What happened, Marie? Were you sick?"

She said, "Hello, Betsy. I'm so glad to see you. Let's have a drink."

It was about ten to twelve. I'm no drinker but I'm not a non-drinker either. We went to an Italian joint on 60th across from the store. Marie ordered us two double scotches. I said if I was going to have a double scotch, then I had to have some food so Marie orders spaghetti *alla matriciana* and she tells the waiter to tell the kitchen to cook it *al fildiferro*. He grins and goes away. Walter didn't trust Italians.

279

After a sip or so we stop talking about the kids because I ask her if she's been sick.

"Yeah," she says. "I've been sick. I'm an alcoholic."

I grab her hand. "Marie, what are you talking about, for heaven's sake?"

"My children are in California with my mother. I hate my husband's work and maybe my husband. I know I hate my life so I got sick. I'm an alcoholic." She stared straight ahead lecturing the past.

"Don't say that. Those things are just phases."

"I start to drink when I get up in the morning. I drink all day— alone. I never get drunk. I've been sick like that for eight months. Since last November."

"But why?"

"I blame it all on my husband. Why not?" She finished the drink and called for another round.

"Marie, would you want your kids to see you like this?"

"They have my mother. They love her. They're nearly grown up. And if my body were sick instead of my mind they'd survive it."

"If you can't respect your husband, then it isn't possible for you to love him. If you're a Catholic or something, and you won't divorce him, you've got to leave him. You told me once that in Harlem they want to be sure they lived before they die. I never forgot that. Booze isn't living. It's turning you into an old woman because you can't respect your husband. So you've got to leave him. Go out to California with your kids, Marie. You aren't going to stay on booze when you're with your kids because you know they have to respect you. Do you need any money?"

"No. Thanks, Betsy."

"Will you do it? Will you go there? Now?"

She began to cry. I told the waiter to hold the spaghetti. I put my arm around her and said, "As bad as it is now, you know how good it can be. Go to California. Will you do that for your kids, Marie?"

She dipped a handkerchief in a glass of water and washed her face. "I'm going to do it," she said. "Charley has his life."

I signaled for the spaghetti and finished Marie's drink.

TO: FIRST DEPUTY COMMISSIONER VINCENT J. MULSHINE

FROM: LIEUTENANT RICHARD GALLAGHER, 17th HSQ

We got a make on the shoes in Bridgeport, Connecticut, last night at eleven o'clock. That is two days after we got the prints on the murder scene. The shoes are specially built, so it would be impossible for anyone to wear them other than the person for whom they were made. These shoes are almost as positive an identification as fingerprints. They are called Murray Space Shoes and they are crafted on plaster-of-Paris molds made by pouring plaster over the feet of whoever is to wear the shoes. Every dimple, wen, and disfiguration of the feet of whoever ordered and wears the shoes are exactly reproduced.

There are about 1,500 casts of individual feet stored at the Murray wearhouse in Bridgeport. These are held for customers who know they will want duplicate shoes made in the future. The owner/wearer of the shoes that made the bloody prints at the murder scene in the Waldorf bathroom has a pair of plastic feet on file there.

His cast and all the others are labeled by full name in indelible purple pencil. The name is also card-filed with full street address, alphabetically by shoe owner name. The customer names and individual specifications are also filed on production cards. Every shoe made by Murray is numbered and cross-relates to the casts and the card files.

For the moment we won't say that the man who ordered and owned these shoes is Slurrie's killer. We won't make any arrest until I see the imminent report on who ordered the special bullets for the gun, where, and whether positive identification of the buyer can be made. We expect the results of that search to be in this morning. The FBI ran down the gunsmith in Omaha, Nebraska, who had received the order for the bullets and who made them on that order. Sergeant George Fearons went to Omaha to interrogate the gunsmith. He is expected back in New York before noon today.

I want to note here that if the man who ordered and owns these shoes is the same man who ordered the special bullets for the murder weapon, we have to understand that he has extreme political clout of an overpowering nature. For that reason I am not going to write down his name in this report inasmuch as the PC believes that his name may well be included in the total circulation of these reports from the Mayor's office. When all this evidence is in, it will stand up in any court of law.

DATE: 12th August 1964
TIME: 9:17 A.M.
BASE REPORTING: Miami   DSP (Semley) Only

EDWARD CARDOZO (continued)

Harry Danzig call me after Wullair's beautiful funeral. The whole world send somebody there to pay a last tribute to this great man. I was at Betsy's house when the call come. Harry say Nudey want to see me at the Jakarta when I can get away. Betsy deen fill like hongeen aronn Dallas anyway. It is a rough couple days for her. She cry a lot. At the funeral she ask the Governor of Texas to proclaim a Walter Bodmor Slurrie Week an he jus stare at her an walk to the other side of the chapel. She is practically jus back from New York, then you people grab her an keep her hyped up to make her talk all night. She is not made of iron.

The kids came in from military school. Franklin look pathetic in his German field uniform. I once say to Wullair he mus wan the boys to grow up like Dad Kampferhaufe, for crissake. The first thing I do after they plant Wullair an I get Betsy back to the house is to tell her that from now on I have something to say about how the boys is gun be brought up and that deeden include military school. She say, "Yes, Eddie."

We fly to Miami. I drive Betsy an the boys out to the house then I go out to the Jakarta.

I wait at the counter in front until Nudey come donnstairs. I fool aronn with the li'l gorl who is obbsolutely *loco* about making *pinche* but I tell her I just come back from Wullair's funeral so we don't talk about sex. Nudey comes donnstairs and sit in his booth. He nod to me so I go over.

"How was the funeral?" he ask me.

"Great."

"What families were there?"

"The Salvadores from Boston. The brother of Chigi Carrastone. I think I see Walyo Amatini and about four of the boys from Vegas was there."

"Very nice. Who did the White House send?"

"Humbert."

"Who else?"

"Is a bewriful turnout. The airplane lobby, the oil people, that banker from San Diego, insurance people, the farm lobby, the Korean ambassador, the Iranians. Betaut was there and the dairy industry. Defense contracts, Charley Coffey, a whole flock of rabbis and priests. It was a very good funeral. I count eight television cameras. There was thirty cops to hold the crowds back. Bewriful."

"They are gonna have to look a long time to find a fixer with Waller's moxie," Nudey say.

I nod my head. I am thinking of the amount of money that Wullair could generate.

"Kiddo, I got a proposition for you."

I show him I am listen.

"You are a prominent banker because you own a bank and I made you a banker. You are rich because I showed you the money and told you to pick it up."

"You are three hunnerd percent, Nudey."

"You deliver. So now I am gonna do something else for you because you deliver. You are a leader in southern Florida, a friend of the great and near great, right? You are big with the charities and on the national scene. In a year or two you'll be marrying the widow of Waller Slurrie, right?"

"If I stay lucky."

"So—I am gonna put you in the Senate. I talked to Betaut. I talked to Charley Coffey. They think it is a very good idea."

I was knock out. It nearly blow me off my feet. Politics, that

284

was Wullair's thing. All I can do is jus nod my head like one of them toy birds they sit on the edge of a glass of gwatter.

"And Betsy can open a lot of doors for you in Washington," Nudey say.

I remember Betsy in Washington twenty-two years ago, when she was alone. It is a bewriful memory.

"When do I start?" I say to Nudey.

TO: FIRST DEPUTY COMMSSIONER VIN-
CENT J. MULSHINE

FROM: LIEUTENANT RICHARD GALLA-
GHER, 17th HSQ

Sergeant George Fearons questioned
city & private gunsmith Faber Emig,
whose licensed premises are at 1257 Ka-
men Avenue, Omaha, at 7:20 P.M. last
night, in Omaha, following a confirmation from the FBI and the Omaha Police
Department that Emig had stated that
he made the bullets that killed Walter
Slurrie, which were made on special order
to fit the murder weapon, a Nambu 7mm,

287

a Japanese Army issue pistol.

Faber examined the weapon found in the NYC trash basket and positively identified it as the weapon he had measured and fitted with special bullets for a four-time client whom he then named. Emig's measurements for the pistol, his record of its barrel markings, his calibrations and specifications for the bullets which will fit only this pistol, were brought by Fearons intact to New York. Faber Emig had met the owner of the pistol, the man who ordered the ammunition, once, had corresponded with him three times. These records and Emig's deposition to Fearons are in hand.

The Ballistics Department NYPD confirms Emig's records.

The owner-wearer of the shoes, and the owner of the gun, who ordered the bullets that killed Walter Slurrie, is the same person. We will make the arrest now.

DATE: 12th August 1964
TIME: 11:20 A.M.
BASE REPORTING: New York

DSP (Semley) Only

CHARLES COFFEY (Continued)

Walter got to New York from Miami a couple of hours before the scheduled campaign strategy meeting at Betaut's apartment at the Waldorf Towers on August 9th. He called me at the office from the airport to see if I could have a late lunch with him. We met at the Cheesa, an around-the-clock Swiss restaurant near the Waldorf at two-thirty. In honor of the Swiss, Walter moved up from frankfurters and ketchup to *kalbsbratwurst* and ketchup. He ate so much *rosti* with ketchup that I knew I was intended to get the check. Why else would Walter invite anyone to lunch?

He chewed ecstatically and said, "You look terrible, Charley. What's the matter?"

"My wife left me."

He stared at me, chewing. He swallowed, then said, "Why?"

"It would be almost impossible to explain to you, Walter.

She—well, she detests politicians so much that it unbalances her."

"She was a difficult woman, Charley."

"What do you know about her?"

"You won't like this but I've always wanted to tell you and I never had the chance."

"Tell me what?"

"You remember the night I came to dinner at your place? How hostile she was? How she espoused the Rosenberg cause? God, that's nine years ago."

"Yes. I remember."

"I had the SP debrief her after that."

"You—*what*?"

"There's nothing to it, Charley. They just stop by the apartment when she's alone and with the marvelous advances they've made with chemicals and hypnosis she didn't even know she'd ever been debriefed."

"But what the hell did you do that for?"

"I thought—mistakenly—that she was a Communist. I had to know because you were handling my most intimate political affairs. Well, she wasn't a Communist. She was just hostile. The report stated that she hated politicians of any kind but that most of all she hated me."

"Jesus, Walter, that is just about the most fucking outrageous story I have ever heard."

"And I happen to agree with her."

"*Agree* with her?"

"I detest politicians."

"*You?*"

"Why not? I detest my life. I detest myself. I know exactly how she feels and why she got out. But I can't get out."

"Get out? What are you talking about, Walter? They're going to make you the next President this afternoon."

"God." He sighed hopelessly. "Oh, my God. What will they make me do when that happens?" He made a choked sound deep in his throat. "You probably thought that nothing more degrading could happen to anybody after the beating Mr. Danzig gave me in the Waldorf last November. I told them over and over again that I would not get involved in that killing—and yet I went along. I merely insisted that they degrade and humiliate me first but after that—out of that recognition of my sense of honor—I went right along with them and flew to Texas for them and persuaded that—that *nothing* to kill their catspaw for them. It was the moment when I began to hate myself, Charley."

I believed him suddenly. I believed his grief over his own life because he was telling it to me *without forcing tears out of his eyes.* He was explaining the bottomlessness of his failure to me and he was not crying.

His eyes became like empty holes in his head. They were black holes far out in space with the power to pull all grief into them.

"Maybe I always hated myself. I don't know. I don't think so. I could have made a life in Salopado because my father was gone. I could have made something there if I turned my back on practising law and tried to build up a grocery business. I was born understanding the grocery business. If I had to know when I began to despise myself without any hope of going back, I think it would be in '46, in that first campaign in Dallas, when my people spread the word that that girl had gonorrhea. The girl who killed herself because of that three years later."

"But you told me you had nothing to do with that! Anyway, that was eighteen years ago."

"I didn't have anything to do with it, Charley. To this day I don't know who ordered it and paid for it. But I knew about it. They told me that it was happening and that it was getting good results and I let it happen so I could get elected. That's when I began to despise myself. The hatred has expanded like a musical note from an oboe ever since then. I haven't been able to look into a mirror for eighteen years. I have to have pills to be able to face getting out of bed every day. That young girl. Oh, dear God, dear God."

"Walter, believe me. They have therapies for treating the past. You've got to let me help."

"Charley, you're only a broker. I'm the commodity. God, all my life I've wanted to leap into the real beautiful world with normal people but I have this compulsion to turn cheap tricks and each trick I turned pulled me in deeper. I *know* how your wife must have felt, living with you, seeing what they were doing to you and waiting in fear for you finally to feel the pain, while you kept telling yourself that politics was only the family trade and there was no need for you to feel it. But you feel the pain now, don't you, Charley?"

"I feel it."

"Then get out! Get out and you'll get her back! I can't bring my six thousand broken ghosts back or I would run away with you."

"Walter, please. This—this will pass. You have to keep telling yourself that you are the next President of the United States until all of this passes."

He shrugged. "It hasn't passed in eighteen years. Do you think what happened last November in Dallas will ever pass? But—I think God tested me with politics to reveal my nature and my intentions to me. He has allowed me to see how I cheated myself because I took whatever was offered. Politics buried me under anything else I might have been intended to feel—if there ever was anything else. The cream of the jest, my friend, is that *you* did it to me. And your share of this loot of pain and sorrow is that you have lost your wife. And here we are. I could say that, except—as you have always pointed out—I am still in Salopado."

I sat in the meeting at Betaut's with Walter and Dr. Huggems, Henri Emmet from the Calumet Bank, who would handle the finance committee, Calvin C. Carma, the pollster, and Packy Hanly who had been handling all the advance work in the grass roots for Walter for years. Betaut wasn't cool to me when I came in with Walter, he merely ignored me. If I had had any interest in what the future would be all about I would have looked behind the arras for the handwriting on the wall.

Betaut ran the meeting. He put Emmet on first because Emmet had an appointment with a conglomerate operator in St. Louis about a contribution. "The earlier they come in, they know the better it will be for them," Emmet said. He was sure that when Walter started moving around the country in October the money was going to begin to pour in. "That's the wonderful thing about being privileged to raise money for Walter," Emmet said. "He attracts money the way a cabbage rose gets bees."

My attention began to wander. I was gone by the time Dr. Huggems began to explain what Walter's foreign policy should be when he got out into the boondocks.

Marie had left me. It wasn't real. The vital, passionate, caring, beautiful woman I had turned into a common drunk had left me; alone and blank, numb and frightened. Four nights ago. The letter. She was going to take a bus to California so she could have plenty of time to think about what she wanted to do with the rest of her life. She saw clearly, all at once, that she couldn't spend it with me. She thought that after she got settled in with her mother and the kids she would file for a divorce. "You have Walter," she wrote at the end. "Forget about me."

We had never been able to get things started again. Not since the night she found out my lie, and not—after that—since the night of the assassination. We had never been able to get back to the way we were before Pop told her I was a political fixer. I would start to blame it on her mental problems but she hadn't had anything like that since long ago, after the war. If she did, I had produced them for her, for the torment of both of us.

I couldn't get it out of my head that someone particular, alive, near her, loving her and being loved by her had died on that beach that morning at Ruaroa. Maybe a Navy doctor. Whoever, what was the difference? It had to be true. *Had* to be that I was just a surrogate for him, the dead lover who had been blown apart before her eyes, sending her almost over the edge of sanity. That was why she was embedded in the blood-red sand back there. That was why she did everything so recklessly the first year we were together in Australia and back here. That was the only possible explanation why she could sustain such a violent hatred of politicians. It would be unaccountable otherwise. The way she saw it, they had ripped her lover from her and had blown him apart for her to see. And because someone, something more tangible than God had to take the blame for her paralyzing loss, I became them, in the end, because I wasn't the man she had loved and possessed only fleetingly, to then lose forever.

I had to know about that. I couldn't understand why I hadn't seen this in all of the years before, so that we could have ducked under the curtains of the fantasy in her mind and dragged out into the sunlight what was destroying us, to talk about death and loss as a substantive thing: self-existent, independent of morbidity, self-sufficient, and capable of contrast with hauntings and visions of blood and flying guts.

I had to have this out with Marie. If nothing else came of it, if she still sent me away, I nevertheless had to hear her tell me whether this was true, that she had never loved me, except as a substitute for the life that had ended.

I was still sitting in Betaut's vaulted living room. Walter was droning on about the dangers of blacks, about the need for law and order, the need for polarization. I was sweating grief and hopelessness, thinking of Marie sending her mind and spirit away to a dead man. Walter was telling us about the welfare state, I think. My mind drifted to a bus rushing away from me to California. I had to be there when she got there. Walter was telling us that Communism was all worn out as an issue. "Even if it

293

still had any voter appeal, which it does not," he said, "it would only offend Russia and China, who are going to be our biggest consumers of products and services."

I shouldn't be sitting here. Marie was already four days away from me. I had to be waiting for her at Angela's when she got there. If I got a plane tonight—within the hour—I could do it. Walter was telling us about building his Presidency on a coalition of the non-black, non-radical, and non-young population of the country, when I got up and walked out of there. Betaut yelled something after me but I didn't hear what he was saying.

As I hurried along Park toward 57th, I decided to call Marie's mother, Angela, to break the news about what had happened and tell her that I would be there in a matter of hours. I wanted to break into a run to get home but I found a cab instead.

Otto, the doorman, said he had signed for a telegram for me and had slipped it under the door. I let myself into the apartment, picking up the telegram and opening it as I crossed the room to the telephone.

The telegram said: MARIE KILLED IN BUS ACCIDENT TODAY, WE NEED YOU, LOVE, ANGELA.

I read the asinine thing over and over again. After a while I began to understand what it meant. I went to the file cabinet in my study and got out the Japanese pistol I had bought in Australia. I filled the clip and slammed the clip into the gun.

I went back to the Waldorf just after seven and killed Walter. When he knew what I was going to do, he seemed happy about it. He asked me if he could be seated in the bathtub when it happened so that he wouldn't make another mess of his life.

3

5

7